Closed Circuit

Marte Brengle

LOGAN BOOKS

Closed Circuit is a work of fiction. Names, characters, places and incidents are either the product of the author's imagination or are used fictitiously. Any resemblance to persons living or dead, actual events or locations is entirely coincidental.

Published in the United States of America
by Logan Books LLC

Second Edition

ISBN 978-0-9829280-0-4

Bought and Sold

The town of Lyric, Iowa (which was pronounced "Larrick" by the eight thousand or so folks who lived there, because it had been named by the town's founder's mother, who knew what she liked but couldn't pronounce it) was enjoying an unusually mild and breezy early summer. In the center of the town square the flowers had appeared in spectacular clusters and even its weatherbeaten old bandstand looked good.

But in a small, warm, and perpetually underventilated store on the northwest corner of the square, one frazzled citizen of Lyric had had enough.

Ruth Peyton pushed the same damp lock of hair away from her face for what felt like the hundredth time that afternoon, and for the hundredth time it promptly fell right back down over her eyes. With a growl, she threw her soldering iron into its stand, smacked both hands flat on her workbench and forced a mental count-to-ten followed by a deep breath. The wall clock, an oversized Mickey Mouse watch, told her that even though at least three hours had passed since she'd last looked at it, the hands had only moved from 4:00 to 4:25.

Somewhere in one of those bins... Ah. A passably clean scrunchie was under that pile of miscellaneous bits. Leaning over, she twisted her long hair into an extremely untidy ponytail on top of her head, careful to keep it away from the debris on the bench in the process. A quick swipe across her face with the corner of her shop apron got her field of vision clear enough that she dared pick up the soldering iron again.

The bell over the front door chimed. Back went the soldering iron, and not gently.

"That's Bill Martin and you don't have his radio done. I told you," groused Chet Walker from the other side of the room. He ran a sweat-stained bandana over his face as he swiveled his drafting stool away from the jumbled insides of an old TV.

"I'm almost finished with it. I'll go tell him what's up." Ruth pushed through the curtain that divided the workshop from the counter area, putting on a great show of bustle and industry that she absolutely did not feel.

But it wasn't Bill Martin. It was someone she had never seen before, a petite, tailored blonde woman in her forties. The visitor wore a dark blue linen skirt, sheer white sleeveless blouse and gold-and-diamond earrings that matched the arrow-shaped pin on her left shoulder. Ruth, in jeans, t-shirt and shop apron, felt more disgustingly scruffy and sweaty than ever. She straightened her shoulders a bit, which made the end of her newly gathered, already forgotten ponytail tickle the back of her neck. *Ohhh boy.*

Not much she could do about it now; making the best of it, she leaned on the counter and smiled at the newcomer. "Hi. Can I help you with something?"

The woman smiled back. "Hello. I'm Lydia Caldwell. Is Mr. Peyton in, please?"

"Well, if by 'Mr. Peyton' you mean Rick Peyton, no, I'm afraid he's not here. I'm Ruth Peyton. Is there something I can help you with?"

"Oh—well, when will Mr. Peyton be back?"

Ruth laughed. "Maybe next year, if we're lucky. If it's something important I can get a message to him when his submarine comes up for air."

The older woman blinked, apparently at a loss. She ran a careful hand over her hair and shifted her grip on an expensive-looking leather handbag. "Well," she said, finally, "I must admit I'm a bit confused. Are you Mrs. Peyton? I'm the new owner."

"Ms. Peyton. Rick is my brother—you're *what*?"

"I'm the new owner of the building—well, one of the new owners, that is. I'm sorry, I thought you knew." She opened her handbag and handed Ruth a business card from a gold card case.

Ruth's mental wheels spun for a moment. "I didn't even know the building was up for sale. I... I'm sorry; this is the first I've heard..." She dropped the business card on the counter without really seeing it. "When did this happen?"

"Last week. How very odd. Mr. and Mrs. Shapiro assured me that you knew what was happening. We did ask that the sale be kept quiet, but I didn't mean it to be this quiet. Is it you that has the apartment upstairs, then, or did your brother sublet to someone else?"

"Upstairs? Oh... Yes, that's me too. This is really bizarre. I had no idea about any of this, and I just saw Mrs. Shapiro at the grocery store yesterday..." Ruth's voice trailed off. She glanced at the card on the counter. The word "Investments" caught her eye. *Investments? Investing in this dump?*

A trickle of sweat down the back of her neck triggered an unpleasant thought. "Um... are you here to inspect the building, Ms. Caldwell?" The counter area was neat enough, but the back... Ruth felt even grubbier than ever, something she hadn't thought humanly possible. She brushed at a splash of solder on the front of her apron.

"Oh, heavens no," said Lydia, smiling, "I wouldn't want to barge in on you without warning." She looked around. "I see you've done some interesting things with the decorating here."

Ruth couldn't tell whether the lady was being sarcastic or not. Did assorted bits of electronic antiquity, souvenirs from Rick's travels and a coat of pale peach semigloss constitute "interesting"? "Um... Thanks."

"You're running the business while your brother's away, then?"

"Something like that. Actually, it's my shop for the foreseeable future. Rick might stay in the Navy. Things were still up in the air the last time I heard from him. So I'm trying to learn as much about electronics as I can. Are you going to raise the rent?" She blurted it out without stopping to think, then bit her lip.

Lydia looked blank for a moment, then smiled. "No, of course not."

"I... that's good to know." *Well, now that you've put your foot in it, stagger on, Ruthie.* "Didn't you need to see the inside of the building before you bought it?"

"Ordinarily we would do that, and if I'd known you were going to be left in the dark we certainly would have come before now. But we were tied up with other things back home and worked this out directly with Mr. Shapiro—he knows my partner. Since he'd had the building inspected within the last year and treated for termites last fall we felt we could take his word for its condition."

Ruth twisted the end of her ponytail absently through her fingers. Something was exceedingly fishy here. And who the heck was this partner?

"Look," said Lydia, "I know you're busy right now and it's obvious that communications have broken down somewhere. So why don't we make a fresh start? Would you like to join me and my partner for dinner tonight? Can you recommend a good restaurant?"

"I... uh, yes, sure, that sounds like a good idea." *Think, Ruthie, where haven't you eaten in a while?* "La Cocina Mexicana across the square is very good, if you like Mexican food."

"I love Mexican food. You must have read my mind." She looked at her watch. "Why don't we meet there at seven tonight?"

"That'd be fine." *Phew, at least that will give me time to take a bath!*

"Wonderful, Ms. Peyton... honestly, that sounds so formal. What did you say your first name was? I'm sorry, I'm terrible with names."

"It's Ruth."

"I'll look forward to seeing you later tonight, then, Ruth." She pulled open the door, jangling the bell again, and walked off toward the west side of the square.

◯ॐ◯

Ruth leaned into the front-window display area and watched Lydia go until the edge of the building blocked her view. She was still looking out the window when Chet came through the curtain behind her. His grey hair had been rumpled straight up. Chet wasn't much taller than Ruth's 5'7", a wiry, angular man who wore old-fashioned rimless glasses and kept the pocket of his faded chambray shirt full of small tools. Ruth noticed that his shop apron was even more disreputable-looking than hers and he had grease on his jeans.

"What the heck was that all about?" Chet rubbed his hands on his apron, leaving a dark streak of sweat.

Ruth turned away from the window. "Looks like we've got a new landlady. She says her company bought the building. And she says she's not going to raise the rent..." She frowned. "*Why* didn't Mr. Shapiro warn us he was selling the place? That makes *no* sense at all."

"That's the problem with this town. Either everybody knows everything or nobody knows nothing. Person can't keep anything straight." He shook his head and pushed back through the curtain. Ruth followed and took a good look at her surroundings, trying to see it as her landlady would.

The building was like most of the others around the square, a turn-of-the-twentieth-century two-story brick box with a decorative facade and a trio of arched windows on the second floor in the front. And, as with most of the other buildings on the square, many years of different and indifferent tenants had left their mark on the interior.

The room was wide enough to hold the two deep workbenches, one on each side, with a cluttered aisle in between and plenty of storage space plus a small bathroom in the corner in the back. Some previous occupant had removed most of the plaster from the inside walls to expose the bricks, which might have looked artistic, but did nothing to help keep out the heat or the cold. Ruth's bench, on the left, had a tall padded drafting stool, a bright yellow long-necked magnifying lamp, and several reasonably tidy works-in-progress. Over the bench was a movie poster from "Raiders of the Lost Ark." It was her brother's favorite movie, and he'd scrounged the poster from somewhere years ago and scrawled across the bottom in black marker "Ruthie, you really pop my whip! XXXX, Harry." Unlike the World-War-Three scene on Chet's side of the room, Ruth's tools were neatly stored and the floor beneath the bench was relatively junk-free. Dusty sunlight filtered through the chicken-wire glass in the large rectangular window halfway up the wall.

But the rest of the place would probably need a team of archaeologists to get everything sorted out. The wide-planked wooden floor hadn't been swept since who knows when and she could see at least a dozen dead electronic components lying around. Cardboard boxes were stacked haphazardly on shelves; rolls of wire hung on nails pounded here and there. The shop's wooden back door was open for ventilation and the screen door had a hole in it near the top. There was a very faint scent of burnt insulation in the air, that bitter scorched-plastic smell that would make any visitor wonder if maybe the place was on fire.

A huge old-fashioned paddle-bladed fan hung limply down from the high ceiling. Ruth had gotten it at what she'd thought was a bargain price at an auction in the spring. She'd thought the fan would look good and add some much-needed air circulation to the workroom, but there it hung, motionless as it had been since the day she'd installed it. She hadn't been able to get it to go, and Chet was still in a snit about the cost of the thing and refused to help her fix it.

Ruth looked at the heap of tools and debris surrounding Chet at his workbench and sighed. "We're lucky Lydia Whatzername didn't want to come back here and look around. She'd probably faint dead away and then call the bomb squad, and I mean to *plant* a bomb." She stood with her hands on her hips and let the breeze from the floor fan in the corner cool her back. "Don't you think we should get started cleaning up back here?"

"Place ain't as bad as all that." Chet was nose-to-nose with the television again and didn't turn around.

"Ain't as bad as... Jeez, Chet, look around you! I can't tell what's TV and what's junk in that pile and I bet you can't either! The place is a dump! We're just lucky she didn't want to come back and look around to see her new... What kind of idiot investor buys a building sight unseen?"

"Uh-huh. So why don't you call old man Shapiro yourself and find out what's what." He dropped his screwdriver and picked up a hemostat.

Her shoulders drooped. Great. She was going to get stuck unraveling the whole mess herself.

Chet put down his tools and swiveled around. "Now look here, you ain't gonna get this place cleaned up tonight and neither am I. Day's been too long and too hot. I'll help you with it first thing in the morning, I promise. But I ain't sweeping no floors tonight. And neither are you. We're both too tired to do anything more'n yell at each other."

Ruth looked up at Mickey Mouse again. It was nearly five o'clock. "Yeah, I guess you're right. But you've gotta help me start getting this stuff squared away tomorrow. If that woman really did buy the building, one of these days she's going to come back here and I don't want a dead landlady on my conscience." She watched as her partner began to put his tools away.

"Worst comes to worst," he said, "I'll just tell her we got high voltage back here and stand in the doorway till she gives up and goes home. You know me, I can out-stubborn anyone."

Ruth laughed. "You can say that again."

Chet had been ready to retire from his jack-of-all-trades job at City Hall when her brother had first asked him to come help start the repair shop. He'd been willing to do the repairs Rick hadn't yet mastered, willing to answer questions when Ruth first started working behind the counter, willing to teach her simple techniques when she asked, and willing to be just as grumpy as necessary to give himself the illusion that he ran the place. It was a good partnership all around.

Ruth wiped her hands on her apron again and brushed a few wisps of hair back from her face as she went through the curtain to the front. The bell gave a soft chime as she pushed the front door firmly closed. She ran a fingertip over the lettering on the glass. *Electronic Wizardry*, the backwards letters said. *R. Peyton.* She pulled down the shade and latched the door.

Tidying up a few odds and ends on the counter, she poked into the shell casing that Rick had sent her and decided that the philodendron trailing out of it didn't need watering tonight.

The beat-up remains of an old wooden console TV stood against the far wall. She took a rag from her apron pocket to wipe some fingerprints off its small, curved screen. The picture tube was long gone; the photo of Captain Kangaroo taped to the inside of the protective glass smiled back at her.

She tossed the rag under the counter and turned to straighten the curtains across the lower half of the window display area. Then she leaned over the heavy brass curtain rod to scoop up her long-haired black-and-white cat from his peaceful perch on the turntable of the old wind-up Victrola in the window.

"When you gonna listen, you silly beast? I keep telling you, Charlie, it's dogs that belong on those things. What would the Victrola people think?" The cat made a sulky sound. She ruffled his fur affectionately and he began to purr. He draped happily over her shoulder as she pushed buttons on the antique cash register. Sighing, she took the till out and tore off the paper strip with the record of the day's meager receipts.

In the back she set Charlie on the floor and poured some food into his dish so he'd stay in one place while she finished closing up. Chet was already gone. The till went into the antique safe. She walked around checking to see what might still be plugged in, then turned off the floor fan and turned on the night light. Charlie gave her a half-hearted "Hey, I'm eating!" hiss as she scooped him up again. Ruth locked the back door, slammed the battered screen door shut and headed up the stairs to her apartment, lugging the cat.

The business card stayed on the front counter where she'd dropped it, its message unseen.

Try to Remember... Or Not.

The sun had dropped behind what passed for Lyric's skyline (all two stories of it) and the sky had begun to fade a bit as Ruth reached the bottom of the worn wooden staircase on the side of her building.

Just this once, she wasn't going to be on time. Let Lydia and her unknown partner sit for a while and eat a few doggone tortilla chips. The warm breeze ruffled her hair. She stopped by the mirrored wall of the old candy store to peer into the dark blue depths and check herself out one more time. Hard to tell if she passed inspection when her reflection looked like Cookie Monster. She sighed.

Getting ready for tonight's escapade had taken more than an hour. She'd gone through five complete changes before she'd compromised between "dress up and impress the landlady" and "to hell with it," donning a bright tropical-print blouse, fashionably faded denim skirt and dark brown leather sandals.

"Everything's fine." She had to say it aloud. "*Fine!*" Firmly ignoring the raised eyebrows of other early-evening strollers, she lifted her chin and walked on.

As she approached her destination on the south side of the square the breeze blew a wonderfully spicy scent and the soft sounds of Mexican music across the sidewalk. Her friend Grace Juarez, the owner's daughter, was acting as hostess tonight. "Hi Ruth! About time you got here. Hey, when did he get back?"

"What? When did who what?"

"Oh come on, don't do that to me, it's been a long day. They're in the back there." She waved a hand.

La Cocina wasn't too crowded yet—just a few people taking advantage of the early-bird specials plus an elderly couple at the bar. Lydia Caldwell was sitting at a table in an alcove on the right, well toward the back of the restaurant. Ruth turned back to Grace with a "*So*?" expression.

Grace folded her arms and tilted the top of her head. Lydia was in profile, in animated conversation. Nothing else registered at first. But then…

"No way. No… freakin'… *way*." He'd grown a mustache, but it didn't disguise him for a moment.

Ruth closed her eyes, then opened them. No use. Damn. He was still there. "Forget about it, Gracie, I'm not going back there."

"Chicken."

Ruth gave Grace a look that should have melted the wall behind her. "I'm telling you, I'm leaving. If they ask, don't tell them I came in."

"And make yourself look like you're still a pissed-off teenager after all these years? Grow up, Ruth. Go wash your face or something. Then go back there and deal with it."

Ruth opened her mouth, then snapped it shut. "Right." Because, damn it, Grace *was* right. Fuming, she marched into the ladies' room and plopped onto the wooden bench inside. Someone had left a small stack of folded paper towels on the end of the bench. With the rough stucco wall at her back, she made an effort to unclench her hands.

಄

It was twelve years ago, she was a high school senior, and she was madly in love with an older man. Adam Talbott, just graduated and gone off to college in Chicago with a promise that he loved her and he'd be home to see her as often as he could. He was the one person in her uncertain life who kept his word.

She'd worn his letter jacket everywhere, pushing up the sleeves, and she'd turned down plenty of invitations from other guys. She was Adam's girl, just as she had been ever since he'd found her on her first day of high school hopelessly lost in the hallway trying to find her biology classroom on the wrong floor. He'd offered to escort her to all her classes. She'd laughed. He'd walked her home. And so it began.

Right after he left for college, his letters came once or even twice a week. But after the first month he wrote less often and never came back for his promised visits. In October he stopped writing completely. She waited, waited, wrote him, asked him if he could come back for Homecoming in late November. Two weeks later the answer came, a couple of lines scribbled on a page torn out of a spiral notebook. *No. Too busy. Sorry. Write again soon. Love, Adam.*

Came the day before Homecoming, her seventeenth birthday...

The school day was over. As she scuffed along, morosely kicking up dead leaves with her worn sneakers, a friend bicycled by and shouted a greeting. Ruth gave a halfhearted wave, hoping she'd be left in peace, but Grace skidded to a stop by the curb and waited for her to catch up.

"So what'd you get for your birthday?"

"My parents gave me some perfume and Rick got me a Judy Collins album."

"Uh-huh. What did Adam get you?"

"Adam who?"

"You're kidding, right?"

"I haven't seen today's mail." She brightened. "Hey, yeah, there's probably something waiting for me at home." On her sixteenth birthday, he'd had a corsage delivered to her sixth period class. A gold heart-shaped locket in a velvet jeweler's box had been at her place at the reserved table at the country club that evening. There probably *was* something waiting for her at home. She took off down the sidewalk. "Gee thanks, Ruthie!" Grace yelled after her. Ruth kept going.

Cheeks glowing, slightly out of breath, she banged the back door open and heaved her armload of books on the kitchen counter. Her mother called from upstairs, "Ruth, don't leave your books in the kitchen. Take them up to your room. You've got some mail."

Mail! I knew it! "Okay Mom, just a minute." An untidy postal heap was piled on the hall table. She scooped it all up—magazines, flyers, bills, and two large envelopes addressed to her in familiar handwriting. But not Adam's handwriting. *Oh well*, she thought miserably, *so much for that bit of brilliant inspiration.*

She sighed and tore open the first envelope with a thumb. It was a syrupy-sweet card and a check for seventeen dollars from her grandparents. The second envelope held a funny card from Eleanor Ward, her best friend. The verse inside was appropriate, kidding her about being over the hill—Eleanor, away at college, was a whole two years older—and Ruth did manage a faint chuckle as she slipped the card back into its envelope.

She picked up the rest of the pile and shuffled through it hopefully one more time. Nothing. Shoulders drooping, she flipped the mail onto the table and turned to get her stuff out of the kitchen.

Wait—! Something on the floor caught her eye. Back under the table were two flyers on shiny paper and a small padded mailer that had apparently slid off with them. She picked it up. Adam's handwriting was on the label. A cascade of tingles went down her back. He hadn't forgotten!

Ruth darted into the kitchen and grabbed her belongings, making record time on the stairs to her room. She heaved everything onto the desk without looking where it fell.

She pried the staples out of the mailer with a thumbnail and squeezed it open. Something heavy and gold slid out into her hand. One heartbeat, two, three, and she saw her own name engraved on the inside of the ID bracelet-- the one she'd given him for Christmas, with his name engraved on the front. It slipped through her fingers and fell to the floor. Was there something else? Another single sheet of ragged-edged spiral notebook paper was stuffed in the mailer. She unfolded it with shaking hands and smoothed it out.

Hi Ruth,

College life is really hectic, and that's why you haven't heard from me in a while. Books, classes, you know how it goes. Plus, there's something else I have to tell you. Remember that girl in my English class I told you about? It seems she's become much more than just a classmate. I'm sending back the bracelet and if there's any photos you want back let me know. I'm sure you'll understand— we knew this might happen—and I'm sure we can still be friends.

Love,

Adam

What happened after that wasn't really worth re-membering.

ᏣᏍᎪ

Neither she nor anyone else in Lyric had heard one word from Adam Talbott since that day. And now here he was. Grace was right; not to deal with him would only revive a stupid teenage past. But damn it, why had he come back to Lyric after all this time? To buy her building?

Ruth sighed. Better get it over with, she told herself. Maybe she'd get at least a few answers and they'd pay for dinner and this would be the last time she'd have to deal with Adam Talbott before he took his new mustache and his tailored blonde partner back to Chicago for good. If ever there were a time to encourage someone to be an absentee landlord, this was it.

As she marched past the counter in the front she heard Grace whisper, "Go get 'em!"

This time they saw her and both of them rose to greet her. She breezed across the restaurant, extended a hand to Lydia and looked coolly at Adam as though he were no more out of the ordinary than the chair he'd been sitting on. She gave him a carefully crafted smile and turned away. There was the very faintest traitorous echo of an old familiar tingle down her back.

"Hello, Ruth, so nice of you to come," said Lydia. "And I gather you and Adam don't need to be introduced."

"Hello, Ms. Caldwell." Ruth gave Lydia's hand a quick shake and backed up to stand beside the one empty chair. She wasn't going to dignify Adam with any more attention than he'd already been granted.

"Oh, please call me Lydia." She slid back into her seat, but Ruth, focusing intently on being cool and controlled, missed her cue. Adam looked from Ruth to Lydia and back again, shrugged and stayed where he was.

There was a pause. Lydia cleared her throat. "Well, why don't we all sit down and Ruth can tell us what's best on the menu."

Adam moved to Ruth's side and pulled out the chair for her. Since sinking into the floor and pulling the linoleum over herself was not an option, she sat down quickly and as gracefully as she could manage under the circumstances. "Thanks, Adam." Maybe he'd think she'd just been waiting for him to be a gentleman. Maybe. She hastily unfolded her napkin and smoothed it out in her lap.

Adam sat down. "You're welcome, Ruth." His voice was still the same, deep and soft with just a trace of a Southern accent. She risked a glance. No, not too much had changed, although the expensive polo shirt was definitely something new. The mustache was just a little darker than his hair, and his brown eyes darker than both.

His parents had moved to Lyric from Atlanta, stayed just long enough for Adam to finish high school and find The Right University, and then they'd moved on. Funny, in all the time she and Adam had been together she'd only seen his parents once or twice. His father had been Dean at the community college, and they just hadn't mixed with the townspeople socially. She couldn't even remember what they'd looked like.

"You know," said Lydia, interrupting Ruth's thoughts, "I imagine this is going to sound pretty silly, but I didn't realize you and Adam already knew each other till just before dinner. We thought the store belonged to your brother."

Ah. That answered one question. Ruth cleared her throat. "Originally it did belong to Rick. He opened it up while I was in college and I used to help out in there during the summer when I was home. After I graduated, he decided to join the Navy and left it to me. When I first started I didn't know a transistor from a trash masher, so you can imagine the time I had." She gave a little that's-a-joke-son laugh. "Really, if it hadn't been for Chet—the technician—I think I probably would have closed the place in about a week." Her fingers were sweaty. *Stop babbling, Ruthie!* "Oh well, that was years ago. I'm a pretty competent technician myself now, or so I'm told."

"Oh, I'm sure you are. The store looks like it's doing well."

"We like to think so." She looked at Lydia and smiled.

"Well," said Lydia, "since you and Adam don't need to be introduced, I guess we need to explain what he and I are doing here. Maybe I should start by telling you how our partnership came to be. My husband..."

Husband? Ruth glanced quickly at Lydia's left hand. Yes, there was a heavy gold ring. *Hmmmm...* This certainly put a new twist on certain small speculations.

"... Chairman of the Business Department..."

Ruth clasped her hands together in her lap and forced herself to pay attention.

"... teaches several upper-level classes in the MBA program and Adam was one of his best students. As you can imagine, my husband is a very busy man, so he recommended that I get in touch with Adam when I wanted to start up this investment company. I didn't understand why he told me to go to a former student for advice." She smiled and patted her partner's hand. "But I found out."

Adam looked down. Odd how very silent he was being tonight, Ruth mused.

"Anyway," Lydia continued, "in the beginning Adam was my advisor since my husband didn't have the time to look over my shoulder. I'd been studying, auditing some classes, taking seminars, that kind of thing, and oh, I was sure I'd learned everything I needed to know. But to tell you the truth, without my partner here I don't think the company would have lasted more than a month. So as businesswomen I guess you and I have a little something in common, Ruth." She smiled. "I mean, going right into the business and learning it as we went along."

Something in common? I doubt that very much, Lydia. Ruth smiled back, hoping she wasn't showing too many teeth.

At that moment, much to Ruth's relief, Grace's cousin Ray bustled by, handed out menus, asked if anyone would like a drink and gave Ruth a big wink behind Adam's back. She held the menu up in front of her face and gave him what she hoped was a very discreet glare. And then she carefully considered every item just as if she hadn't there often enough to know the whole menu by heart.

※

As Ruth made a great show of reading, Adam watched her thoughtfully over the top of his menu. Lydia had really dropped a bomb on him that evening. He'd been expecting to have a quick and fairly casual dinner with his fellow football team member Rick, and then he'd heard who the owner of Electronic Wizardry really was.

Not in a million years had he ever expected to find Ruth running an electronics repair store—or, for that matter, still being anywhere near Lyric after all this time. But here she was. What could he say?

Amazing that Lydia hadn't nailed him with a cat-got-your-tongue comment long since. Was she watching him? No, thank goodness, she was reading the menu. He looked at Ruth again. She seemed a little taller and her figure had filled out a bit since high-school days, but those beautiful green eyes, heart-shaped face, honey-brown hair and full mouth hadn't changed. The brightly colored blouse suited her well. It was a far cry from the ratty old t-shirts he remembered.

He turned his attention to the menu as well.

They ordered dinner, and then, feeling that he should at least try to contribute to the conversation, Adam spoke up. "So Rick's in the Navy? I'm sorry to miss him. I was looking forward to catching up on old times."

Ruth pulled her chin slightly back and frowned. "Really? I didn't remember you and Rick being such good friends. Especially... um, never mind." She flushed.

"Especially what?"

"Nothing. Yes, he's on a submarine. You couldn't get me on one of those things, but he seems to love it."

"I know what you mean," said Adam, appearing not to notice Ruth's discomfort. "I'm sure glad I'm not 'full fathom five' for months at a time. I'm much too fond of fresh air and open spaces. Is he planning to be a career Navy man?"

"Who knows? I guess he'll decide when it's time for him to re-enlist."

There was an uncomfortable silence. Lydia spoke up. "Ruth, is the ladies' room there by the front door?"

"Yes. Just look for the signs with the bull and the cow."

"As long as I don't need a cape to go in there, I'm sure I'll manage." She rose. "Well, if you two will excuse me for just a second..."

Trying for a neutral topic, Adam asked what had happened to several of their classmates. Most of them were still in town, she told him, and many had married their high school sweethearts. "I'm not surprised," he said, which pretty much killed the conversation. Lydia's return from the restroom broke the silence. He sought a safer subject.

"Are your parents still here?" He turned to Lydia before Ruth could answer. "Ruth's father teaches Spanish at the high school. Honestly, if it hadn't been for him beating it into my head I wouldn't be even passably fluent now." He turned back to Ruth. "We have some investments in

Puerto Rico and your dad's discipline has really come in handy. I'd like to tell him that if I get the chance."

Ruth took a sip of water and set the glass down. "No, they're not here any more."

"Oh? Are they…."

"They left several years ago."

Adam waited for more, but that seemed to be all she wanted to say.

Ray came by with a pitcher of sangria. Lydia and Ruth let their wine glasses be filled, but Adam turned his over on the table and waved Ray off. He turned back to Ruth. "So you're here all alone now? Why did you stay in Lyric?"

"I like it here."

"You've been here since high school, then?"

It was hard for Ruth not to sigh in utter exasperation. "No, Adam," she answered as pleasantly as she could, "I went to the University in Iowa City, and I got a degree in English. After I graduated, things were…" She took another sip of water. "I didn't have any particular plans for the future. Rick offered me the store and I liked the idea of running my own business. And here I am."

At that point, to Ruth's great relief, the food arrived. They all turned their attention to dinner and the conversation tapered off.

By the time they finished the main course Ruth was finally beginning to relax a bit. But as they prepared to order dessert, Lydia, trying to make conversation, piped up with "When I told Adam that it was you and not your brother who was running the store, he said that you and he had been friends in high school."

Ruth raised both eyebrows and turned to give Adam one long look. He flushed and turned away. Ruth cleared her throat softly and hoped that her smile wasn't as phony as it felt. "Friends? Why no," she said, "I wouldn't have called it that."

"Ah," said Lydia, who didn't look as though she understood at all. "Well. I'm sorry I brought it up, then. What would you recommend for dessert?"

Once they'd ordered, Lydia quickly took up the burden of conversation again.

"We've been partners for... what, six years now, Adam?"

He nodded.

"We've tried to find unusual investments, and for the most part we've succeeded. This guy,"--she patted his hand—"has an amazing instinct for business. He's picked up on things no one else has seen, and I hope it doesn't sound too much like bragging..."

Oh no, we wouldn't want to brag, thought Ruth...

"...to say that we've made a lot of money. Of course, once people realize the value in some of these things, everyone wants to jump on the bandwagon. But usually by that time we've moved on to something else and we can sell to the newcomers." She took a sip of her sangria. "We've been very successful, and I don't know where we'd be without Adam's talents. I know we've got great times ahead."

Ruth looked down at her plate. *Mmmm-hmmm.* What kinds of "talents" had Adam used on Lydia, she wondered? And exactly what kind of "great times" would they be having, and where? *Oh, shame on you, Ruthie. The lady's buying your dinner and you've got no call to be so catty*. She glanced at Adam, who was eating his dessert with his entire attention apparently focused on his plate. Feeling that she should make up for her unkind thoughts, Ruth said "It's good to know your company has been so successful."

"Thanks. I'm going to have to find out why you weren't notified of the sale of the building. Mr. Shapiro assured me he'd told you. I'll definitely check into that with him tomorrow."

"Yes," said Ruth, "that really is strange. We must have gotten our wires crossed somewhere." No point in mentioning that she'd tried dialing the Shapiros repeatedly herself this evening and had gotten no answer.

Adam chimed in. "I didn't realize that there was enough business in Lyric to support an electronics repair shop."

Ruth was suddenly very tired of all the tap dancing. "Oh, what, you figured there were only ten people left in this one-horse town and we all get our entertainment from watching the chickens? We do just fine, thank you."

"Oh, I didn't mean…" His voice trailed off. He cleared his throat. "I… What I meant was, it's nice that there's a place for a shop like yours."

"Oh yes," said Ruth, tightly, "very nice indeed. Amazing what we hicks can do if we put our minds to it." She looked at her plate again. *I shouldn't let him make me angry.*

Hastily he tried another approach. "I'm sorry. Let me start over. I'll be here in Lyric for a while, and I'll do my best to catch up with everyone and make up for lost time before I make any more dumb comments. How's that?"

"I hope you can manage it, Adam." Something occurred to her and her eyes widened. She covered for that by pressing her napkin to her mouth. *Oh, crap. She said Mr. Shapiro knew her partner. Adam was his right-hand man at the hardware store, two summers in a row. No wonder he could pull this off. Duh!*

Lydia excused herself again, making a light comment about the effects of the sangria. Ruth kept her eyes on her plate, not trusting herself to say more. Damn the man. She had hoped to be able to deal with him coolly, or at least neutrally. Fat chance. She chased an errant fragment of dessert around the plate with her fork.

"And, um, speaking of catching up," said Adam, "do you ever drive out by the lake on weekends any more? Does anyone?"

Ruth loosened her death grip on the fork and set it down. "Oh, it's still popular, but I don't get there very often myself unless some friends want to go. It's a bit too long a ride."

He looked blank. "Ride?"

"Ride my bike. My car finally gave up the ghost a couple months ago and I haven't gotten around to replacing it yet."

"Ah." He seemed to be considering something. "So the kids still hang out at the lake?"

"Some of them do. But someone's been selling pot, so the cops have been doing random checks and hassling the kids. There's a lot fewer cars out there at night. Or so I hear."

"Oh? No clue who the dealer is?"

"No. They've been trying to figure that out for nearly a year now, but no luck. It doesn't look like that's a high priority for the cops or the sheriff and they haven't really busted anyone yet. I'm sure that'd change pretty quickly if they caught any of the younger kids with the pot."

"I'm surprised they're that laid back about it."

"Well, they do have a few other things on their minds. Pot's not the major deal it was when we were in high school."

"That's interesting." He looked thoughtful.

Lydia seated herself once again, looking from face to face and not seeing obvious signs of danger. "So, Ruth, the reason I wanted to talk with you… Yes?"

Ray held up the coffee pot.

"No, thank you."

Adam pushed forward his coffee cup and Ruth gave Ray a "no thanks" wave. Grace showed some newcomers to a table in the next alcove. The restaurant was fast filling up and the noise level was increasing. Ruth looked around, hoping none of her friends would wander in tonight. How soon could she escape? Would Lydia ever get to the point?

"We were hoping…"

"Adam! Adam Talbott? What the hell are you doing here?"

"Hey, Craig! Bet you thought I'd never catch up with you, turkey. Lydia, meet Craig Nakamura, my locker mate from senior year. I think he's the one who threw my homework down the trash chute."

Lydia smiled and made the appropriate noises, but Ruth saw her drumming her fingers on the table.

"Hey, come on over here and meet my wife."

Adam looked at his tablemates apologetically and got up. Lydia shrugged. Ruth sighed. Maybe she should have a cup of coffee after all, just to occupy her hands. She looked around for Ray, who was nowhere to be seen. "Lydia, if you don't mind, I'm going to go get some coffee. I'll be right back."

Ruth picked up the coffee pot from the warming stand and waved at Grace's father in the kitchen, who waved back and called out something in Spanish over the rattle of pots and pans. This had been the longest hour of Ruth's life and it showed no signs of ending. She picked up a cup, considered, put the cup back down and put the pot back down. If she drank the coffee it would just drag things out even more. She went back to the table.

"You know what?" she said, picking her purse up from the floor, "I wasn't keeping track of the time. I have quite a day tomorrow, so I'd better head on home now. Thanks so much for dinner."

"Oh..." said Lydia. "Well..." She looked over at Adam, who was paying no attention. "Uh... I'll call Mr. Shapiro in the morning and let you know what I find out. Thanks so much for joining us. This is really a nice restaurant—and to tell you the truth, the food was better than we usually get in Chicago." She smiled. Ruth smiled back, thinking, *of course, and the bridges here are so much less expensive than that one in Brooklyn, too.* Lydia rose.

Adam finally noticed the ladies standing and hurried over. "Are you leaving, Ruth? Would you like me to walk you home?"

"No, thank you, I think I can manage that on my own. Goodnight." As she passed the cash register Grace raised one eyebrow. Ruth just rolled her eyes and sailed on out the door.

Once she'd escaped into the warm summer night she slowed her pace a bit. The full moon had risen over the trees and the night was so welcoming that after a moment she changed her mind and her course; it would be better for both mind and body to stroll around the square for a while, instead of cutting straight across to get home.

⊙੩୫⊙

Lydia paid the check, adding a generous tip. Then the partners went out the back door to the parking lot.

"Here, let me drive. I know how strong that sangria can be." He held out a hand.

"You worry too much." She rummaged in her handbag and tossed him the keys to the maroon Mercedes. "Ruth seems like a nice girl. I'd think someone as bright as that would have a million other places to go."

Adam started the car and headed west. "It never occurred to me that she'd stay here. Hell, who knows why anyone does anything? I never thought I'd end up as a businessman. When Ruth and I were dating, sports were my life…"

"Whoa, wait a second. *Dating?*"

"Oh, crap." He smacked his palm on the steering wheel. "Didn't mean to let that out. Uh… well, we started dating when I was a junior and she was a sophomore. I said we were friends because I really didn't want to get into that. I treated her pretty badly and we both know it."

"Ah." Lydia looked thoughtful. "Is this going to cause problems?"

There was a long silence. "I don't know. I never talked with her again after the breakup. I have a pretty good idea how she felt, though, because my parents told me that just before they moved out of Lyric—which would have been shortly after Ruth and I broke up—they found

28

my letter jacket on the front lawn, cut to pieces and covered with tire tracks. Someone must have been pretty mad. Or maybe someone's brother. Or both. I don't know."

"And you never asked." They sat in silence for a block. "You'll have to mend your fences with her. We need everyone's good will if we're going to carry out this project."

"Yeah. I'll do my best." He stopped for a traffic signal, then turned the car onto the highway.

After a minute or two of silence, he said "Classes. I wonder what would have happened if Professor Caldwell's Business Essentials hadn't been such an easy A for all the jocks? Did I ever get lucky."

"Both our luck, partner." She turned to look out the window. "I think you've made another score—we can do great things for Lyric."

"I hope so." And after that, the two of them were silent till they reached the motel on the edge of town. Adam parked the car and he and Lydia wished each other goodnight before they went off to their separate rooms.

Grapevine

The next morning Ruth took one look at herself in the mirror and headed straight for the shower to wash away her restless night. Or at least that was her intention. Charlie jumped off his end of the bed, twining himself around her ankles and purring, which meant she had to make one brief detour. But as soon as the food hit the dish and his nose hit the food, it was *"Human? What human?"* as far as Charlie was concerned. Ruth laughed as she ran a hand down the cat's back to the end of his fluffy white-tipped tail and left him alone with his breakfast. She wasn't usually a shower singer, but this morning she went through every cheerful song she could think of, trying to get a sense of equilibrium back. By the time she'd finished the third repeat of "I'm Henry the Eighth I Am" she was giggling and life was looking better. The sun was just peeking through her front windows from the east side of the square as she fluffed her hair up to dry, folded the newspaper to the advice columnists and dug into her cornflakes.

A little after 8:30, she scooped up the cat and went down to the store. Chet came in a few minutes later and Ruth listened to his early-morning growling with amusement. Not much chance of having a two-way conversation with him until he'd finished the coffee in the stainless steel Thermos bottle he slammed down on the bench. He brought his own—didn't trust anyone else in the world to prepare coffee right, and didn't trust any coffee-making device but the ancient machine in his own kitchen.

While she was waiting for Chet's digestive system to attain the proper maintenance level of caffeine and sugar, she readied the cash register, turned on the lights in the front and unlocked the front door. She'd just gone back to finish up the repairs on the previous day's neglected radio when the door bell chimed.

A compact, muscular blonde man waited by the counter and Ruth greeted him with delight. Kyle Hartmann was a friend of Rick's who'd always been a favorite of hers. Like Rick, he'd kicked around town for a while after graduation, then took off—in his case, to Texas for a couple of years. When he returned, he'd opened up a small feed, seed and farm-implement store on the south side of town and seemed to be doing well.

"Hiya Kyle, what's up?"

"Oh, not much." He lifted two battered, dusty six-foot fluorescent light fixtures onto the counter. "Could you or Chet take a look at these? I bought a bunch of 'em at a damaged-freight place down in Davenport over the weekend. Figured it'd take too long to check all of them out, so I brought the two worst-looking ones. If these work I figure I got a chance the others will too."

Ruth ran a fingertip over the filthy white-enameled metal and brushed the resulting layer of ick off onto her apron. "Not much can really go wrong with a fluorescent light. If the ballast and starter work and the light sockets aren't damaged they should do OK. Do you need these back right away?"

"Oh shoot, no. I gotta figure out where I'm gonna put 'em first. Why don't you just give me a call when you're done? I might even have some extras left over if you want to put them up by the famous fan." He grinned and winked at her.

Ruth laughed. "Just what this place needs, more dead junk hanging from the ceiling. Our reputation will be ruined."

"Yeah, but most of us Lyricals got worse reputations of our own, don'tcha know. Hey listen, I gotta run. Just give me a call when those things are ready, OK?"

"No problem." She waved goodbye and wrestled the light fixtures back through the curtain one by one.

It took only about half an hour after that to fix yesterday's radio and the control unit for a remote-controlled dragster. She was running the little car around the obstacle course of junk on the floor of the workshop when the bell over the front door chimed again. Thinking that it might be the car owner's mother coming in to pick it up, she aimed the bright yellow racer at the curtain and followed close behind it.

Today Lydia wore white sandals, white slacks and a lacy pink cotton short-sleeved sweater. Ruth hastily scooped up the racer and put it on the counter with its controller. "Oh—Lydia, I thought you were Billy's mother come to pick up the car."

Lydia laughed. "I'm afraid not. Although I wouldn't mind having something like that to play with. I'll bet—Billy?—will be pleased to see his car on the racetrack again."

Ruth smiled. "This kind of repair work is fun. If Billy just remembers not to stomp on the controller when the car crashes it'll work just fine."

"Do you do all the repairs yourself?"

"Oh no, just the easy ones. Like I said last night, I'm still a beginner. Chet does the complicated stuff. He's the real Wizard in Wizardry, but don't tell him I said so."

"I heard that!" came echoing out of the back, and both women laughed. Ruth put the car and its controller in a paper bag and set it on the pickup shelf.

Lydia opened her handbag and took out a leather-covered address book. "I tried calling Mr. Shapiro earlier this morning but he wasn't in. If you don't mind, I'd like to try again. May I use your phone?"

"Sure." She pointed to an ancient pay phone on the wall beside the counter. Lydia reached into her handbag again.

Ruth spoke up quickly. "Oh no, it doesn't take coins. Rick found it in a junk store and fixed it and put it up there as a joke." Would Lydia spot the real joke, a small bell-shaped frame on the phone's face plate, holding a photo of William Shatner dressed as Captain Kirk over the legend *Iowa Bill*?

But if Lydia noticed anything she gave no sign. Ruth shrugged. So much for Rick's sense of humor and Captain Kirk's Iowa home town. She snagged a broom from just inside the curtain and went out front to sweep the sidewalk.

Charlie was already curled in a neat circle on the turntable of the old Victrola, eyes closed, basking. Ruth tapped on the glass. The cat merely twitched the tip of his tail. 'Hmf," said Ruth. "Guess I've been told, you dumb cat."

She swept some leaves into the street and tossed some candy wrappers and a paper cup into the city's wastebasket on the corner, wishing she too could spend a little time basking somewhere. Fat chance. There just weren't enough broken appliances in the county to finance a vacation. And here were Adam and Lydia, far from home, rolling in money, up to who knows what... She swung the broom fiercely down the walk, nearly clipping an elderly lady passing by. By the time apologies had been made and ruffled feathers smoothed, she could see that Lydia had hung up the phone and was waiting by the counter.

"Well," said Lydia, as Ruth slipped back inside, "there's a mystery here. Mr. Shapiro said he sent three or four letters, since he thought that a letter would be, as he put it, 'more like legal than a phone call.' He said he hadn't gotten any answer so he figured you'd had no comments. But when I said that you'd told me you hadn't heard a thing, he said 'No, I sent 'em to the boy. He runs the place.' I gather that by 'the boy' he means your brother?"

"Ohhh..." Ruth's mouth twitched. "Mr. Shapiro is, uh, kind of old-fashioned. Rick was the one who started the shop and I guess Mr. Shapiro still thinks he's the owner even though Rick told him he was leaving and I've been running the place for years now." She thought for a moment. "I bet I know what happened." She put the broom back inside the door to the workroom and ran her hands through her hair. "Rick's on a submarine and he's out to sea for months at a time. Cathy at the Post Office must have seen his name on the envelopes and just merrily forwarded everything to his FPO address. So I guess Mr. Shapiro actually did tell the boy." She shrugged.

"Ah. That would certainly explain it. Well, at least in the future you can be sure your landlords will know who you are."

Yeah, I'll bet, Ruth thought, picturing Adam.

Lydia put her address book back in her purse and snapped it shut. "I have some errands to run now, but I'd like to talk with you about some of the plans that we have, since we got sidetracked last night. Could you possibly meet me for lunch? Is there some nice quiet place where we could talk a while?"

"Sure, if we go to the coffee shop after one o'clock, there's almost never anyone in there. Would that be all right?"

"The coffee shop? I... Oh, I suppose that would do. It's just around the corner, isn't it?"

"Is that not good for you? We could try the steak house."

"Oh no, no, the coffee shop will be fine. I'll see you a little after one, then."

Ruth watched her visitor walk off across the street, then leaned back against the counter and scratched her head, frowning. Something wasn't right, but she couldn't quite put a finger on it.

Chet came through the curtain. "What on earth did that dame want?"

"Lunch, I guess, so she can tell me what they're planning. I hope we don't get sidetracked again like we did last night—I'd really like to know what she's up to."

"I heard she's working with that no-good Adam Talbott. Never liked that boy. Always too darn full of himself."

35

Ruth reflected sourly on the efficiency of the Lyric grapevine. "That's exactly the kind of thing that drives me nuts. Telephone, telegraph, tell a neighbor. Nobody in this hick town has any privacy!"

"Don't you get all huffy with me. Not my fault people talk."

"You're right. I'm sorry. It's not you I'm mad at. But if you've heard about Adam then half the town's heard about Adam and I'll bet half of *them* call us up and ask me about Adam and I'm not interested in spending half the day talking about you know who!" She wiped her hands on her apron and sighed. "Are you about done with the Allisons' stereo so I can call Miriam and tell her to come get it? If I'm going to be tied up on the phone all morning I'd better get busy."

Chet refused to be diverted. "I'll get to the stereo in a minute. Long's we're taking a break, there's something I been meaning to talk to you about. You remember my nephew Eddie? Big guy? Senior in high school this fall?"

Ruth made a noncommittal sound. She remembered Eddie all right.

"Well, reason I bring it up is, he's in with the wrong crowd. And my sister, she thinks he might be taking drugs. Worries her to death. So what I thought was I'd try to find something to keep him busy for an hour or so in the afternoons, maybe come in and help get this place cleaned up, maybe teach him to fix things. Thought I'd check with you first before I roped him in here, though."

"Uh... Chet, I'd love to help out, but..."

"Now don't you worry about paying him. I'll take care of that. I figure he'll think a few bucks an hour is better than nothing. This way you get the junk cleaned up, I get some help and Eddie gets some money and gets away from those punks he's been hanging out with. Be willing to try it out for a week or so?"

"Do you think he really is on drugs? Because if he is..." she waved a hand around at the contents of the shop.

"Nah. My sister, she's always thinking the worst. She's been raising Eddie all alone since he was five years old and he's been a handful all his life. Far as I can tell, about all he does is drink beer when he thinks he can get away with it." He stopped for a moment and then said, "Besides, fact is, there ain't anything back here that'd be worth stealing."

Ruth had to ruefully admit to herself that this was true. "Oh... well, all right, Chet," she said.

"I'll keep an eagle eye on him anyway, don't you worry. Ain't the kid been born can outsmart me."

Ruth knew this was true as well. "When do you want him to start?"

"Thought I'd catch him today. He's just been hanging round the bowling alley, cruising with his friends and what-not. I'm going to call my sister, get her to send him on over here when he gets home. How's that sound?"

She sighed. "Whatever. But Chet..."

"Problem?"

"No. Not really."

She must not have sounded like she believed that, though, because Chet immediately tried to reassure her. "Don't you worry, Ruthie. He's not a bad kid, once you get him away from those friends of his. We'll be all right."

The rest of the morning passed quickly. They each took care of several small repairs and Ruth spent about an hour making what should have been five minutes' worth of phone calls to ask people to come pick things up. As she'd predicted, everyone asked how Adam Talbott was doing these days. It was very hard to carry on a pleasant chat through gritted teeth.

Finally she was ready to go get cleaned up for lunch. Chet was already munching on a rather drippy tuna-salad sandwich he'd pulled out of a crumpled paper bag. Between bites, he wagged a rosin-stained finger at her. "You take care of yourself with that lady."

"Oh Chet. Don't be such a worrywart!"

"Don't you get all 'Oh Chet' with me. There's times when a body needs a few friends to look after 'em."

Ruth sighed. "I know. I'm sure everyone on the square will be keeping an eye on me the whole time. It's just that I wish they wouldn't."

◌৪৫

Lydia was waiting for her in front of the coffee shop. "I'm glad you could make it. What do you recommend for lunch?"

"Oh, anything that doesn't look like it'll bite back," Ruth deadpanned. Lydia frowned, then realized that Ruth was teasing her.

"No, ah, rattlesnake specials or fried cowboy boots?" They both laughed as Ruth pushed open the doors.

Only three people still sat at the glass-topped tables in the front, munching the last remnants of lunch or dawdling over cups of coffee. The ceiling fans lazily circulated the aroma of burgers, onion rings, fries, mustard, coffee and pie. Lydia looked around rather dubiously. The waitress was deep in conversation with a man at the counter and didn't look their way. "Do we need to wait to be seated?"

"Not this time of day," said Ruth. A few clanks and rattles came from the direction of the kitchen. The man at the counter got up and ambled toward them and the waitress waved at Ruth and made a "be right with you" gesture. "Why don't you pick a table?"

Lydia mulled over the choices and then headed for a booth in the back by the windows, well away from the few lingering diners. The two women sat down and picked up smudged plastic-covered menus from a wire rack that also held ceramic salt and pepper shakers, a glass sugar container and small, well-used plastic squirt bottles of ketchup and barbecue sauce. Ruth pointed out several choices on the menu that tasted considerably better than the owner's literary skills might imply.

The waitress bustled over. Lunch ordered, Lydia reached across the table and patted Ruth on the hand. "Ruth, I like you," she said quietly, "and I'm sorry you were surprised by the sale of your building. I hope I can make it up to you, because we have some wonderful plans for Lyric. May I ask you, please, not to talk about any of what I'm going to tell you?"

Surprised, Ruth said "Sure, but if this is going to be something wonderful, why the secret?"

"It's just that it involves some important business plans that aren't quite final yet. I would hate to raise people's hopes too early, that's all. I would really appreciate it if you'd keep this completely to yourself. It's very important."

"I'll do my best." *Why on earth is she talking about it in a public place if she doesn't want it spread all over town?* Again she had the uneasy feeling that something just didn't add up.

The waitress brought their orders. "Hey Ruth, did you hear what happened at Dr. Ryan's office the other day?"

"Uh, no, Jolene, I didn't. Can you, um, tell me about it later?"

"No problem. But just wait'll you hear... You'll just never be-*lieve*... Oh! Aren't you the lady who's here in town with Adam Talbott? I didn't recognize you before."

"Why, ah, yes," said Lydia, with a rather excessively toothy smile.

"Thought so," said the waitress. "Nice to meet you."

"Nice to, ah, meet you too," said Lydia. She looked at Ruth with a raised eyebrow as the waitress bustled off to take care of another table.

"You'll get used to it in time," said Ruth. "People are curious. Nobody means any harm, but word does travel." She took a bite of her club sandwich.

"Hmmm, yes, so I see." Lydia's tone was sour. "Perhaps this isn't the place to talk about this after all. Maybe I should have been more specific—I gather my idea of a 'quiet place for lunch' doesn't quite mesh with yours."

"This is about the quietest place there is, once the lunch rush has passed. If you'd asked me where we could eat in a public place in a soundproof room I would have told you there was no such thing in Lyric."

"Oh, I didn't mean—" She looked down and poked at her Chinese chicken salad with her fork. "I mean, I just had hopes of going someplace where people wouldn't eavesdrop."

Ruth shifted in her seat and tried not to let her growing irritation show on her face. "Nobody's eavesdropping, Lydia. But people can't exactly switch their ears off. If you'd wanted to talk with me absolutely privately I do wish you'd said so. I could have made lunch for us in my apartment easily enough, or ordered something in. Let's get to the point. What is all this 'top secret' stuff anyway? And why involve me?"

"Because we need your help. You're a part of this community and a friend of Adam's."

Ruth dropped her sandwich on her plate and put both hands flat on the table, eyebrows at maximum elevation.

Lydia hurried on. "I know, I know. I guess 'friend' isn't the word for it at the moment. But we did make part of our plans based on the knowledge that your brother owned the store. And we do hope that you can help us."

Ruth took a deep breath and let it out slowly. If they really thought she was going to help Adam Talbott do anything but get out of town with all deliberate speed, preferably thoroughly sticky, well feathered and sitting on a rail...

Lydia pointed at something in midair with the tines of her fork. "Let me give you some idea of what we plan to do. Lyric could be... *aii!*" The fork clanged onto the tabletop and she clapped her napkin over her mouth. She hadn't heard the waitress, coffee carafe in hand, approaching her from behind, and the sudden appearance caught her completely by surprise.

"Everything all right with you ladies?" Jolene looked curiously at Lydia, whose face had flushed dark red.

Ruth quickly said "We're fine. Would you like some coffee, Lydia?" Lydia, making quite a show of dabbing her mouth with the napkin, waved her other hand in a negative gesture. Ruth gave the waitress a surreptitious thumbs-up beside the table where Lydia couldn't see. "Guess we don't need anything right now."

"OK, ladies, just call me if you do." She backed up a few steps and raised an eyebrow at Lydia's back. Ruth gave the barest shake of her head in response. Lydia, now making an elaborate production out of smoothing her napkin out in her lap again, missed the quick exchange. Jolene sat down on a stool next to the cash register and opened a thick paperback book.

Ruth stifled a sigh as she glanced at her watch and started eating again. Sandwich or no sandwich it was getting close to time she should get back to work.

"Isn't there anywhere in town we can eat and talk privately?" Lydia's voice was petulant. "All I wanted was to have a conversation without every blessed cook and waitress in town listening in."

Ruth swallowed the bite of sandwich and took a sip of her drink. "I guess not," she said, "unless you want to take your chances with my cooking in my apartment and trust me not to bug the place. I'm sorry, but we just don't have enough wheeler-dealers in Lyric to make the isolation-booth business profitable."

Lydia drummed her perfectly-manicured fingernails on the table. "I can see this is not the time and place to get into specifics. But I would like to say that we've done some studies and we've made some plans, and if we all work together we can make quite a difference for Lyric. That's the basics. And quite frankly, I think Lyric needs our help."

Ruth's patience was at an end. "Lydia, what on earth— You haven't been in Lyric for so much as a week, and you're saying it needs—" She cleared her throat. "How do you know what Lyric needs? And for that matter, what gives you the idea that this town needs your kind of 'help'?"

"It's true that I haven't been in Lyric long, but Adam used to live here, and—"

That did it. "Adam Talbott lived in this town for less than five years," Ruth snapped. "He left for college twelve years ago and he never once came back. Nobody in Lyric ever heard one word from him till now, so what makes you think he knows any more about it than you do?"

"He said things haven't changed much—"

"Oh, he did, did he? And how the hell would he know?" Ruth slid to the outside end of the booth bench, trying to keep from losing her cool completely. She was grimly pleased to note that behind them all conversation in the room had come to a dead stop.

Lydia tried for a soothing tone of voice. "Ruth, please don't get so upset. When you've seen more of the world you'll understand that progress doesn't always come in the forms we expect it to."

"I've seen rather more of the world than you think, Lydia. Are you two planning on buying up the whole square, or what?"

"Oh, no, just a... "Her mouth snapped shut. "No. Just... No."

Ruth's eyebrows felt like they'd gone halfway to the back of her head. "Oh really? Just what? Would you care to elaborate on that, Ms. Caldwell?"

"No. No, I would not. And I can see quite clearly that our conversation has come to an end. Thank you for your time." She scooped up her handbag, took out a bill and tossed it on the table, slid out of the booth and turned to the other people in the restaurant. Her voice was not loud, but it carried. "And I hope you all enjoyed the show. May it provide a month's entertainment for you."

Ruth watched the older woman's brisk and surprisingly dignified march out of the restaurant. As the door closed behind her the soft buzz of conversation began again, with an undercurrent of laughter. Jolene scurried over.

"What on earth was that all about?"

"I couldn't begin to explain it. I just hope she left you enough to cover lunch."

The waitress picked up the crumpled bill from the table. "My gosh, I should hope so, this is a fifty! Do you think she wants her change back?"

"I have no idea. Probably not. She's rich enough to afford a good tip. I'd say keep the change." She took a deep breath and let it out with a sigh. "Can you wrap up my sandwich and put a lid on this drink? I need some fresh air before I go back to work."

⊙੪౩⊙

She crossed the street to the grassy center of the square, slipped off her shoes and socks and plopped down on a bench, bare feet swinging, while she finished her lunch. Then she made a perfect two-pointer into a wire wastebasket with the sandwich wrapper and cup and set off walking around the perimeter of the square, working out the tensions of the morning. The grass felt surprisingly cool under her bare feet. She stopped at the corner across from the shop and bent over to touch her toes, then sat down on the grass to slip her socks and sneakers back on. By the time she reached the front door of Electronic Wizardry, she was feeling pretty good.

Two steps inside the door she stopped dead in her tracks. Adam Talbott was standing next to the counter talking with Chet. Chet looked grumpier than usual.

"Hi Ruth," Adam said with a smile, "I was just asking about you. Chet said you'd gone to lunch with Lydia. If I'd known she was going to invite you to lunch I would have asked if I could come along." He paused and looked from Ruth to Chet and back again. "Since I missed the chance to join you for lunch, would you like to have dinner with me tonight?"

Ruth couldn't believe her ears. "No, I wouldn't be interested," she said coldly. "And now if you'll excuse us, Chet and I have quite a lot of work to do this afternoon. I've taken too much time away from the job as it is." She brushed past him, went around the counter and through the curtain into the workshop. The good feeling had thoroughly evaporated. *Wait a second...*

She pushed back through to the front. "Adam, tell me, just exactly why did you and Lydia come to Lyric? The truth."

"Didn't she tell you? We're doing some geological studies. I think there's a good chance of finding some valuable minerals around here."

Ruth snorted. Chet laughed outright. "Oh sure, tell me another one," he said. "Minerals. This county doesn't have one damn thing that's valuable buried out there, unless there's money in cowflops."

Adam brushed back his hair with one hand and leaned an elbow on the counter. "Last time this county was thoroughly surveyed was in the forties, and they didn't find anything then. And nobody's had the ambition to look for anything since. But I've got some geologists coming in, some people who really know their business, and..."

Ruth cut him off. "Is that what Lydia meant by 'studies' at lunch today? Geologists?"

"Uh, sure, that's it."

"Mmmm-hmmm. Geologists. Right." She turned to go back to the workshop.

"Ruth?"

"*What*, Adam, I've got work to do!"

He cleared his throat. "OK. Look, can I trust you two?" Ignoring the supremely skeptical looks on both faces, he lowered his voice. "Truth is, the story about mineral exploration is just a cover. We've found reliable information that leads us to believe that Jean-Claude Mercredi's treasure is buried somewhere in the county, I'm not at liberty to say where."

Ruth and Chet looked at each other and burst out laughing. Ruth leaned up against the counter and whooped, and Chet slapped a palm against the side of the cash register and pointed at Adam, tears running down his face. Adam folded his arms and scowled. "All right, don't believe me. But it's there."

Ruth sniffled and wiped her eyes. "Oh... geez, Adam, don't tell me you fell for that old story about the crazy Frenchman and the governor's gold. What'd you do, buy one of those genuine treasure maps out of the back of some men's magazine?" She started laughing again. "Oh please!"

His face reddened. "All right, fine, and now I suppose you're going to spread it all over town!"

"Love to, boy," said Chet, somewhat breathlessly, "but you're gonna have enough trouble convincing people you're not a total dip without that. Nah, we'll just keep it to ourselves for the next time everything goes wrong and we need a good laugh. Now you go on about your business. Jean-Claude Mercredi, oh my God..."

Adam whirled and stalked out, yanking the door shut behind him. But the minute he was out of view of the window his face lit up with a big grin.

಼಼಼

Ruth wiped her eyes with the back of her hand and went back to her bench, still chuckling. Chet pushed through the curtain a moment later. "That boy's worse off than I thought, Ruthie."

"Yeah." She tapped the handle of a screwdriver absently against the bench. "But you know, I still have a funny feeling about all this. This business about the minerals and the treasure hunting just doesn't fit in with the way Lydia was acting at lunch. Now, maybe she *was* just acting, but she let slip that they were planning on buying up something around here. I asked her if they planned on grabbing everything on the square and she said 'No, just...' and then clammed up. And the worst part is, I can't tell if she was putting on an act or not. I'm inclined to think not, but I just don't know."

"Ehh. I think the two of 'em are just shining everyone on so they can have a little fling out here in the boonies where they think they can get away with it. Fat lot they know, but there it is as far as I'm concerned."

Ruth considered. "Mmmm. Could be, but I don't think even Adam is stupid enough to try that."

"Talk about stupid, I bet that dame thinks if she's seen talking with you enough, people will start to believe you're in cahoots with her."

Ruth snorted. "Let her go on thinking that. It just means that much less time till she gets a big fat pie in the face."

CRBO

Eddie, all six feet, hundred and ninety pounds of him, arrived at four that afternoon, his black hair suspiciously clean and his expression more than a little surly. His uncle didn't give him much chance to sulk. Within five minutes of his arrival he was steadily, if sullenly, picking up rolls of wire from the floor and stacking them neatly on a shelf in the back. Ruth tried to stay busy on her own side of the shop; beyond greeting Eddie when he came in, she wasn't sure what to say to him.

"Good work, boy. Reason I wanted all them rolls moved, wanted you to have space to sit here by me. I'm gonna teach you how to solder."

"Aww, Uncle Chet—"

Whatever Eddie had started to say was cut off as if by a guillotine. Ruth hadn't dared watch, but she knew from experience that an industrial strength glare had been called into action. Probably now would be a good time for her to find something to do out front.

As she finished wiping down the top of the counter with glass cleaner, the door banged open and two young men in torn cutoffs, sweaty tank tops and backwards-facing baseball caps slouched in. Ruth blinked. "Can I—"

"Eddie here?"

"He's busy right now. If you'd like to talk with him I'm afraid you'll have to come back—"

"I wanna see Eddie *now*, man. He in there?" The young man started to walk through the opening in the counter toward the curtained doorway. Ruth stepped over and blocked his way.

Amazed at how calm her own voice sounded, she looked the young man right in the eye and said "Sorry, you can't go back there. Employees only. You can come by at closing time if you want to talk with Eddie."

"Look, you—"

Chet shoved the curtain aside and stood in the doorway, slapping a large pipe wrench into the palm of his hand. "I suggest you take your business elsewhere, sonny. Eddie's busy learnin' somethin', which is more than I can say for you two baboons. Duane, Aaron, your folks know you're loose?" Snorts from the teenagers. Chet snorted back. "You two get lost before I have the cops come pick up what's left of you."

"You don't scare me, old man—" the boy started, but his companion butted in.

"C'mon, Duane, it ain't worth it. We'll come back and see Eddie later." The two teens stood and looked at each other for a moment, and then snickered.

"Yeah, we'll come back at *closing* time." They sauntered out of the store, middle fingers held high.

Ruth sagged against the counter. "Thanks, Chet."

"That's what I'm here for, Ruthie. And I'm betting those monkeys don't even bother to come back. They wouldn't know what to do with an educated friend. Now let's all get back to work."

49

They pushed back through the curtain and nearly ran over Eddie by the doorway. "Hey, man, those were my friends. I can talk to them if I want to." He tipped his chin up in his best imitation of a cool-tough stare.

Chet slapped the pipe wrench into an open palm again. "Not on my time, boy. Now you sit down over there and let's get back to business." Uncle glared at nephew. Nephew put up just enough resistance to save face and then stomped back over and plopped himself down on the stool. Chet followed, set the wrench down against one leg of the bench and picked up his soldering iron. Ruth wiped her damp palms on her shop apron, shook her head and got back to her own repairs.

Released from the store at closing time, Eddie zipped out the back door, looked around to find no one waiting for him and loped off toward the courthouse park. Ruth watched him leave and shook her head. "Are you sure this is going to be a good idea, Chet? I don't want to have to do battle with every teenage loser in town every day while Eddie's working here."

"It'll be all right, Ruthie. I know who those boys are and who their parents are, and they know I know. If I let the mayor know his precious Aaron's a juvenile delinquent, he'll take care of it in no time flat. I think maybe I'll make a few phone calls, see if I can't line up a few more part-time jobs. Who knows, I might just be the man who cleans up Lyric."

She laughed. "I hope you're right, Marshal Walker."

C3✸EO

Ruth slipped her supper dishes into the water in the sink. It was still too warm to think about actually washing them. She leaned her elbows on the box fan whirring away in the front window and looked out over the square in twilight. How peaceful it all seemed, how stubbornly immune to any real ripples in the current of life. Was this where she wanted to spend the rest of her days? Or was it finally time to think of moving on, starting over, finding a place where no one had known her forever?

What a time to get philosophical. The day must have been longer and warmer than she'd thought. She pulled her tank top out and let the fan's breeze play over bare skin. Maybe there'd be a good junk movie on TV tonight, some old cheesy science fiction movie or maybe one of those Abrahams-Zucker comedies.

She plopped down in a chair and leafed idly through the TV listings, but found nothing sufficiently rotten or dumb or amusing enough to justify taking her little TV out of the antique trunk that usually hid it and hooking it up to the cable. She tossed the magazine aside and stretched, then turned the chair so she was facing the breeze from the fan.

So what was she going to do about the Adam Talbott Situation? Like it or not, it looked like she'd be dealing with him one way or another till he made up his mind to get out of town. And Lydia. Now there was one strange lady. What were those two up to?

She settled herself more comfortably in the chair. Could someone from a big city really be so ignorant or stupid as to think that a restaurant in a small town was a good place to talk about matters that she wanted kept entirely confidential? Ruth scratched her head and twisted her hair up into a knot on top to get it off her neck. No. That whole thing had to have been done deliberately.

So, if Lydia's performance at lunch today hadn't been outright stupidity but in fact a very clever act, then what? What if Lydia had decided to test her out by saying, or almost saying, the kinds of things she thought would be most upsetting? What if Chet's assessment of Lydia's motivation was correct?

Ruth mulled that over for a moment. The real question was: Did Adam know everything Lydia had said and done at lunch, because he'd planned it?

She sighed and shook her head. It had been too long a day. She'd just have to think about it some other time. But if those two thought they could play her for a fool, the more fool they.

◌ॐ◌

The man set down one last tray of tiny seedlings. He moved down the aisle between the tables, poking at the soil in the trays to see if the plants needed water. So far so good. This new arrangement was going to work out just great. Another week's work and the room would be absolutely perfect.

He picked up the hose and adjusted the nozzle for a very fine spray, swinging his arm in an arc so that all the plants got misted. Once he'd finished with the seedlings, he twisted the nozzle closed and dragged the hose across the room to the lower tables where the bigger plants were already flourishing in their new home. They were really beautiful, tall, intensely green under the lights, with large fan-shaped sprays of leaves and the buds just beginning to form on top. He'd been worried about the move but it had all gone perfectly and as far as he could tell he hadn't lost a single plant. As he turned the hose back on again he started whistling the theme from "Green Acres."

Unsettled Weather

Rain sluiced down the front windows. Well, so much for "Sunday go to market." Ruth moodily swiped the glass to clear the fog where she'd breathed on it.

A flash from somewhere out beyond the other side of the square lit the buildings, briefly. By force of habit, she counted off the seconds. Nine, ten... *Ka-rumble*. Two miles away. Better not plan on doing anything involving electricity in sustained quantities for the next few hours. In Lyric, one good flash of lightning and the whole town went dark. Everyone talked about fixing the old power system, but somehow no one ever wanted to pay the taxes to do it.

Oh well. Rotten day, a good time to do rotten work. She changed into torn cutoffs and a paint-splattered sweatshirt and pulled her hair back into a ponytail. Nearly an hour later, as she applied the final touches to a fresh coat of wax on the kitchen floor, the phone rang.

"Hi Ruth, it's Adam. I hope I'm not interrupting?"

Oh brother. Tomorrow, so help me, I am getting Caller ID! "Well, as a matter of fact I'm in the middle of cleaning house right now..."

He cut in. "Oh good! Hey listen, I just heard on the radio that the weatherman says the rain should clear up pretty soon. Would you like to hit the hot dog stand with me for dinner tonight and then take in a movie? Just like old times?"

Ruth pulled a chair away from the table and sat down. *Old times! Fat chance!* But instead of snapping back at him, she steeled herself to be exceptionally, exquisitely, Miss-Manners-ly polite. "No, I really wouldn't be interested, thank you very much for asking. Now, if you'll excuse me please, I have to get back to work. Goodbye." She reached to put the receiver back on the hook, but Adam's voice came tinnily through the air.

"Wait! Please don't hang up!"

With a sigh, she brought the phone back to her ear. "What *is* it, Adam? I *really* don't have time to spend talking right now."

"Ruth, please. Look, all I'm asking you to do is have some chili dogs and go see a movie." A faraway flash lit the window glass; there were a few faint crackles on the phone line. "Just as friends. Nothing more."

The thought of being stuck in a dark movie theater with... *Ick.* She shivered. "No, thank you, Adam. And now I really do have to get back to work. Goodbye." She put the receiver down firmly, giving herself a mental pat on the back for not slamming it into the cradle. *Just like old times, hah.*

Five seconds later the phone rang again. And again, and again, and again, and... Ruth grabbed her rain poncho from the coat tree, slipped into her flip-flops and went out. She could hear the answering machine pick up, but before the message was done she was all the way down the stairs.

Adam held the receiver in a death grip. "Answer, damn it!" When he heard the machine he slammed down the handset and backhanded the slim Lyric phone book across the motel room.

∞

Flip. Flip. Flip. Flip. Ruth's rubber sandals slapped lightly against her heels as she headed north toward the courthouse park. The rain had almost stopped and the air smelled wonderful, washed clean of dust and full of wet grass and flowers. She took a deep breath and exhaled happily.

She splashed through a puddle, scrunching up her toes to keep her flip-flops on as she covered the last half-block of sidewalk to the park. A few cars went by, their tires spinning trails of water off the street, but it looked like she'd have the park all to herself. She'd always loved coming to the playground after a good rain, when she could swing and swirl to her heart's content without feeling as if she were displacing half the little kids in town. She kicked off her sandals and stuffed them toe first into the large pocket in the front of her poncho. As she turned to look around she could see clear blue sky in the south. She danced on bare toes in wet grass just for the joy of it. Then with a whoop she ran the rest of the way to the swings. It took just a moment to dump water out of a rubber sling seat and fold her poncho under herself to keep her shorts dry, and then she started pumping the swing to the sky. The old metal hinges screeled and moaned at first, but as she gathered momentum they settled down to just an occasional squeak. The long chain links clinked together lightly as she paused at the top of the arc then plunged down again.

Up, pause, down, up, pause, down, high as she could go. Up, and what was Adam up to? Down and back, and why was he back? Up, and what did he want from her, why was he asking her out? Down, and what was Lydia after? Up, and pause, and down again, and why was she ruining a perfectly good swing by worrying about things like that? "I wish I could read minds for just ten minutes," she muttered, and then she let it go. And back again, and pause, and forward, and feet to the sky, pulling with all her might on the long straight links of the chain.

Then she coasted, holding her feet out straight in front of her, watching the wet green world rise and fall. The swing slowed gradually, and finally when it was only reaching half its ultimate arc she jumped out, soaring to a soft landing on the damp sand.

CRXO

Across town, three people stood in the large room full of flourishing marijuana plants. The irrigation system trickled in the background and the whole room smelled like a meadow, with just the very faintest underlay of something burnt. Two of the lights near the back wall flickered and buzzed. One in the center of the room was not quite as bright as the others.

"Boy, this is some setup. You really did a great job on it," said one man, looking around him.

"Yeah," grinned the owner, "and here *you* said it'd never work. I think we can just about double the profits, and best of all, there's no way anyone will know this is down here. No more worries about the cops."

"No kidding. So, that's the dryer over there?"

"Yeah, come here and I'll show you." He led the way past the rows of plants to a work area where a large scientific balance scale sat on a stainless steel counter. He patted an oversized commercial clothes dryer beside the counter. "I got this from a coin laundry over in Grinnell that was being torn down for a parking lot. Put its power through one of those big industrial dimmers they took out of the high school when they modernized the stage last year. I can control how fast the motor runs and how hot the air gets."

One of his companions looked dubiously at the huge Bakelite knob and assembly mounted on the wall. "Are you sure that's safe? I don't think those things are designed to work that way."

"I think it will—it has so far. I'm not exactly planning to get an electrician to come down here and check on it. And if it blows up, I've got another one of those dryers and six more dimmers in storage. I've got plenty of smoke alarms and this is all concrete, so I don't think there's much danger."

"You sure you want smoke alarms down here? What if they go off when you're not around? Those guys gonna try to break down the door?"

He waved that off. "C'mon, it's not going to happen."

Another dubious look. "If you say so."

"Will you quit worrying? As hard as we worked on this place, nothing's going to go wrong."

"Whatever. When's the first harvest?"

"Probably in about a week. Be prepared."

"Oh, we will, we will."

The three threaded their way back through the plants and tiptoed up the stairs. The owner waved a hand at them for silence as they reached the top. He pressed an ear to the door, listened, heard nothing, grinned and opened the door.

ဆာ

Shortly after noon on Monday, Ruth put down her tools and swiped sweat off her forehead with her forearm for what seemed like the millionth time. It felt like a hundred and five in the workshop even though the old tire-advertisement thermometer on the back wall said only eighty-nine. She flicked the bulb with a finger but the red column didn't budge. "Liar," she snapped, as if that would help. She glared at it and huffed back to her bench.

But she knew it was no use trying to go back to work on the boom box she'd been pecking away at for the last hour. She'd already soldered the same wire in the same wrong place twice. Time to take a break before she fried the whole thing. Who the heck still wanted a boom box fixed in an MP3 world?

She threw her apron on the bench, hung the "OUT TO LUNCH" sign on the front door, locked up and told Chet she was going outside. Chet was unusually agreeable. "Sure, go ahead. I'm just about done with the TV here. Can't find a darn thing wrong with it. I'm gonna eat lunch just as soon's I get it back together. See you when you get back."

The breeze made it seem cooler outside, even though the sun was directly overhead in a nearly cloudless sky and the clock-thermometer on the bank was blinking ninety-three. There had to be some way she could persuade Chet to quit being so stubborn and fix that stupid ceiling fan. She started off around the grassy center-square at an easy trot, threading a path through the clusters of shiny green-painted park benches and small circular brick planters. By the time she'd gotten halfway around she was feeling a lot sunnier about life in general. She danced on the grass and waved to a couple of friends who were window-shopping in the shade of a store's awning across the street. They waved back, and beckoned to her to join them. She scooted across the crosswalk.

And was immediately greeted with "Hi Ruth, I hear good old Adam Talbott's back in town."

Ruth had to laugh. "I might have known. I've spent more time talking about that guy these past few days than I have in ten years. So what else have you heard?"

Amy exploded, "You're asking *us*? We were going to ask *you*!"

"Oh great. Since when did I become the source of all knowledge? Don't you guys know anything?"

"Hey, you're the one who's actually seen him. All we know is what we hear from every old biddy in town—especially the ones who just *never* gossip."

Ruth sighed. "Well, go on, what's the latest dirt?"

Carolyn pushed her sunglasses back up into place and considered. "Well," she said, "my mom heard he was going to open up some kind of offices here in town. I'm surprised you haven't heard all about it from Eleanor, because apparently Ron from her office took Adam and that woman to look at that empty building across from the library, the one where the kite store used to be, and it sounds like they're going to buy it."

"Huh," said Amy, pushing her shiny black bangs out of her face and mopping her forehead with a tissue, "if they're really buying that place they've got their work cut out for them. It's a mess. Old Mrs. McFarlane has been looking to sell it forever."

"Now that's interesting," said Ruth. "They want to buy that building from Mrs. McFarlane, and they already bought our building from Mr. and Mrs. Shapiro."

Carolyn dropped her shopping bag on the sidewalk. "They did *what*? Are you kidding? Tell me you're kidding."

"Nope. No kidding. Unfortunately. I thought Mr. Shapiro was going to hang onto that building till the day he died, but obviously not. They must have made him *some* kind of offer."

"Geez, that's terrible! Adam Talbott as a landlord. Eeewww, Ruthie. If I were you I'd move, quick."

"Believe me, I would if I could. I'd have to call in a team of archaeologists to deal with all that stuff in the back first, though. I still can't figure out why they want that building in the first place. And now it's *two* ratty old buildings. It just doesn't make any sense."

"Well, if it were *my* store and *my* luck, they'd be looking to tear the whole place down. Be glad you're not me," Amy said with a wry smile.

Ruth sighed. "Yeah, I've been thinking the same thing. I can't see how owning our building 'as is' would be profitable for them, especially if they paid enough to change Mr. Shapiro's mind about hanging onto it forever. That's what's got me worried."

Carolyn cut right to the real topic of interest. "So tell us, Ruth, what's that woman like?"

"Well, uh, she's blonde, she has nice clothes, she's older than Adam and she's married, that's about all I can say." She shrugged.

Her two friends snickered. "Well," said Amy, "he must be doing *something* right if he could get her to follow him all the way out here in the sticks."

"Chet had pretty much the same idea. Speaking of which, I'd better go eat lunch so I can get back to work. He's probably already wondering where I am."

"Honestly, Ruth, you'd think Chet ran the place and not you."

Ruth laughed. "What do you mean think? He does! And on top of everything else he's got his nephew working for us now."

"Oh Lord," said Carolyn, pushing damp blonde curls away from her plump face. "You mean Eddie? Eddie the gang wannabee? Poor you!" She patted Ruth sympathetically on the shoulder.

"So far he hasn't been so bad, knock on wood." She rapped her forehead lightly with her knuckles. "Chet's mostly had him cleaning up in the shop. Heaven knows it needed it."

"You beat me to it, Ruthie." Laughter all around. But then Amy got serious. "Listen, though, you be careful. I'll bet the only reason he's cleaning up is so he can find out what's worth stealing. Me, I'd be calling the cops to check his pockets every night before he went home."

"That's the very first thing I thought of when Chet asked about having Eddie come in. Chet said he'd keep an eye on him and so far he has. Oh well," she shrugged, "who knows, maybe I'll just take off for the South Pacific and it'll be Chet and Eddie's Electronic Emporium and *they* can worry about the rent."

"Still looking to get out of here?" Carolyn shook her head. "That's what we all say, but we never leave. And hey, on top of everything else, hasn't *anyone* else noticed that here we've been out of high school all these years and nobody's ever talked about a reunion?"

"My how time flies." Ruth snorted. "Sometimes it seems like we're all just coasting."

"Well, why don't we do something about it?"

Ruth smiled. "Good question. Why don't we all do a little asking around and see what people think?"

"Sounds like a plan. Why don't you come over sometime this weekend and we'll figure something out?"

"Sure. Maybe we'll be able to salvage something out of this summer after all."

By the time she rounded the corner toward the back door of the shop she was already making mental lists of people to call. This might be just the thing to take her mind off what Adam and Lydia were up to, and give her something constructive to do.

Chet was sitting at his bench drinking coffee, the remains of his lunch mixed in among bits and pieces of the insides of the television set he'd been working on.

"It's a wonder we don't get complaints about tuna fish in the picture tube, Chet."

He chuckled. "This old TV, might improve it some. I sure couldn't find anything wrong with it otherwise. You might's well eat your lunch now if you haven't already, because I doubt Jerry's mom is going to let him have that boom box back any time soon. Fact is, when she brought it in she asked me could we keep it at least a month."

Ruth laughed. "In that case I will definitely eat my lunch. I was just talking to Carolyn Charles and Amy Kim and we came up with the idea of a class reunion. I was going to write down some names and think about who's got the patience of a saint and more time on their hands than they know what to do with."

"Tough assignment any time." Chet crumpled the wax paper his sandwich had been wrapped in and flipped it into the wastebasket. "Well, I got another TV waiting for me after I finish this one, so I better get busy. You go ahead and eat and I'll open up the door and watch the counter."

❀

Thursday afternoon, with Chet and Eddie excavating deep inside a VCR behind her, Ruth sat down at her bench and looked at the carcass of an ancient wooden-cased table radio that had been brought in by an elderly friend of her mother's. Although she had cheerfully assured Mrs. Lewis that she'd do her best, after looking at the battered, water-stained remains she wasn't so sure.

"OK, boy, now I don't think there's anything wrong with this VCR but I'm gonna show you how it works. Now, hold this steady. We need to adjust—" There was a clatter from the bench behind her and a petulant "Sor-REE" from Eddie.

Chet sighed. "All right then, let's take a break. Time to stretch my legs anyway. Never have seen such a mess of things that don't need fixing." He strolled over to Ruth's bench as Eddie popped the top on a can of soda.

Chet ran a hand over the top of the radio and brushed a thick layer of dust off his fingers onto his pants leg. "Holy smokes, talk about things that don't need fixing. What in tarnation did you take that thing for? Just call the old biddy and tell her to buy herself a new radio. Cost her less than what it's going to take you to fix that'n. I bet the last time she used it was to tune in Roosevelt. *Teddy* Roosevelt."

"Why Chet, don't you think people should use every old thing they happen to find when they clean the basement? Besides, she said she'd pay me whatever it cost, and you don't hear *that* from a customer every day." Ruth turned around on her stool. "Speaking of which, how are you and Eddie doing on that VCR?"

"Doin' fine. Eddie's gettin' the hang of it real fast. But I don't think there's anything really wrong with it in the first place. Been real strange—first two TVs and now this VCR and I can't find a darn thing wrong with any of 'em. But at least it's something for Eddie to learn on."

Ruth leaned sideways to see around Chet and raised an eyebrow. Eddie looked sullenly down at his sneakers and swirled the can of soda around.

"Although if he gets pop in the works..." Chet let the sentence hang. Eddie glared at his uncle's back, chugged the rest of the can and let out a gale-force belch.

Ruth forced herself to keep a straight face. "So what seems to be the problem?"

"People bring 'em in, say they're getting nothing but snow and the picture keeps changing sizes. But when I look at 'em they work just fine. It's driving me nuts. Makes me think maybe I'm losing it." Chet scowled at her, then at Eddie, then moseyed on back to his bench and muttered something. Ruth reflected that it was probably just as well she couldn't hear him.

The screws that held the back on the radio were corroded in place. Ruth dabbed some penetrating oil on them and set the radio aside to let the oil do its work. Nothing else on the bench needed her immediate attention, so she got up, stretched, and after a moment's consideration decided to use the time to do some paperwork.

She took a ledger book and a small pile of cash-register tapes from the file cabinet in the corner. A brief excavation in the back of the drawer unearthed a small calculator. She cleared space on her bench and sat down to copy figures into the book, wishing she could afford to buy a computer to do the bookkeeping for her. Oh well, if she did buy it, it would just mean one more thing for Chet to get peeved about. She finished copying, did several subtractions, sighed at the total and tossed everything back in the drawer and locked it up.

The bell over the front door chimed. As Ruth pushed through the curtain her insides churned for an instant when she saw that her customer was a teenager, but it was someone she knew and not one of Eddie's friends. The young man held up a small MP3 player. "Any chance you can fix this? It won't play."

Ruth looked it over. "If the hard drive isn't damaged I can probably fix it. What happened to it?"

"Dropped it."

"I'll have to open it up and take a look, then. No guarantees if it's been dropped. Why don't you leave it here and I'll call you when I know what's what?"

"I guess so. Can't use it the way it is. OK." As he turned to leave, the door swung open and a woman came in, deftly maneuvering around the hapless teenager so that he walked smack into the door frame. The young man yipped in anguish and fled. The woman laughed.

Ruth sighed. "Jodi, that really wasn't nice."

Jodi Diamante laughed again. "I know. But them's the breaks if you can't ogle and walk at the same time, right?"

Jodi had been a classmate of Ruth's in high school, but as far as Ruth could remember this was the first time she'd ever set foot inside the store. A petite, brown-eyed blonde with a cute, elfin face, Jodi was wearing abbreviated khaki shorts and a soft short-sleeved shirt with an abundance of pockets and not quite enough buttons. Ruth looked down at her solder-splashed apron and old t-shirt and reflected grumpily on the all-too-apparent differences between "recent divorcee" and "still-single small-business owner." Doing the bookkeeping was depressing enough without that.

Jodi dug into her canvas tote and pulled out a pack of cigarettes and a gold-plated lighter. Ruth cleared her throat loudly and pointed to the NO SMOKING sign on the wall. "Oh, right, sorry." Jodi breezily tossed everything back in the bag and got to the point. "Hear your old boyfriend's back in town."

Aha! "Oh, you mean Adam?" Ruth made herself laugh lightly. "Yeah, I had dinner with him the other night, and he hasn't changed a bit. So, ah, what else have you heard?"

"Well, I was talking with Lucy over at the hair stylists' and she said that she'd heard that Adam's involved with some older woman and the two of them are running around town looking for a place to build a high-rise. Can you believe that? A high-rise in Lyric?"

"A high-rise?" said Ruth. "What's that, *five* floors?" The two women laughed. "Seriously though, Jodi, do you think it's true?"

"Who knows? Maybe they're just here in town to set up their own rumor mill?"

Ruth snorted. "Well, if that's the case then it's working out just fine."

"Well, you know Lyric was always long on rumors and short on reality. Hey, when are you going to move out, anyway? You're kind of all talk and no action yourself these days, Ruthie."

Uh-huh, thought Ruth, *and how would you know? I haven't had a five-word conversation with you in the past ten years.* She chose her words carefully. "Sometimes the big decisions take a little longer, Jodi."

"Well," said Jodi, listening not at all, "gotta go. I just stopped by to check in with you, seeing as how you'd be most likely to keep up with old Adam."

"Old Adam," said Ruth with just the barest trace of heat, "can keep up with his own self as far as I'm concerned." But then, considering the most reliable sources of gossip and Jodi's usual haunts, she added "Hey, listen, Jodi, if you hear any more about what they're up to, stop by again, ok?"

"Oh, you bet. In fact, I think maybe I'll just do a little investigating on my own."

As the door closed, Ruth found herself wondering why on earth the thought of Jodi's "investigation" should irritate her so.

Chet's comment when Ruth pushed back through the curtains was a mild "A person might think you were still interested in that fool Talbott boy." Eddie looked at her with interest.

Ruth bit off an indignant denial. Instead, she managed a neutral noise and sat back down at her bench, pretending she didn't hear a very faint chuckle behind her.

Instead of getting back to work on the old radio, she fiddled idly with a pair of pliers, flipping the jaws back and forth, staring off into space. The past few days, she reflected, she'd been wasting an awful lot of time doing something she usually scorned more than anything else— seeking out gossip. What was wrong with her? Who *cared* what Adam and Lydia were up to?

Ruth's mind drifted, the clink-clink-clink of the pliers stilled, and Chet and Eddie's voices faded into the background. Coming all the way from Chicago to buy two crummy, rundown buildings in Lyric and talking about "studies" and "help" just didn't add up, and that baloney about minerals and the old treasure legend was just plain laughable. She shook her head, sighed, and got back to work.

⚬⚬⚬

A few days later she sat talking after a late lunch at the coffee shop with her best friend Eleanor Ward, who was the office manager at the one local real estate agency. There was nothing for either of them to hurry back to work for that day, so they were enjoying the rare luxury of dawdling over the remains of chocolate sundaes. Eleanor, taller than Ruth, with a round face, brown eyes, and dark brown hair that she wore in a nearly waist-length braid, was sitting across the booth bench with her feet dangling over the edge. She'd kicked off her shoes and was wiggling stockinged toes.

"So," said Ruth, feeling that now was as good a time as any to pump her friend about the real-estate doings of Adam and Lydia, "any truth to the rumor that they've bought up half the town?"

Eleanor laughed. "Well, they got your building without our having anything to do with it, and they bought that old building across from the library. That's it as far as I know, but they might be trying to make any number of 'Shapiro deals' without involving us. Oh, and since Mrs. McFarlane was so eager to get rid of that building, she told them to go ahead and move in even before they close escrow, so they've hired people to remodel the old kite store into an office—and, get this, fix up that apartment upstairs. Now, *what* do you suppose those two will do with an apartment upstairs?"

"I can imagine," said Ruth, who could, and who was surprised to find the image faintly annoying.

"Some of our handymen are doing some of the work, and I hear it's going to be quite a place. Oh, and the *office* is nice too." A knowing chuckle. "Hey, you ought to just casually go return some library books in a week or two and take a look at it. I hear that half the single women in town are reading a *lot* more books these days. Looks like Adam's still a hot number around here, but I still can't understand why."

"Me neither. Well, I suppose I could always go check out a few more Agatha Christies just to while away these warm summer nights." Both women laughed. Ruth thought of something else. "Hey, listen, speaking of the old days, what did you guys do for your reunion? We never had one and we're talking about it now."

"We didn't do much of anything, really. Had a dance at the Elks Club, a dinner and a class photo taken. I should show you mine sometime. They sat us down around the bandstand with the sun in our eyes and the picture looks like something that ought to be hanging on the post office wall." Eleanor held her braid across her face to imitate a mustache and put on a fierce outlaw expression, or as much as she could manage with her pleasant, usually smiling features.

"Doesn't sound like it'd take much to put something like that together," said Ruth. "The thing is, Carolyn and Amy and I have been batting ideas around, but none of us really wants to take on the responsibility for planning it. We all have enough to do without making ten gazillion phone calls."

"Well, the idea is not to do the work yourselves. Spread the news around a bit, see how people feel about it, and then fix it so the person who thinks it's the best idea is the one who gets stuck organizing it. That's what we did. And we think maybe Mike Harper will forgive us in ten or twenty years." Both women chuckled.

"Not a bad idea," Ruth agreed. "I'll get Carolyn and Amy to start asking around. But you know, even if we do put something together, there might not be time to get word to all the people who've moved away. Maybe we've missed our chance."

"There's nothing that says it has to be in summer. A lot of the classes have done it then, but I think some of them have planned it around Homecoming."

Ruth grimaced. "Homecoming. Ewww."

Eleanor scowled. "Oh Ruth, come on. After all these years." Ruth looked away and made aimless circles on the table top with the tip of one finger. Eleanor looked at her in exasperation. "You know what your problem is, Ruthie?

You're acting like that's the only really bad thing that's ever happened in your life and you won't get over it."

"What are you *talking* about? My parents…"

"OK, point taken," Eleanor cut in, hastily. "Your parents were idiots and behaved like baboons. They had a big fat messy divorce and kept the gossip mill running overtime. That was years ago, they've both left town, and not even the worst gossip ever thought you or Rick had anything to do with it. But here you are, still carrying a grudge about getting dumped in high school. That's ridiculous. That wasn't your fault either, and I'm amazed you're still letting it get to you after all this time."

Ruth sat, speechless.

There was a stretch of silence that went on just a little too long. Then Ruth sighed. "I think all of that crap with our parents was harder on Rick than it was on me. He was always flying off the handle at pretty much nothing and everything. He took my getting dumped personally, too." She stared at the table for a moment. "Well, water under the bridge. Anyway," she said as she picked a crumpled napkin off the table and stuffed it into her empty ice cream dish, "it'd be a real shame if we piddled away the entire summer and never planned a reunion at all. Wonder who'd be the best person to hint around to?"

Eleanor let the subject be changed. "Good question." She tapped idly on the table with her iced-tea spoon. "Who's got plenty of time and plenty of ego?"

"Hey, now that you mention it, Jodi Diamante stopped by the store the other day for the first time in her life. I wonder…"

"Mmmm, that has possibilities. She's certainly got enough time on her hands since Sonny ran off."

"Yeah. Next time she stops by the store I think maybe I'll just kind of casually bring it up."

"You think she'll be back by? Two visits in ten years, I don't know, Ruthie."

"Oh, she'll be back. She was going to do a little 'investigating' on Adam Talbott and 'get back to me' if she found anything out. Now you know how that woman's mind works; she'll be back to gloat and purr the minute she even *imagines* she knows something."

"Ahhhh… good point. Well, have at it. I doubt she'll have much trouble corralling other people to do the real work, since she's not about to get her manicure mussed. Maybe Adam will turn out to be worth something after all."

"First time ever, I think," Ruth grinned. "But it's too bad we'll have to wait till old Jodi catches up with him to find out what he's really up to. I'll bet he'll tell her everything just to get her to go away."

Eleanor chuckled, then looked thoughtful. "I'm surprised he hasn't asked you out, just for old times' sake."

"He has. I turned him down."

"Oh? You might think about changing your mind on that. If you and he went out together a few times you wouldn't have to wait on Jodi. You could get the lowdown straight from the horse's mouth."

Ruth whooped with laughter. "The other end of the horse is more like it!"

"Well, there is that. Hey, maybe those two are behind whoever's selling pot around here, did you think of that? I've heard that rumor a time or two. You could find out if that's what they're up to."

"Oh please. Give me a break. I don't care if they're the French Connection, I'm not going out with him. If you think it's such a great idea, why don't you do it?"

Eleanor waved that aside. "Besides the fact that nobody's asking? I've got twin ten-year-old excuses, and that's more than enough. Look, all I'm saying is that it might not kill you to let him take you out to lunch a few times. Who knows, he might just spill the beans."

"No chance. One Dear Jane letter from him was enough."

"Ruthie, for pity's sake, aren't you ever going to let that go? I'm not telling you to marry the guy. I'm just suggesting that your social life could use a little more social and a lot more life."

Ruth was getting more and more nettled. "I can't help it if all the guys around here are married, gay, dating someone else or long gone." She rapped a finger hard on the table. "No way. Besides, if I thought my social life was so all-fired rotten you'd have heard me complain about it long since. Have you? I ask you, now have you?"

"No, but..."

Ruth cut her off. "There, you see? If and when I get to feeling like I'm that bad off, I might consider letting Adam buy me a few lunches. But don't hold your breath. I wouldn't get involved with him again if he groveled on his knees and begged me in front of the whole damn town. And that's the truth."

෴

Lydia pointed at the shimmering screen of her laptop computer and smiled. "There's the first of them, Adam; I've got the printout for you over there."

"Good work! Great! Not long now and we'll really be on our way. I hope they hurry up with the office construction so we can get you a desktop computer and a printer and plenty of storage space. This looks like a winner. Remind me to send him a bonus, would you? This is first-class work."

"Well, you've always known where to look. And the rest of them will turn up—shouldn't be too long now. I'll zip back home once we've gotten settled into the office and get the rest of this taken care of. Do we have enough money in the operating account?"

"I'll have to check on that. If not, I'll make the transfer." He plopped down on the lumpy chenille bedspread that covered the motel bed, lay back and crossed his arms behind his head with a sigh of satisfaction. "Yes sir, we're on our way. This is what I've been dreaming about..." He blinked. "Uh, ever since we got here," he went on quickly. "Amazing how fast the time passes when things are going your way."

Lydia swiveled on the plastic-seated chair and looked at him thoughtfully, but he'd closed his eyes. She shrugged and went back to work. Sooner or later he'd talk about it; he always had.

Dreams and Schemes

Adam polished off the last bite of his sandwich, then crumpled the plastic wrap into a ball and stuffed it inside the brown paper bag beside him on the park bench. Leaning back, he took a deep swallow of soda from a can and let out a sigh.

His companion, Ted Ross, a former high-school classmate and fellow football team member who was now a vice president at the bank, upended a small bag of potato chips over his mouth to get the last salty flakes, crushed it and stuffed it inside a white paper bag. He wiped his mouth with a paper napkin and resettled his expensive gold-framed sunglasses.

There was a companionable silence. They'd been talking business between bites as they ate, but by now their attention was only hazily connected to affairs of high finance.

Adam took another sip of his drink and looked dreamily out over the square. Then, with a start, he realized that Ted had asked him something.

"Sorry, I was daydreaming." He waved a hand. "Good day for it, I guess. What were you saying?"

"Never mind, it wasn't important. Guess I never really appreciated how nice it is to be able to sit here in the square and have lunch. I haven't brown-bagged it in years—Jolene at the coffee shop will have my hide if this keeps up." A pause. "Bet there's nothing like this in Chicago."

"No," said Adam, thinking of a lot more than the beautiful summer day in front of him, "there sure isn't. Just another good reason for me to stick around for a while."

"Oh, will you be staying? I thought you were going to set up the corporation and head on back to the city."

"Well, here's another little bit of fuel for the gossip mill. My partner's going back tomorrow, but I'm staying, at least for a while. You can spread that around with all the other stories." But he said it with a smile.

"Who, me? I never gossip. Pass on little bits of valuable information yes, gossip no," his friend grinned. He looked across the square to the northwest corner. "So, you've got three buildings already?"

"Two, but I have feelers out on some others."

"Oh? Huh. The gossip mill must not be as efficient as I thought it was. Hadn't heard about that."

Adam grinned. "I'm not dumb enough to make the offers directly. I have people working on that. Precisely because I don't want the news spread all over town before we're ready."

"Ah," said Ted. Looking across the square again, he waved a hand in the direction of Electronic Wizardry. "Speaking of gossip, heck of a thing about Rick and Ruth's parents, wasn't it?"

"I wouldn't know, haven't heard anything about it."

"Oh, that must have happened after you left, then. Dad thought Mom was having an affair, Mom thought Dad was having an affair, who knows what was really going on, but they pulled out every last bit of dirty laundry during the divorce proceedings. Must have been absolute hell for the kids. Ruth had just started college, and here her parents were fighting each other to the death over every last cent, so she had to run get financial aid on her own so she could stay in school. The parents finally got tired of slugging it out and settled, and then both of them moved out—who knows where they are now. Rick came back and opened up the store and helped Ruth pay her bills. You gotta admire both of them for surviving all that."

Adam was silent for a moment. "I had no idea."

"Well, you had no reason to keep up with the local soap operas. Hey, listen, how'd you like to come on out to the country club Saturday? Play a few holes, maybe go swimming, knock back a few and have an early supper? Some guys you probably remember from high school, we get together as often as the wives will let us."

"Uh... Sure, that sounds fine. What time do you guys usually show up out there?"

"Oh, eleven-ish, thereabouts. You remember how to get there? You did drive out there in the daytime once in a while, didn't you?"

Adam didn't answer. The soft-drink can in his hand made a soft crunching noise.

"Adam? Yo, Adam, you daydreaming again?"

"Wh... Oh! Yeah, yeah, can't keep my mind on anything today. Uh, yeah, I remember how to get there. Haven't been there since..." His voice trailed off. He shook his head slightly. "Since senior year. I, uh, I imagine a lot of folks out there remember my parents?"

"No idea. Haven't heard them come up in conversation anyway. So, you gonna to be there on Saturday then?"

Adam grinned. "You bet. Saturday at eleven. I'm a rotten golfer but I'm a good swimmer—be nice to get away from that crowded city pool."

"Well," said his companion, looking at his watch, "you big city executives have all the time in the world, but this small town vice president has to get back to work. I like this proposal of yours and I'll bet the guys you'll meet on Saturday will too, if you feel like discussing it with them. Just out of curiosity, what are you telling everyone else?"

"Mineral studies is one story. I've even got a prospectus, got the print shop to run me off a few copies. And I've told another story or two here and there, so don't be surprised at what you might hear. Especially if you hear we're after buried treasure."

"Buried treasure? Oh geez, you didn't tell people you were after that French guy's gold? Who the hell did you think would fall for that one?"

"Guess they didn't, if that didn't get spread around town yet. I'm kind of surprised it didn't. I'll have to rethink who I tell tales to."

"Hey, wait a minute—so how do I know you're giving me the real poop on this deal?"

"You don't, of course." Adam grinned and swatted his friend on the arm. "Look, I have to give out some kind of plausible story. Even I don't have enough money to pull the whole thing off, which is why I need a few very select investors. I really am going to have a geologist come out next month. But you and a few others are the only ones in on the real investments."

"Well, that's good to know. Because you're not going to be able to sell this idea to just anyone."

"Yeah, I know. But I think we 'inner circle' guys can make it work." He slapped both palms on his knees. "Well, as the saying goes, someday we'll have to quit meeting like this. But you see what I mean about getting real privacy by sitting out here."

Ted waved to a couple of strollers on the other side of the square. "You're right. As long as we're in plain sight we're not up to anything. I'll have to keep that one in mind."

The two men got up, brushed themselves off and put the wrappers from their lunch in a nearby wastebasket. Adam said goodbye to his friend, then looked over at Electronic Wizardry's corner of the square. *Hmmm...*

Charlie the cat was curled up in his usual place on the turntable of the Victrola with his chin on the tonearm. His tail was draped over the side, twitching in response to some feline dream. Adam put the edge of his hand against the window and peered into the shop. There was no one behind the counter. He stood for a moment watching Charlie snooze in the sunlight, then pushed open the door.

In the workshop Ruth looked up from putting what seemed like a hundred microscopic screws back into a computer keyboard. Why anyone would want her to fix it rather than just buy a new one... She slid off her stool, stretched, shook her head and hands to get some of the tension out and went through the curtain to the front. Her smile froze when she saw Adam reaching into the window to pet the cat.

She cleared her throat. "Hello, Adam."

He turned around. "Hi Ruth. Hey, I was just having lunch in the square and I wondered if you'd like to join me for dinner tonight. Nothing fancy, just the buffet at Christopher's in Blue River. I could pick you up after work if you'd like."

"That's... ahem... very nice of you, Adam, but I'm busy tonight. Maybe Lydia would like to see what the buffet is like."

"Lydia is packing to go back to Chicago tomorrow. And packing is a major event for her. She wouldn't want to be interrupted for two hours just to go eat." He put on his most charming smile. "If you'd rather not go alone I can include a few other people in the invitation. Maybe we could make it a 'Lyric Attack' on the buffet?"

"No thanks, Adam, not tonight." So Lydia was leaving? Well, well, well. Things were looking up. One down, one to go. In that case, maybe a little polite evasion was in order. "Ah... maybe we could go some other time, though. Can I take a rain check?"

"All right, a rain check it is. I hope you're not just saying that because it's only rained once since I've been back."

"No, really, I'd like to go sometime. But right now I have what looks like fifty million screws to put back into a keyboard, so if you don't mind I need to get back to work."

"Wouldn't want to take you away from a task of that magnitude," Adam said, mock-seriously. "I'll give you a call next week sometime, how does that sound?"

"Oh sure, fine." She could always arrange to be busy. Or invite half a dozen friends and get him to foot the bill. No problem.

He took a card out of his shirt pocket and scrawled something on it with a gold Cross pen. "I'm reminding myself to write this down in my calendar."

"What, you don't have a smartphone? Who'd believe that?"

He laughed. "Oh, I've got one," he said, taking it out of its holster on the back of his belt to show her, "but this is not just about the phone call. It's to commemorate the first time since I've been back that I've asked you out and you haven't chewed my head off."

"Well, we all have our off days. This must be one of mine." But she managed to say it with a smile.

CR&O

As the bell chimed behind Adam, Ruth went back to the shop, frowning. Chet turned from his workbench and looked at her. "Now what?"

"Nothing. I need to get that dumb keyboard back together, that's all."

"Uh huh." He turned back.

She waited, but he had apparently decided to say no more. She went over to see what he was poking into. The bench was amazingly free of debris.

"What are you going to have Eddie work on this afternoon? I can't see any more cleaning that needs to be done." The shop was so tidy it was hardly recognizable these days. Eddie had been a major surprise in that regard.

And his friends hadn't come back either, although it was a sure bet that the spray-painted obscenities on the wall facing the alley hadn't appeared there by accident. When Eddie ran out of other things to do she'd have Chet make him clean off his friends' little masterpieces. That might put a halt to it for a while.

"Today I'm teachin' him how to align a tape machine." Chet patted a hulking contraption that the local radio station had given him to haul away when they'd installed new equipment years before. It was one of many long-lost items that had emerged from under layers of debris during the cleanup.

"Chet, nobody uses those things any more. You got after me for fixing a Teddy Roosevelt radio, well, that's a Harry Truman tape recorder."

"I know, I know, but the boy says he might like to go into radio station repair one day and this here's the safest thing I got for him to practice on. If he messes up it ain't gonna be a customer in here screaming for his scalp."

She had to concede that. Well, at least Eddie was thinking about the future, which was more than she would have given him credit for. Now if someone could only do something about his friends. Today, spray paint. Tomorrow, what?

She sighed and sat wearily back down at her bench. Just one more thing to worry about, and she couldn't afford to do much about the ancient alarm system, or stable and feed a king-size dog.

Ruth cupped her chin in her hands and stared moodily off into space. Everything seemed to be going wrong. Adam's dinner invitations. Eddie's friends. The increasing number of items that Chet couldn't seem to find anything wrong with, and that she felt guilty charging the customers for. Why did everything have to hit her all at once?

She closed her eyes and let her imagination wander, trying to conjure up pleasant images to get herself back on track. Eddie cleaning spray paint off the bricks with his toothbrush. Chet finding a really complex piece of machinery with twenty things wrong with it that he could fix at premium prices. Adam walking up to the door of her apartment to take her out to dinner. Adam walking through the door of her bedroom when he brought her home. *Whoa!* She hastily picked up her screwdriver and fished another tiny screw out of the jar lid she'd put them in.

When Chet got up to get a part from the cabinet fifteen minutes later he saw her sitting with her chin on her hand again, staring off into space. He shook his head but for once said nothing.

෨෨

Dozens of small zip-sealed plastic bags full of marijuana sat next to a pile of dried greenery on the stainless steel counter. Beside them was a stack of folded brown paper grocery bags printed with the name of a local business.

"You sure you want to do that, man?" He pointed to the paper bags. "Seems to me that's just asking for trouble."

"How many stores around here do you know of that don't put their name on the bag?"

"Uh..."

"Right. So if someone's carrying a plain brown bag, where did it come from?"

"Oh come on, who's going to notice?"

"Maybe nobody. But all it takes is one. In this business you never take chances."

"Yeah, but why put *that* on the bag?"

"Diversion. Nobody's going to put their business name on a bag that's full of pot, right?"

His companion scratched his head thoughtfully. "You got a point there."

"Damn right. Now help me fill the rest of these baggies. I gotta go back upstairs. They think I've gone to the bathroom and they'll be wondering if I fell in."

"OK, but I can't stick around too long. I'm supposed to be back at work at three."

"Well, next time don't let Her Majesty brush you off. There's only the four of us, and we've all got to work."

"Oh now come on, it's not my fault that…"

"Don't give me excuses. You go over there the next time, you make sure the both of you come back, and don't argue with me."

"Yeah yeah, whatever you say."

There was silence for a few minutes as the two of them weighed and measured, scooped and filled. Then the second man tossed a bag on the pile and stopped long enough to light a cigarette. "You know," he said, "I still think we should consider expanding the operation. Did you think over what I was saying the other day?"

"If you mean about the hard stuff, yeah, I thought about it, but let's get real. None of us are going to risk a meth lab in the basement, and for anything stronger than pot we have to buy from God knows who. Plus, think— even the cops are kind of going, oh, it's just pot. They've been hassling people, but have you noticed nobody's really gotten busted yet? If people listen when we keep reminding them to hide the stash and not have any more than a joint or two on hand, then it's likely to stay that way. And the cost of production is as low as you can get. This is about as close to ideal as we can make it."

"What about at least getting a few more people as distributors?"

"I don't think that's a good idea. One of them gets busted, we all get busted, and we'll take the biggest rap because we're the ones in charge."

"Yeah, but look at all the weed we've got here. If we try to sell it all ourselves we'll be putting ourselves in the same kind of danger just because there's so much of it. Get a few more people to peddle it way out in the county and we'll be farther from where the cops can find us."

His companion put down the bag he'd been filling and scratched his head. "Well, yeah, that's a good point. To tell you the truth, I hadn't planned on such a big harvest—using the hydroponics has really made a difference. Do you have anyone particular in mind?"

"No, not really. I'll think about it, though, and I'll ask a couple of the current distributors. I'm sure we can find at least one or two more people we can trust."

"Let's both think about it. But don't let Her Majesty in on this one—first thing you know we'd be up to our eyeballs in freshly recruited narcs."

"Yeah," he said, rolling his eyes, "you said a mouthful there, boy."

⚜

Ruth leaned her elbows on the counter and sighed. They'd had precisely two customers since lunchtime, and the man who'd just left had brought his TV set back in, insisting that Chet hadn't fixed the problem and demanding that he do it over and do it right this time. Which of course meant that they wouldn't be able to charge him for opening it back up again. Chet had tried to insist that there'd been nothing wrong with the TV, but the customer was having none of that. Snow, and lousy reception, and it wasn't the antenna because he'd checked that. In the end, Chet had grabbed the TV off the counter and stomped off into the workshop with it. Ruth sighed again.

She pushed through the curtain to the back, sat down at her bench and fidgeted with her screwdriver. But it was no use. She couldn't get herself back into a fix-it frame of mind. Well, maybe she should do something that didn't require much concentration.

She went back out front, got out her cleaning supplies and swabbed down the countertop and the top of the old TV, rubbed fingerprints off the glass in front of Captain Kangaroo and the glass in the front door. She sprayed a feather duster with dust attractant and went after the horn on the Victrola in the window. Charlie snoozed on undisturbed. She tickled his nose with the feather duster and he sneezed, opened his eyes and glared at her.

"Hey, just spreading the bad mood around, cat. You got a problem with that?"

Charlie got up, stretched, humped his back, turned around the other way and settled back in again with his tail covering his nose.

"Well, if you want to breathe tail fur all afternoon, be my guest." Ruth sighed again. She put the cleaning supplies away and went back into the workshop. Less than half an hour had passed. The day was going to last an eternity at this rate. She plopped back onto her stool and forced herself to concentrate on finding the problem with the toaster oven whose corpse lay on the bench.

She took out a few screws, then upended the toaster oven onto the old newspaper she'd spread on the bench and gave it a good smack. Five years' worth of crumbs and dust and general ick cascaded down. Her eyes watered. "Well... ker-*CHOO!* ... I guess I've... *ker-CHOO!* ... found half the problem with this thing." No comment from Chet, who was glaring at the insides of the TV on his bench. She smacked the oven once more for good measure, shook it, put it right side up, sneezed again and folded the crumbs plus—*Eeewww!*—a few old roach carcasses into the paper. She sneezed twice more as she hustled the paper back to the trash bin.

After that, though, it took only a minute to find and replace a blown fuse. She put the oven back together, checked it, added an extra charge for "cleaning" to its work order and carried it out to the front.

And that, she realized, was really all she had to do for the day. The only remaining item to be repaired was a portable CD player on the back of Chet's bench, and he'd said he'd fix that. She cleaned off her workspace and got out her bookkeeping.

After a few minutes she heard Chet put down his tools. "Ruthie," he said, swiveling his stool around, "I... I think we really got to talk." She turned to face him, eyebrows raised. This didn't sound like Chet. He looked down at his shoes for a moment, then continued. "Look, I got to be honest with you, I'm worried. Things have been real slow around here this summer and no matter what you think, I ain't so sure Talbott ain't fixing to raise the rent. Are we going to be able to make it?"

Ruth was touched. "Chet, I don't want you to worry. Rick is sending me money every month so we're not in danger. We'll manage."

"Well, it ain't just that." Chet got up and walked over to her bench. "The point is, we've got to find something new to do. I'm glad to hear about Rick, takes a load off my mind, but we can't sponge off him forever. So I been thinking. Maybe we should take up computer repairs, more than just broken keyboards and blown fuses. Seems like everybody in town is buying computers these days and nobody in town is fixing them. I know I can't do much with 'em now, but I could take a class or something, learn how to do it right. Or you could. What'dya think about that?"

Ruth looked thoughtful. "You know, Chet, you're absolutely right. Honestly, I've just been letting things go on from day to day and not considering the future at all." She gave him a brilliant smile. "I'm sure glad one of us has some sense."

"Awww, now..."

She held up a hand. "No, I mean it. Computers are too expensive for people to just throw out. And a lot of people in town are buying them these days, so why should they have to drive to the next county to find a repair shop? How'bout you look into it, see what we'd have to learn? I'm sure there are classes at the community college for things like that."

"Yeah, I'll do that." He pulled an old bandana out of his back pocket and mopped his face. "Hot in here today."

"Hot in here every day." Ruth laughed as Chet swiftly turned away to keep from seeing her pointedly look up at the wilted, motionless ceiling fan. "Hey, I don't have anything left to fix and I sure don't have enough receipts here to keep me busy till five. Should we just close up the place and go on home? It's not like we've had customers stampeding in here today. We could both use the afternoon off to rejuvenate."

"Not a bad idea. Why don't you go close up the front and get that dim-witted cat out of the window."

Ruth chuckled. "Poor Charlie, he gets no respect." She went to the front and scooped the cat up onto her shoulders. Charlie gave a sleepy *mrow* of protest, then purred, looking like a big fluffy black-and-white fur collar. Ruth closed out the cash register, locked the front door and carried the cat into the back. "I think maybe I'll go swimming, Chet. Soak some of this worry out in the pool."

"They got enough pollution in that pool as it is," said Chet, but he was smiling.

⚬⚬

Twenty minutes later, beach bag slung over her shoulder, Ruth was on her way. She considered riding her bike, but decided she wasn't in the mood to unlock the store again to get it out of the back. Besides, it was perfect weather for a walk.

By the time she reached her destination her spirits were much improved. In the women's locker room she slipped off her oversized t-shirt and faded shorts to reveal an iridescent green two-piece bathing suit. It hadn't been her choice of color, for sure, but there hadn't been much choice at last year's after-season sales, and it fit perfectly.

Anointed with sunblock, clothes safely stashed in a wire basket, she took her equally bright green beach towel and looked around the pool to see if any of her friends were there. Not surprisingly, the water was filled mostly with kids. Ruth spread her towel out in a small patch of shade where a locust tree overhung the chain link fence near the shallow end.

She threaded her way past a row of simmering sun-bathers to the deep end of the pool, selected a fairly un-populated area of water and dove in. The water was colder than she'd expected and she came up gasping. Then she began making her way across the pool, trying to dodge the splashers who weren't paying any attention to would-be swimmers.

As Ruth was completing her third crossing of the pool, trying to get around yet another splash-fight without getting an elbow in the head or a face full of water, Adam walked out onto the deck from the men's locker room. He wore a form-fitting maroon tank suit and carried his towel draped around his neck. As he handed his basket to the attendant he looked at the crowd in the water with a sigh of irritation. He'd been coming to the pool almost every day in the vain hope that he'd find it uncrowded enough to actually swim. No chance of that—again—so he found a place to spread out his towel near the diving boards, sat down and began to smooth on sunblock. After he'd gotten himself thoroughly covered he lay back on the towel, ad-justed his sunglasses and closed his eyes.

A few minutes later, Ruth climbed out of the pool on the other side and headed for the diving boards, pushing her hair straight back from her face. The deep end had cleared out enough that she thought maybe she could try a dive or two without landing on half a dozen children. She bounced experimentally a time or two on the farthest reaches of the low diving board, and then—*Aiii!*—suddenly catching sight of Adam lying on his towel, she yipped, tee-tered, staggered, waved her arms frantically and fell in rear end first with a huge and extremely undignified splash.

Mortified, she sank to the bottom and stayed there till she was very nearly out of air. The only way out was to swim underwater toward the side of the pool away from Adam. When she finally came up, gasping, she kept her face carefully turned away and fervently hoped he hadn't opened his eyes to see who was cannonballing off the board. Without looking back, she swam quickly to the ladder and climbed out, pushing back her hair again as she stepped onto the warm cement to a chorus of appreciative hand-claps and hoots from the kids. A quick glance in Adam's direction showed her that—oh, thank God—he hadn't moved; she heaved a huge sigh of relief as she sped down the pool deck. She scooped up her towel to dry her hair, and since her face was pretty well hidden she risked another glance in Adam's direction.

He still hadn't moved a muscle; still lay flat on his back on the towel, a light film of sweat on his smooth, beautifully tanned skin. Even from this distance she could see he was in great shape. *Must work out with weights or something. Look at those muscles...* Her eyes moved downward to the brief, tight tank suit. When they were in high school he'd always worn the baggy surfer-style trunks. She'd never had a view quite like this. Her eyes widened; then, suddenly realizing where she was and what she was doing, she whipped around to face the fence and began scrubbing the rest of herself dry with the towel, her face blazing red.

Time to get out while the getting was good.

As Ruth scurried toward the locker room, Adam opened his eyes and sat up. Time to toast the other side. He set his sunglasses on the towel, turned over and stretched out again on his stomach, head cradled on his folded arms.

Inside the locker room, Ruth quickly showered and stuffed her suit and towel into the beach bag. After she'd pulled her clothes on and returned the empty basket to the front counter she looked cautiously out the entryway. Hooray, he wasn't there. She zipped across the street and headed for home.

Wow, what a sight Adam had been, though. An image of a long-ago warm summer night in the back seat of Adam's parents' car came back to her...

The blare of a horn rudely shattered the picture. She'd stepped off the curb right into the path of a pickup truck. Her face blazed red and she scurried back to the sidewalk. Now the journey home seemed to stretch out for a hundred miles and she wished that she'd ridden her bike. She looked both ways and hurried on, picking up the pace considerably. After what seemed like an eternity she reached her apartment and ran up the stairs. What on earth had gotten into her? Hot nights in parked cars, indeed.

ꆸꆹ

Adam jumped as the drops of cold water splashed on his back. He'd drowsed off. Another drop hit him and he flinched again and turned over to look for the source.

A very wet blonde woman in a hot-pink bikini stood next to him, arm outstretched to dribble still more water. He blinked. *Who the...* He shaded his eyes and looked up at the woman again. "Ah... Jodi, isn't it?"

Jodi laughed and plopped down beside him. "You got it! I didn't think you'd remember me. How are you, Adam? I heard you were back but I didn't expect to find you at the pool."

Adam sat up. "Sure I remember. You've changed your hair color, haven't you? And you've, ah..." his gaze moved up and down her lush figure appreciatively. The wet bikini clung like a thin coat of paint.

"Changed since high school, uh huh—on purpose." She gave him a brilliant smile. "Blondes do have more fun. And I've been going to the gym three times a week for a couple years," she said, extending her right arm and looking down the length of it as she turned her hand over. The bright pink polish on her nails matched her bikini exactly. "Like those muscles?" She batted her eyes at Adam, with a smile and an exaggerated deep breath that indicated that it wasn't exactly her arm muscles she thought he should appreciate.

"Very, ah," Adam cleared his throat, "impressive." He grinned. "So, what brings you to the pool in the middle of a work day?"

"Oh, well, since Sonny and I got divorced—you did know I married Sonny Diamante, didn't you?—I've been taking some time for myself. Worked my fanny off at the drugstore," —and here she wiggled the anatomy in question— "and put away a little nest egg, so I figure I'm past due. How'bout you? Everyone wants to know what brings you back to Lyric after all these years."

Adam laughed. "I'm sure they do. Well, you can tell everyone that I'm back here on business, and I hope to do some great things for my former home town."

"Oh? Like what?"

"Oh, this and that. You'll see. I wouldn't want to spoil the surprise," he said easily.

Jodi considered this for a moment, then shrugged. "Can I use some of your sunscreen? I forgot to bring mine."

"Sure." He handed it over. "Do you go swimming often? I don't think I've seen you here before."

Jodi rubbed sunblock on her arms. "No, this is the first time I've been here this summer. I usually sunbathe in my back yard. Today I just had a feeling that going to the pool would be worth while." She smiled. "Here, let me put some of this on your back, it looks a little red."

Adam obediently swiveled around and sat cross-legged on his towel facing away from her. Jodi began rubbing the sunscreen into his back, using slow, lingering strokes. She leaned in closer to smooth the thin white lotion over his shoulders and onto his chest, and he could feel her breasts pressing lightly into his back. He caught a faint whiff of stale cigarette smoke and wrinkled his nose. He rotated his shoulders slightly and leaned away from her just a bit as she poured more of the sunscreen onto her hands and rubbed it down his back right to the top elastic of his bathing suit.

"How's that?" Jodi leaned against his back again, asking the question softly.

"Mmmm. Very nice." Adam was amused. But his body definitely wasn't getting the message she was trying to send. *That's a first,* he thought. He let her rub his shoulders for a few minutes more, then turned to face the pool. Jodi knelt beside him, breathing rapidly—he glanced sideways at the shape of her nipples visible through the thin fabric of the bikini top. He thought for a moment, then brushed the side of her face softly with his hand.

"Thanks, Jodi. I'm going to go swim for a while now. I think you've rubbed that in enough that it won't wash off. Would you like to join me in the pool?"

"Swim... You mean you're really going to go swimming?"

"Yeah, it looks like some of the kids are clearing out, so I might be able to actually swim. That's why I came to the pool. Join me?"

"No, actually, I've gotten just as... wet as I want to be today." She smiled and leaned against his arm. "Sure you *really* want to go swimming?"

He smiled back. "Yeah, I really do need to cool off a bit. Plus you know how it is when you don't get your exercise."

"Mmmm-hmmmm," she purred. "I could help you keep in shape, you know."

"I'll bet you could." He patted her hand. "Maybe I could take a rain check?"

She sat back on her heels and pouted. "You know how many times it's rained this summer?"

Adam burst out laughing. "Now, where have I heard that before? Seriously, Jodi, some other time? I'd really like to try to swim while I can."

She sighed, then got to her feet. "Don't you forget now."

"I won't, don't worry."

He sat for a moment, looking dreamily at nothing in particular. Then he turned and watched as Jodi rounded the end of the pool and sashayed up to distract the young summer-blond lifeguard from his duties. Adam chuckled. *Might have known.*

He got up, stretched his arms upwards to their limit, bent down to touch his toes and did a few jogging steps. Then he dove into the blissfully cool water.

CRID

Eddie opened the car door and slid across the back seat. "Move it, man, I gotta dump my stuff at home before I head over to the store or my old lady'll never shut up about it."

"Awww, mama's boy, whassamatta, scared you'll get a whippin'?"

"Knock it off, Duane, or I'll knock *you* off."

His friend held up his hands in mock horror. "Oh yeah, man, like I'm just really, truly scared."

"Look, you want me to keep on doing this or what? I got better things to do than keep an eye on the shit in that place. I don't think we could get twenty bucks for the whole pile. It ain't like she's fixin' iPhones in there."

"Yeah, you just keep on doin' it, long enough she thinks maybe we forgot about her. You think you can do that, Eddie boy?"

Eddie spat out the car window onto the street. "Yeah, I can do it, Duane. But I'm tellin' you, you better make it worth my while."

"Oh, listen to the big bad man. Yeah, Eddie, I'll make it worth your while. Now let's hustle your ass home before mama comes lookin' for you."

As Eddie tossed his bowling bag on the couch in the living room his mother called to him from the back yard. "Eddie? Come out here a minute!"

"Aww Mom, I'm busy, whaddya want?"

"Eddie, I'm not standing out here in the yard yelling at you. You come out here so I can talk."

"Yeah, right, in a minute!" He lounged into the kitchen and took his own sweet time getting a can from the refrigerator. Then he ambled out the back door. His mother was hanging underwear on the clothesline. "What,

Mom, I don't got time to help you with the laundry, I gotta get to work."

"That's what I need to talk with you about. Your Uncle Chet called, they closed down the store for the rest of the afternoon, you don't have to go today."

"Aw sh..." he cut off the offending word. "Why didn't you call me over at the bowling alley? I got things I coulda been doing if I hadn't had to come home!"

"Never you mind that, young man. I have things for you to do right here. And you can start by taking the basket inside to the washer and putting the wet clothes in it. And then fill up the machine and do another load. It's just about all your clothes anyway."

"I'm not gonna do laundry! I got better things to do!" Eddie turned and stomped back into the house. His mother stood for a moment and then shrugged. She was too tired and hot to argue. She went back to pinning up pairs of socks.

Inside, Eddie took a quick look out the window to make sure his mother wasn't watching and quietly picked up the phone.

Just for Reference

The ancient coffeemaker gurgled and spat and began the laborious process of dribbling water into its basket of grounds. Chet glanced up from the newspaper spread out across his chrome and Formica kitchen table to check the progress of the brewing. A tall glass flecked with bits of orange pulp and a bowl with traces of cereal stuck to the bottom sat on the counter along with a few odds and ends of silverware and a couple of empty root beer cans.

He turned to the sports section and looked at the box scores, only to find that his team had lost. Again. He made a disgusted noise and pushed his chair back from the table. As he ran hot water into one side of the worn white porcelain double sink and squirted in some dish detergent, the coffee-maker gave one last burp and quit perking. He slid the dishes into the water and picked up the carafe.

As he sipped his coffee, Chet turned the paper over one more time to scan the headlines. There was not much news of any kind today, so it didn't take long. Dropping the newspaper into the recycle bin, he poured the rest of the coffee and a healthy shake of sugar into his Thermos bottle.

As he walked through the living room he noticed that the only decoration on the walls was hanging crooked again. He gave the heavy gold frame a nudge on the lower right corner. And then he stood for a moment, as he always did, looking at the portrait taken of him and his new wife in 1963. She'd talked him into having that portrait made; got a good deal on it because her best friend was the photographer's receptionist. How he'd fussed at the time, portraits, foolishness, and he didn't look exactly thrilled in the photo either. Who could have known, on that day of wedding clothes and careful poses, that in less than a year she'd be gone? He shook his head. Leukemia. No way for such a young woman to die.

Now what was he getting so all-fired sentimental about this morning? Lorraine was gone and he'd long ago made his peace. Ruth taking up with that Talbott boy, that's what he ought to be fussing about. He slapped his hand on the back of the sofa and raised a small cloud of dust.

It was a gorgeous day outside. By the time he'd walked the four blocks to work he was feeling a lot more chipper, but it wouldn't do to let Ruth think he was getting soft. She was just coming down the stairs from her apartment as he crossed the street.

"Morning, Chet! How's things with you today?"

"Hmf. Let's cut the cackle and get to work."

"Oh, the Pirates lost again?"

"Wouldn't know. Haven't been following. C'mon, get that door open and let's get busy."

Ruth laughed. And so the day began.

CRANGD

Lydia folded her nightgown neatly and put it on top of the rest of her clothes in the suitcase that lay open on the bed. She checked the bathroom one more time to make sure she hadn't forgotten her cosmetics bag, then pulled the zippers on the suitcase around.

All the shades in the bedroom were drawn and the air conditioner hummed away on "fan" in one of the windows. She considered for a moment, then decided to leave things as they were. Adam could adjust the shades and the a/c controls to suit himself when he moved in. She knew he'd be as glad to get out of that seedy motel as she had been. It was so nice of him to insist that she be the one to spend the first night in the new apartment.

She stretched, yawned, bent over to touch her toes and slipped on her shoes. There was a long drive ahead of her today. She pulled the suitcase off the bed and rolled it over to the door, where two matching smaller suitcases sat waiting. As she stepped outside onto the mat on the landing, Adam came through the office door below, glanced upward and walked out into the parking lot so he could see her. "Sleep well?" he said.

"Wonderfully well. You won't believe the difference that bed makes. Thanks so much for giving me first crack at it." Gingerly she started down the rickety metal stairs, making sure she kept her eyes fixed on the building across the alley. If she looked down she'd never be able to keep walking. Just as well she wasn't staying, if it meant dealing with those stairs every day.

"Hey, no problem. Are you finished packing? Want me to bring the bags downstairs?"

"Yes, and yes. Then let's go get some breakfast, and I have two or three more phone calls to make before I leave."

He waited for her to finish inching her way down the stairs before he started up. He'd have to see about getting someone to come and reinforce the attachment to the building, but it was a low priority. The view straight down through the metal bars that formed the stair treads didn't bother him in the least.

Lydia was already deep in conversation with some-one on the office phone by the time he got back with the bags. She waved a hand at him in an "I'll be with you in a minute" gesture. He grinned. He knew how long "a min-ute" could be when Lydia got to talking business. But rather than twiddle his thumbs and listen in on her con-versation he gave her a "be right back" wave of his own. This was a good time to make his usual trek to the news-stand for all the out-of-town papers. He pulled out the handle on the biggest bag and used it as a dolly to wheel the smaller ones across the office. It was going to be a beautiful day.

⚇

The sound of crashing bowling pins kept drowning out the country-western music from the jukebox, and Eddie had punched five dollars worth of buttons and he was not pleased. He tipped his glass high, gulped down the last few foamy swallows of beer and slammed it back on the table. The waitress looked around from her conver-sation three tables over and yelled "Eddie, you break that, you pay for it, you hear?"

"Yeah yeah, sure sure," he muttered. Eleven o'clock and where the hell was Duane anyway? He was supposed to be here almost an hour ago. Eddie considered his chances of wheedling another beer out of the waitress and shrugged. Being seventeen was the pits. But at least he had a little money to spend for a change. He shifted in his chair and pulled a sweat-stained, dog-eared brochure for Harley-Davidson motorcycles out of his back pocket and unfolded it on the table. Yeah, someday...

He failed to hear the footsteps coming up behind him and nearly knocked the table over when Duane gave him a swift poke in the ribs. "Damn it, Duane!" He cocked a fist, then let it drop as his friend laughed and pointed.

"Oh, ain't you tough. What're you doing, Eddie boy? Dreaming again?"

"Gonna buy me a Harley."

"Oh sure. You and who else? You ain't never gonna have that kind of dough."

"I'll get it, don't you worry."

"From where?"

"I'll figure something out. I ain't as dumb as you look."

Duane shook a fist, but without much malice. He pulled a chair out, flipped it backwards and plopped down in it, leaning his arms on the chair back. "Not many places to latch onto a buck these days, not without half killing yourself. I sure wish I could find some way to make some easy money for a change."

"Yeah, me too. Hauling junk in that damn store just don't cut it. And that's all that's in there is junk."

"Well, we keep our eyes open, I bet something'll come along. Least my old man's paying for the insurance on my truck, that's all I care about. Now if he'd just get off my back about gettin' a real job..."

Eddie looked moodily down into the fading traces of foam on the side of his glass. "Yeah, I know what you mean."

Duane slid his chair over a bit closer to his friend. "Listen," he said, and then looked around to see if anyone might overhear him, "tell you the truth, I just might have a line on something. Aaron said he heard that Jack Bicknell was selling weed."

"Oh go on. Mr. Tight-Ass the Professional Lawn Jockey. And what else is he doing, robbin' stagecoaches?"

"No, man, I'm serious."

"Well, what if he is? What's that got to do with us?"

Duane moved over even closer. "If it's true, he might just need a couple good assistants. Big money in weed these days."

"Uh huh. So what do you plan on doing, go out and play a round of golf and chase him around the putting green asking him if he wants some help? Gimme a break, Duane."

Duane sat back and grinned. "You just wait. You'll see."

CXEC

As Adam set the newspapers on his desk, the phone rang. Lydia was typing up a few last notes.

"Would you get that, please, Adam? I'll take the bags out to the car."

Adam picked up the phone. "Caldwell and Talbott," he said, watching Lydia roll the stack of suitcases out the door. "Oh, hi Jodi. Ah, well, I'm in kind of a hurry right now..."

"Were you by any chance planning to go to the band concert tomorrow night?"

"Band concert?" He shook his head. "I'd forgotten all about those. A couple guys invited me to play golf tomorrow afternoon and I haven't played for such a long time that I'll probably be a basket case by suppertime."

"Then what you need after a long hard day on the golf course is a long leisurely evening doing nothing, right?"

He grinned. *Not too obvious, no, not at all.* But what he said was "Right."

"Well, what better way to do that than to sit and listen to the band? There's nothing on TV tomorrow night."

He chuckled. "You've convinced me. Do the concerts still start at seven?"

"Yeah, still at seven. Amazing you remember that after all this time! You must have a terrific memory," she cooed. Adam could hear her sucking on her cigarette. He held the phone away from his ear and grimaced. "I always sit on the bench in the back on the west side," her voice said tinnily, "and I'd love to save you a seat."

He swung the receiver back. "Well, let's see how things work out, OK? How about we say that if I'm not wiped out by the golf game I'll be there."

Another draw on the cigarette. "That sounds great. I'll definitely look forward to it."

"I have to go now, Jodi, thanks for calling." Adam hung up without listening for a reply. He laughed aloud at the thought of Jodi and her cigarettes waiting on a park bench for him. Oh brother, what a way to spend a Saturday night. But still, he hadn't exactly said no.

Lydia was just shutting the trunk of her Mercedes. Adam went through the usual departure ritual. "Got everything? Maps, sandwiches, keys, purse, four hundred and sixty-five suitcases?"

Lydia laughed. "Oh dear, I only counted four hundred and sixty-three. I guess you'll have to ship the others to me when you find them."

"You just drive carefully so you'll be there to get them, OK? And I should have some good news for you by the end of next week. I'm expecting a few phone calls that should have the answers we need for this project."

"Oh, Adam, that's wonderful!" Lydia hugged her partner tightly. Adam held her and patted her on the back. "Just a few more weeks," she whispered into his shoulder, "and we'll have it!"

"I hope so. Now, you better get going or you'll never get there." He let her go.

She clung for a moment, then stepped back and smoothed her hair. "You're right. I'll call you tomorrow."

Lydia started the car and pulled away from the curb. Adam stood on the sidewalk and waved at her, watching for her answering wave, then turned and went back into the office.

CBEO

Ruth finished putting a new power cord on an old vacuum cleaner and tossed her screwdriver into its rack. That was her last project for the morning.

"Chet? You busy?"

"What's it look like?" But she could tell he wasn't as grumpy as he pretended to be.

"I'm going to take a long lunch today, got some errands to run. That OK with you?"

"You get that vacuum finished?"

"What's it look like?"

He grinned. "Got me. Yeah, sure, go ahead. Put the sign on the door and I'll open back up when I'm ready."

"Great." She produced a terrible Terminator imitation. "Oll be bock."

Upstairs she flipped around the radio dial till she found a station playing really lively music and did a few dance steps to try to work out some of the creaks and groans caused by sitting on a stool all morning. There was nothing new to read while she ate her lunch, which was as good a reason as any to stop by the library before going back to work.

Lyric's public library was half a block south of the square, facing the street that formed the square's east side. The building itself was the long-standing object of much regional amusement. It had been built before the turn of the 20th century, designed by an over-imaginative Victorian architect who'd read a few more Arthurian romances than was good for him—and who, unfortunately for posterity, was also the brother of the mayor. The red brick structure looked like nothing less than a miniature, massively overdecorated castle, with turrets on all four corners. It had arrow slits in the walls, a wide, arching entrance that looked as if the drawbridge had just been temporarily removed for repairs, and the suggestion of a very shallow moat in the landscaping of the lawn. There'd been plenty of talk over the years about tearing the whole blessed thing down and starting over, but the Library had gotten to be such a local conversation piece that no one but the eternally hopeful library staff ever took the notion seriously.

Ruth climbed the steep front steps and pushed open the heavy, ornately carved oak door. The building was air conditioned about as well as it was heated—a haphazard matter indeed—and her friend Karleen stood behind the main circulation desk looking rather wilted.

Giving Karleen a wave, Ruth headed for the shelves where the newest books were kept, and within a few minutes had found a new thriller, a mystery by one of her favorite authors, and, to her surprise, a brand new book on computer repair and maintenance. Things were definitely looking up. She went to check them out. "Things OK with you, Karleen?"

Karleen sighed. "The floor fan's out again. But otherwise, yeah, things are all right. How's things in the shop?"

"Would you believe our floor fan's working, but other than that I know exactly how you feel?"

"Uh huh. And this isn't even a warm summer. I suppose we should be grateful for small mercies." Karleen scanned the books and handed them back across the counter. Ruth carried her new acquisitions outside and stopped dead in her tracks as soon as she'd heaved the heavy door around on its hinges. Across the street, a maroon Mercedes was parked in front of Adam and Lydia's new office building. Lydia, dressed to the nines as always, was just lowering a suitcase into the trunk. As she closed the trunk lid, Adam—dressed in body-hugging dark blue t-shirt, faded jeans and scuffed white running shoes—emerged from the building.

Ruth froze. Maybe if she just stood still in the archway they wouldn't see her. The whole area was in deep shadow because the sun was almost directly overhead. No problem, she'd just wait a few minutes till they went back inside...

The library door swung ponderously shut behind her and part of its ornate carving poked her sharply in the fanny. She let out a startled squeak and very nearly dropped her books. Heart pounding, she flattened herself against the door, but Adam and Lydia never looked her way. They chatted for a moment, but they were too far away for Ruth to catch what they were saying. She forced herself to stand still. Lydia threw her arms around Adam, and Ruth seized the opportunity to make a swift retreat. She heaved the ridiculous door open again and zipped back into the library. Karleen gave her a questioning look. Ruth put on a smile, waved and quickly pretended that she'd only come back in for a drink of water from the antique fountain in the entryway. After she'd spent about as much time pretending to drink as she thought would look natural, she straightened up, shouldered her book bag and told herself firmly that she was going to walk down those steps no matter what.

All the courage-gathering was for naught, though, because by the time she got outside, the Mercedes was gone and the door to the office building was closed. Adam was nowhere in sight.

◌⃝

Adam sat down at his desk and shuffled some papers for a while, then leaned back in his chair, put his feet up on the desk and folded his hands across his middle. He was expecting some calls, but they weren't anything he really had to be there to answer personally. He had a few errands to run that afternoon and he was feeling lazy, and definitely less pressured without Lydia looking over his shoulder.

He decided to grab a bite to eat at the coffee shop before he got his butt in gear to run his errands—some reports to deliver to a businessman in a neighboring community, a jacket to pick up at the cleaners on the way out of town, groceries to buy and a quick trip to the drugstore to pick up shampoo, toothpaste and a couple of other domestic items he'd need now that he was taking over the apartment upstairs. *Boy, it'll be great to get away from that cheap motel.*

After a few minutes more of drowsy idleness, he got up and stretched, locked the front door, turned on the nightlight and went out the back. The old wooden door stuck and it took a good hard yank to slam it shut. He told himself for about the hundredth time since the renovation was completed that he really ought to get those workmen to come back and fix the damn thing so that it would close properly. He turned to his left and went up the rickety stairs to what he and Lydia laughingly referred to as "The Executive Suite."

His good clothes were still in his garment bag and suitcase, brought over from the motel that morning. *Damn, I should have hung them up to de-wrinkle.* Oh well, he'd just put on his blue sport coat and hope that the wrinkles in his dress shirt weren't too obvious. Adam knew perfectly well how to iron a shirt, but he just wasn't in the mood at the moment. *I don't know where Lydia put the ironing board*, he told himself, as though there were more than just two possible places to look for it.

He slipped out of his running shoes and jeans and pulled his shirt over his head, looking critically at himself in the full-length mirror on the bedroom's closet door. *Time to start working out again,* he thought, patting himself on the stomach. *No more piddling around at the pool, pretending. Wonder if there's a gym somewhere around here besides the one Jodi goes to*? He picked up a pad from the nightstand and wrote himself a note to look into that.

As he drove along the street that formed the south side of the square, he glanced over at Ruth's building on the northwest corner, wondering if she'd be at the band concert. A horn honked behind him; the light had changed. He waved cheerily at the other driver and then turned his full attention to his driving.

☙

Eddie slouched through the door at the usual time. "Hi Uncle Chet, what'll we do today?" His tone of voice implied that he was hoping the answer would be "Nothing, boy, g'wan home."

No such luck. Chet pulled out a stool next to his and said "Today I'm gonna teach you how to fix a TV. Or at least get a start on it. Bumped into Roger at the tavern and he gave me this one. He bought a new one. Said if I could fix this I could keep it, but I got no use for another TV. So I figured I'd show you how one worked. Then if your mom says it's OK you can have it."

"That sounds great." Eddie might have been looking at something putrid stuck to the bottom of his sneaker.

"Don't give me that, or I'll just get you to sweeping floors again. I thought you said you wanted to learn something." Chet's tone was mild enough, but the message was quite clear.

Eddie capitulated. "Yeah." He pulled the stool closer to the bench and leaned his elbow on the newly-cleaned surface. "OK, open it up, Uncle Chet, and show me what to do."

Through all this, Ruth had been being extravagantly diligent about carefully prying an old iPod apart. Amazing just how easy it was to look Real Busy while doing a job like this. She made sure her face was turned away from the other bench when she allowed the grin to break through. And then of course there was the major production number of putting on headphones to see if the iPod was working. Why, a person just couldn't possibly listen to what was going on across the room while she was doing all that. She sneaked a quick peek at the other bench. Chet was pointing with his screwdriver and Eddie was actually leaning close and looking—well, if not exactly interested, at least not as surly and bored as he usually did. Ruth grinned again and turned back to her own task quickly lest one of them turn around and catch her. Eddie was undoubtedly thinking of testing out the TV repair job by using it to watch porn. But at least he was thinking. Things were looking up.

෬෮

Twenty miles to the northeast, Adam shook hands with another young businessman, someone Ted Ross had recommended as a possible partner. "Take some time to look over the proposal," he said, "and give me a call collect if you'd like to talk about it."

"I'll do that, Adam. But I must say I'm surprised how little local backing you've gotten for this deal. I'm not sure you're going to be successful if most of your investors are from outside the community. The project itself may go through, but if you haven't got any local cooperation you may be in trouble."

"I'm being very selective about the people I approach on this, because of the nature of the project. I've mainly stuck with people I know, or people like yourself who come highly recommended." Adam put a pile of papers back into his briefcase and closed it. "I haven't talked to all the potential investors yet. That's why the list seems a little unbalanced."

"Ah, I see," said the other man. "Well, I'm willing to take a chance on it because your proposal looks good. But you're going to have to be very careful about how you go about this. Probably the first thing you should do when things start to move is hire yourself a good PR person and give him or her plenty to do. If you don't get those people behind you, you're looking at a major disaster instead of a major improvement."

Diplomatically, Adam said "I'm sure you're right." Then, looking at his watch, "Well, I mustn't keep you any longer. I appreciate your taking time to meet me today, and I appreciate the advice. I'll get back to you later in the week if anything comes up. And please, be sure to call me any time."

The trip back to Lyric wasn't as pleasant as the trip out. He had to loosen his grip on the steering wheel several times to keep his fingers from cramping up. *Damn. I'm going to have to work on my sales pitch.*

CಚಿO

The shop phone rang and Ruth answered it. "Oh, hi Eleanor, what's up?

"My mom said she'd take the twins tonight. Want to get together for dinner and a movie?"

"Gee, you asking me out on a date?" Both women laughed. "Seriously, El, have you seen what's playing? Yet another teenage stink bomb. How about you come over here and we can chow down on hot dogs or something and rent a couple DVDs?"

"Hey, that sounds like a deal. I'll bring some German potato salad and ice cream, and you go rent the DVDs and pick up the hot dogs and soda, how's that?"

"You going to trust my taste in movies?"

"Sure thing. Because you know if you pick a bad one I'll never let you hear the end of it."

Two hours later Ruth stood in the supermarket perusing packages of hot dogs. Which ones looked like they had the fewest floor sweepings in them, and which wouldn't taste like reconstituted cardboard, and...

She jumped as Adam's voice came from behind her. "Hi Ruth, I see we're both in pursuit of a Cordon Bleu dinner tonight."

"Cordon Bleu hot dogs, now there's a thought." She waited for the momentary flash of adrenaline to die down. "You got any recommendations?"

He looked at the selection. "Mmmm. Not much choice, is there? Hey, how about we both forget the hot dogs and I'll buy us a pizza over at Diamante's?"

"No thanks, Adam, I... uh, I have a date tonight. Maybe some other time."

"Date? That's... uh, that's great! Would it be too nosy for me to ask who is the lucky guy?"

She gave him a sweet smile. "Yes, it would definitely be too nosy. Oh..." she looked at her watch, "I have to run." She scooped up the closest package of hot dogs and tossed it into her basket, praying that the wieners would be at least halfway edible. "Nice to see you, Adam. Bye!"

She scurried off toward the front of the store, leaving him frowning at her back.

CRXEED

The pickup truck was parked rear-end-first in a space at the drive-in. The three young men lounged in the back, ostensibly watching the movie. They had the speaker turned up as loud as it would go. Duane shone a small flashlight on the newspaper in his lap. "Now look here, Aaron, the country club is advertising for an assistant groundskeeper."

"So?" Aaron took a final swig of his beer and flipped the empty can toward the tailgate. It bounced off and rolled across the metal bed of the truck. He lifted the lid on the cooler and rummaged inside.

"So you're gonna apply for the job, buddy boy. Nobody's gonna turn down the mayor's kid."

"*What*?" from Eddie.

"Like hell!" Aaron sat up straight. "No chance! No way am I working as a lawn jockey! Piss off, Duane!"

"Will you shut up! Aaron, if you were any dumber they'd have to lead you around on a leash. You apply for the damn job, you get it, you work with Jack for a while and then you tell him we want to help him in his *other* business, see, stupid?"

"If it's such a good idea, dickhead, why don't *you* do it?"

"Oh yeah, right, like the dweebs at the country club are gonna believe I want to be an assistant groundskeeper. I've never set foot in the place my whole entire life. Sorry boy, it's gotta be you."

"He's got a point there," said Eddie, elbowing Aaron in the side.

Aaron gave Eddie a shove. "You keep out of this, ass-hole."

"Hey, who you calling..."

"Shhhh! Cut it out!" Duane shoved Aaron into Eddie, hard. "You guys don't knock it off, they'll come and throw us outta here!" The young men gave each other a few half-hearted shoves and subsided. "Now listen, Aaron, I know it's just gonna kill you to get off that fat ass of yours and get a job, but once we start making the real money with the weed it ain't gonna matter any more. Just keep that in mind, pinhead."

"Oh yeah, you bet I'll keep it in mind. Because if Jack turns us down, I'm gonna make you eat a bag full of grass clippings blade by blade. You keep *that* in mind."

"Oh yeah, boy, I'm *reeeeally* scared. You just get yourself cleaned up and go on over there and apply and make sure you mention your dad five or six times while you're talking to 'em. Won't kill you to ride around on a mower a couple days a week. Think of it as an investment in your future."

"Eat shit, Duane." Aaron shook up his can of beer and popped the top so it sprayed all over his friends.

⊗

There was a quiet knock on the back door, a pause, then another knock. That was the signal. The lights were already out.

"OK, bring the stuff in and put it downstairs."

"You can put it downstairs your own damn self, since you didn't do any of the work."

"Now look, I *told* you why..."

"I don't want to hear all those damn excuses again. They didn't cut much ice with me the first time around. Just pick up the bag."

"You're an asshole, you know that?"

"Yeah. And I learned everything I know from you. Now get moving. I got things to do tonight and I don't want to hang around this neighborhood any longer than I have to."

"I can't believe I got involved in this. You guys are a bunch of small-time pricks."

"Yeah. And you needed the money. Big time principles don't pay the bills, now do they?"

"You go to hell."

A chuckle in the darkness. "Just pick up the shit and carry it down the stairs."

The Best Laid Plans

On Saturdays Electronic Wizardry's hours were eight to noon. Today, noon couldn't come fast enough to suit anyone. Ruth had burned her hand on her soldering iron right off the bat, absentmindedly reaching to pick it up while trying to figure out what Charlie was chasing along the floor in the back corner. Chet had dropped a jar lid full of microscopic screws. They'd had precisely zero customers all day and two people who'd promised to come in and pick up their appliances never showed.

Ruth had given up on fixing anything and spent most of the morning trying to put the store's accounts in order. She'd gotten about halfway through the receipts when she was startled by the phone ringing—a wrong number, as it turned out—and knocked her little calculator to the floor, where it promptly disappeared into the dust balls under the bookcase. And when she'd finally fished it out, she found the display was cracked and no longer readable.

She gave up and threw the whole mess back in the file cabinet and slammed the drawer shut, and then had to pick up a shower of miscellaneous fasteners that flew from a plastic box that had been set too close to the edge on top. She'd had to count to ten several times while she reminded herself quite firmly that it was not her usual custom to employ that kind of language, really it wasn't.

When she was finally able to close up and head for home it seemed only fitting that the telephone inside the store should start to ring just as the latch on the back door clicked into place. Habit took over. She couldn't ignore a ringing business phone.

Her keys stuck obstinately in her pants pocket lining, and the fact that she was carrying a large cat with her other arm was no help. By the time she wrestled the keys free her hand was sweaty and the keys fell to the sidewalk twice before she finally got the door open. Charlie, affectionate companion that he was, saw a golden opportunity to thank her by leaping out of her arms and twining himself through her feet. It was all she could do to keep from kicking his blissfully purring butt out of her way.

When she finally reached the phone it had quite naturally stopped ringing. But it did draw her attention to the fact that she hadn't turned on the answering machine when she left.

Ruth squeezed her eyes shut and let out a wordless yell. Seething, she kicked the wall, then marched back to the door just in time to catch Charlie climbing up the screen. He'd already gotten halfway to the hole in it when she took the most instinctive course of action—grabbed him by the tail and pulled.

The indignant cat yowled and whipped around to swipe at Ruth's hand. She un-snagged his hind claws from the screen and slammed the wooden door. Charlie flattened his ears and hissed. "All *right*, you stupid cat!" Ruth yelled and dumped him on the floor. Charlie's claws scrabbled briefly on the floorboards as he accelerated. He quickly reached warp speed, zipped under the curtain and disappeared. Ruth leaned wearily against the wall.

She looked at the four parallel scratches across the back of her wrist. They stung. She sighed deeply and went into the tiny bathroom to wash. Patting her hand dry with a paper towel, she caught sight of herself in the mirror and winced. She dampened another paper towel with tepid water and used it to wipe her face. Then she went to make amends with the cat and scooped him up from his perch. When she finally got outside again, she leaned her head against the door as she turned the deadbolt.

A friendly voice came from behind her. "Hi Ruth, didn't think you'd still be down here. Things not going so good today?"

"Oh... Hi Eleanor, no, oh man, it's been one of those days." She shifted the cat to the other shoulder and shook her head, wearily.

"Oh dear, sorry to hear that. Well, hey, here's something that will make you laugh—heard the latest?"

"No, what's up?"

"I forgot to tell you last night. When I was collecting the kids at the pool last Thursday I saw Jodi Diamante rubbing suntan lotion all over Adam Talbott. And I do mean *all*. Fast mover, that girl."

"Really? I was at the pool for a while and I saw Adam but I didn't see Jodi. She must have gotten there after I left."

Eleanor smiled. "Must be nice to be able to take off work in the middle of the day and go swimming."

"I don't know about those two, but Chet and I didn't have enough to keep us busy that day so we closed up early. I figured a swim would do me good. But I ended up not staying very long. That's probably why I missed all the good stuff."

Whatever Eleanor had planned to say was drowned out as the clock in City Hall rattled, wheezed, clanked and finally bonged out the Westminster chimes for the half hour, startling Charlie, who gave it a half-hearted hiss. Ruth looked at her watch. The clock kept its own kind of time, so it was always prudent to double check. "Twelve-thirty already and I have yet to get one damn thing done today. I give up."

Her friend patted her on the shoulder and skritched Charlie. "Spend the rest of the day flaking out. I won't tell. If anyone asks me, I'll say you're inventing perpetual motion or something. Oh—hey, how about we go out to the band concert tonight?"

Ruth considered this. Usually she (and sometimes Eleanor and the kids) watched the Saturday-evening band concerts from her living room window, which had a great view of the square and the bandstand—and easier access to food and cleanup for the twins. But after today—yeah, she needed to get outside. "You know, that's not a bad idea. Shall I meet you down in the square someplace?"

"Yeah, I'll grab us a bench and get the kids to defend it for us. See you around seven, OK?"

⋘⋙

The First Vice President of the Community Bank of Lyric, attired in his birthday suit, bided his time. He kept a careful eye on his unsuspecting prey, junior partner in the law firm of Wallace, Exner, McGreevey and Nakamura. Whistling tunelessly, Ted Ross made a great show of toweling off his hair and looking at his teeth in a small mirror stuck to the inside of his locker door. The prey finally quit drying off his back and put one foot up on the wooden bench, leaning over to dry off his toes. The hunter grabbed his own towel by diagonal corners, whirled it around...

CRACK!

"*Yeeeeowww!*" The victim jumped a foot in the air and grabbed his backside. "Ted, you're *dead meat!*" He whirled his own towel tight as his attacker danced out of sight behind a row of lockers, pointing and laughing his head off.

Adam emerged from the shower just as pursuer and prey (roles now reversed) went streaking by. "Hey Adam, help me *get* this guy!"

"You're doing fine on your own, Craig. Go get 'im!" Adam grinned and sauntered over to the bench and pulled another towel out of his gym bag. There was a flurry of splatting footsteps, a skidding sound, a crash from a row of lockers on the other side of the room and another loud *CRACK!*

"*Yaaaaa!* No fair, no fair! Hit me while I was down!"

"Give up?" This time there came the sound of a wet towel snapping on an empty locker. *THWANNG!*

"Awright, you got me, you got me. Geez, you lawyer types are *so* damn sneaky."

Kyle Hartmann sauntered in, carrying a blue gym bag with KYLE FEED & SEED in white letters on the side. "Hi Adam, how you doing? Those two losers at it again?"

"Hey, hi Kyle, how's it going? Yeah, they're back there smacking each other around. What's the latest?"

"Not much, really. Just brought out a load of grass seed, thought maybe I'd stop and take a swim. But I don't know that I dare drop my drawers with those two running around loose."

Laughter. The two men came back into view, both rubbing their backsides. "See what you've been missing all these years, Adam? A chance to work at the bank and get your behind assaulted by cheap shysters day and night. Hi Kyle!"

"Not to mention being taken to the cleaners by shady bank officers," said Craig Nakamura, punching his friend on the arm. "I still think you cheated on the seventeenth hole."

"Hi Craig, Ted. You guys cheating again?"

"Always, Kyle, always." More laughter.

Adam buttoned his polo shirt, tucked it into his jeans and zipped up. "You guys both beat me by a landslide, so what are you griping about? I told you I was no golfer."

"Yeah, you said it." Ted slipped into his underwear.

"Aww, all you need is practice, Adam. Hey, let's go get some lunch, I'm starving. You wanna come too, Kyle?" Craig pulled a blue and black striped rugby shirt over his head.

"Yeah, sounds good to me." Kyle opened his locker and stuffed his gym bag inside.

Ted zipped up his slacks. "Just like a lawyer to go on out in public wearing nothing but panties and a shirt."

Craig grabbed his towel off the bench and swirled it again and snapped the air.

"Lunch sounds real good to me about now," said Adam hastily to forestall another battle. "Shall we hit the snack bar?"

"Nah, let's go eat in the dining room. They should still be serving. I'm sick of snack bar food."

"Uh... OK."

"Problem?"

"No, no, not at all. Just been a long time since I ate in the dining room, that's all."

"Well, the food hasn't changed a bit; it'll be just like old home week."

"That's what I'm afraid of," Adam muttered as he followed his companions out of the locker room.

∽◌∾

The waitress smiled at Ted and batted her eyelashes. "Hey, whad'ya say, Patti," said Ted, smiling back at her. "I think I'll have a beer and a burger. How'bout you guys?"

Craig agreed, but Adam said "I'll go with the burger, but give me a big glass of iced tea with a couple extra lemon wedges on the side, OK?"

"Iced *tea*?" Craig looked him with exaggerated disbelief.

"What can I say, I'm thirsty." Adam grinned. "And I don't want to spend the rest of the afternoon in the can."

"I'm with Adam on the iced tea, and I want a club sandwich. Unlike some lazy bums of my acquaintance, I do have to go back to work this afternoon." Kyle swatted Ted over the head with the menu.

"Two beers and two iced tea, three burgers and a club sandwich, got it." The waitress sashayed off in the direction of the bar. Ted pushed his chair back slightly and watched her go, only to swing around to face the table again in a hurry as the hostess, a gray-haired woman in a pastel pink blouse and slacks, approached the table.

She arched a brow at Ted from behind her glasses. "Hello, Ted, how's Cindy?"

"Uh... she's fine, thanks, Lynne. Out shopping with her mom this afternoon."

"That's nice. How's Aileen, Craig?"

"Doing fine, thanks." Craig shifted slightly in his chair. "And how are you today, Lynne?"

"Fine, thank you. And it's always nice to see you, Kyle." She turned to Adam. "I don't believe we've met... oh, wait a second, you're... let me think, I'll remember it... Adam, Adam Talbott, right?"

Adam coughed into his napkin. "And here I was so sure no one would remember me after all these years."

"Well, you've grown that mustache, that's what threw me. If you'd tried to sneak in here in a bathing suit I would have known you right away. How are your parents?"

"Uh... they're fine, just fine. Living in Arizona. My dad's retired."

"Arizona? That must be a nice change for them. I remember how your mother's allergies used to bother her." She gave Adam a thoughtful look.

Just then the waitress arrived with the drinks. Adam took his time squeezing the extra lemon into his tea, took a long swallow and put the glass down with a sigh. He looked up. The hostess was still watching him, her expression unreadable. "Oh, uh, yeah, she..." He forced a smile. "She doesn't have allergies any more."

Lynne watched him for a moment. "That's good to hear," she said, and turned and walked away. Adam took another long swallow of his tea.

As the three men were polishing off the last remnants of lunch, Ted waved at someone who'd just entered the room. "Ooo baby," he said *sotto voce*, "look who's here."

Adam's back was to the door, but before he could turn around he felt a hand on his shoulder. "Hi guys," said Jodi. "Kyle, I was just over at the store looking for you and they said you'd come on out here. And as for you two, Ted, Craig, might have known I'd find you out here goofing off instead of doing housework. Adam, are they corrupting you too?"

"Looks like. So Jodi, you come here often?" He grinned. She swatted him on the shoulder playfully.

"Yeah," said Craig, "she comes out here to keep an eye on us for our wives. We always try to give her something juicy to report." He pushed the empty chair at their table back with a foot. "Have a seat, Jodi, and we'll see what we can come up with today. Did you know that Ted here was running around the locker room buck naked for at least half an hour?"

She looked him over. "Oh really? Men's or women's?"

"*You* guess." They all laughed.

"Something specific you wanted at the store, Jodi?" Kyle swirled the ice cubes around in his glass and upended it.

"Um, some of that crushed wood stuff for under the deck. I couldn't remember what kind you gave me the last time and Mel didn't know. No big deal, I can pick it up later."

"OK, I think I know what you're after. Stop back by in an hour or so and I'll get it for you."

"So Adam," Jodi said, leaning forward on an elbow and giving the assembled multitude a glimpse down her shirt, "how did the golf game go?"

"If I'd been playing basketball it would have been a very respectable score."

Ted pushed his chair out a bit and tilted it on its back legs. "We're going to keep dragging him out here till he gets the idea. Or until we clean him out of every last dime, which is what we hope comes first."

Adam looked solemn and started counting on his fingers. "Well, let's see, at the current balance in my checkbook... My God, we'll be playing every Saturday till 2253."

"Modest, isn't he?" Craig turned to Jodi. "Once we clean him out I think I'll buy a yacht."

Jodi whooped with laughter. "And sail it in the bath-tub!"

Craig slapped a hand on the table. "I *knew* I was for-getting something. Hey Ted, check that out!" He pointed.

As soon as Ted turned to look, Craig slipped a foot behind the legs of the tilted chair and shoved. Ted's arms flailed wildly and his feet came up under the table with a crash that sent cutlery flying and tipped over Adam's nearly empty iced tea glass. The legs of the chair slid smartly under the table and Ted went down on his back with a whump. He lay there limp, eyes closed.

Adam jumped to his feet and backed up clear to the next table, stopped only by running into the table's edge. Kyle got up slowly and watched as Jodi ran around the table and stood beside Ted, hands clasped over her mouth. Two waiters and the busboy came running. Craig knelt down by Ted's limp form and patted him on the face uncertainly. "Ted? Ted? Ted?? C'mon Ted, say something!"

Like a striking snake, Ted's hand came up and grabbed Craig by the front of his shirt. "Now who's the dead duck, Nakamura? I'm gonna *sue* you!" He burst out laughing and rolled over, pulling his friend with him.

"Oh ho ho, you forget who's the lawyer around here!"

As the two men wrestled on the floor, laughing and trying to poke each other, Adam went back to the table and started setting it to rights. His face was very pale. He picked up Ted's chair and pushed it back into place. The dining room staff was yelling at the combatants to break it up, knock it off, quit horsing around. Kyle sat down again and polished off the last bite of his sandwich. Jodi backed out of the path of the scuffle and laughed and laughed and laughed.

Adam patted her on the shoulder. "Listen, when those two come to their senses would you tell them I had to run? I've got a whole list of stuff I have to do this afternoon."

The two men were getting to their feet, swatting at each other playfully and dusting themselves off. "You can tell them yourself, I think." Jodi grinned at the warriors. "I'm leaving now, boys, and you can bet I'm burning up the phone lines as soon as I get out the door. If you know what's good for you, you'd better run. Kyle, I'll see you at the store in an hour." She sauntered off toward the door, flipping open her phone.

The hostess came steaming in from the other room with three more waiters in tow, her face furious. "You two horses' heinies get out of here and don't come back! Go on now, *get out!*" she shouted, pointing at the door.

The two men made a great show of slinking away, elbowing each other. Adam shook his head and used a napkin from the table to wipe his face. Behind him, the busboy was picking up silverware, muttering.

"Say, Adam," said Kyle, as they walked toward the parking lot, "did I hear right, you're planning on making some substantial investments around here?"

"Uh... something like that, yeah. Mind my asking where you heard about it?"

"Craig came in to get some weed killer yesterday and I kidded him about spending more on his lawn than he did on law school, and he said that he had a line on something good. Didn't mention any specifics, though, if that's what's worrying you. You got a few minutes to talk? I came into a little money a year or so ago and I've been looking at a lot of possibilities for investing it but haven't decided on anything yet. Would you be interested in another investor?"

Adam rubbed his face thoughtfully. "It's all in the planning stages now. We're trying to line up some partners. If you're interested, I've got an information packet. You could stop by the office any time and we can talk about it and I'll show you what I've got."

"I'll do that. The bank sure isn't paying diddly in interest these days. I'd like to put the money to some real use."

"Well, that's what we have in mind." He pulled out a business card. "Give me a call any time, just to make sure I'm actually in the office, and then stop on by. I think this'll interest you."

"Sounds great." Kyle put the card in his pocket. "Well, I better mosey on back to the store, make sure Jodi gets her shredded stuff for under the deck." He rolled his eyes.

"Right. Look forward to seeing you."

As Adam reached his car he looked back and saw Lynne watching him through the plate glass window. She met his gaze steadily and then turned away.

osto

Ruth's favorite spot on breezy summer afternoons was the fire escape at the rear of the building, an ancient structure that made a tiny balcony beneath her bedroom windows. Underneath the bathroom window, stairs led from the platform to a complicated mechanism that was supposed to fold down to ground level should she ever have to use the fire escape for its intended purpose.

Fresh from the shower, she slipped into one of her oversized t-shirts and a pair of shorts and opened one of the bedroom's back windows all the way, unlocking the heavy protective screen so she could climb out. The screen latch seemed unusually stiff; she made a mental note to put some graphite on it later. Stepping through the window, she let the screen swing back into place.

An old seat cushion from a lawn chair was on its edge against the wall, and several plants in terra-cotta pots hung from the railing and screened her view of the dusty alley. Ruth laid the cushion on the metal bars, sat down and leaned back against the warm bricks. She fluffed up her hair so it would finish drying. Here on the north side of the building there was no direct sunlight at this time of day and the breeze was better than any hair dryer. She smiled and closed her eyes.

The phone rang. And she'd turned the answering machine off. With a sigh, she got to her feet and went to open the screen. It wouldn't budge. "What the..." She pulled harder, but the screen was firmly latched. She rat-tled the metal frame and smacked it with the palm of her hand as the phone continued to ring and ring and ring in-side. Kicking the wall in frustration just hurt her toes.

Well, now what? She gave the fire escape stairs and the folding mechanism the fish eye and drummed her fin-gers on her leg. The phone kept ringing. Whether she an-swered it or not, there was only one way off the balcony and she was looking at it.

She put a cautious foot on the top step and ever so slowly shifted her weight. So far so good. Inch by inch, step by step, clutching at the railing for support, she worked her way down, then took a deep breath and stepped onto the folding part. This was where it was sup-posed to do its thing. She hung onto the bars and waited. Nothing happened. *Oh great.* She bounced up and down on the mechanism, fully expecting yet more Nothing to continue to happen.

With an ear-splitting, rust-rendering shriek, the hinges crackled into action and Ruth was thrown off bal-ance, almost lost her grip and clutched wildly at the bars. Slowly, protesting noisily all the way, the stairs folded downwards with Ruth hanging on for dear life near the top. A shower of rust particles fell on her and she blinked frantically, shook her head and sneezed. The stairs hit bot-tom with a resounding thud that nearly knocked her off her perch. It took a moment for her to gather courage; then, knees shaking so that she could barely get her feet from one step to the next, she scurried down rear-end-first. She reached the ground before she was ready for it and staggered backwards, landing on her fanny in the dirt just as the stairs slowly and noisily began to fold them-selves back up again.

Temporarily immobilized, Ruth sat on the ground and watched. After a moment she realized that her mouth was open and quickly shut it. The stairs reached their normal position and screeched into place, quivering and dropping flakes of rust. The plants on the balcony rattled and several dead leaves fell off. Finally all was quiet again. Ruth shook her head and got unsteadily to her feet. Her hands were covered with dirt. She looked at them for a moment and shrugged, then brushed them together to get at least some of it off. Well, now at least she knew the stupid fire escape worked.

She shot a glare at the treacherous mechanism and turned to go around the corner and up the main stairs to her front door. A flake of rust dropped from her hair onto her nose. She brushed it away and two more fell. *Oh geez...* She leaned over and shook her hair like a wet dog. Dirty brown particles flew everywhere. She growled in frustration.

At least her front door wasn't locked. She gave the now-silent telephone a murderous look and punched the switch on the answering machine. In the bedroom mirror she surveyed her rust-covered, dirt-streaked shirt, shorts, face, hair, hands, feet...

Ruth let out a wail of complete and utter misery, pulled her clothes off, heaved them into the laundry hamper and stomped off into the bathroom.

When she emerged she toweled herself reasonably dry and did the absolute bare minimum to get her hair untangled. Then she turned on the box fan and threw herself on the bed. Within a few minutes her breathing evened out and she drifted off to sleep.

CgED

Adam crossed the center of the square with a bag from the hardware store scrunched into one hand. Someone from the city maintenance department was sweeping the floor in the bandstand. A large metal cart filled with folding chairs stood at the foot of its stairs. Yeah, the band concert might actually be a good way to spend the evening, even on a bench with Jodi. He needed a break.

But first, more than anything he needed a nap. The day at the country club had tired him more than he realized. He crossed the street at the south-center of the square, turned left, looked up at the bank clock as he walked under it and checked it against his watch. Four-fifteen. He had time for a nap, a shower and dinner somewhere. Tomorrow he'd stock up the apartment kitchen. It'd be good to get away from restaurant food.

He trudged up the rickety old stairs to his apartment. What a treat not to have to drive back to that godawful motel! He tossed the bag onto the kitchen table and turned down the thermostat on the window air conditioners in the living room and bedroom. Then he peeled off his shirt and slacks, set his alarm to wake him in an hour, stretched out on the bed and closed his eyes.

ᏣᏍᏋᎧ

Jodi put down the phone and scribbled a note to herself on the pad beside it. After stubbing out her cigarette in an already overflowing ashtray, she stretched languidly, her bare legs making faint squeaking noises against the leather cushions on the couch. The breeze from the air conditioning duct quickly dispersed the last of the smoke.

She looked at the wall clock, a large golden starburst on the paneling. Five-thirty. Plenty of time, she thought, to take a nice long bubble bath with that gorgeous scented stuff she'd just ordered from Marshall Field's. She held out one hand, then the other and squinted at the nails critically. What outfit would go best with hot pink polish?

She aimed the remote control at the flat screen TV that took up most of one wall and snapped off the baseball game that had been playing at low volume. One of these days she'd break the habit of automatically turning on the ball games on Saturday afternoons. Sonny was long gone and she could un-learn a lot. She dropped the remote control next to the ashtray on the glass-topped coffee table and yawned. Probably be a good idea to get a cup of coffee before she started the bath or she'd fall asleep in it for sure. She swung her bare feet off the couch and sat up and stretched again.

In the kitchen she started the coffeemaker and then took inventory of the essential supplies. Did she have enough liquor on hand? Or did Adam drink beer? Maybe she should pick up a six-pack. There were several un-opened bags of chips in the pantry and half a jar of salsa in the refrigerator next to four cans of Diet Mountain Dew. She bit her lip and considered. Oh hell, it would have to do. With any luck at all there wouldn't be much time for munchies. She picked up the Kyle Feed & Seed bag from the counter by the back door and took it down to the basement.

As she sipped her coffee she decided to skip the bath and just take a quick shower. The perfume that matched the bath oil would do well enough. Then she'd have that much more time to clean the place up, get a few scented candles and some 40-watt light bulbs. She fished another scrap of paper and a pen out of a basket on the counter and started making a list.

The Boys and the Band

Ruth struggled blearily back to consciousness, not sure at first if it was morning or night. The City Hall clock was whanging out the last of the chimes for the quarter-hour. After a few foggy moments, enough light dawned in her brain to allow her to correlate the digits on her clock with the chimes: 6:15 PM. She stretched, swung her feet over onto the floor, stood unsteadily up and yawned.

Her reflection in the mirror stopped her in midgape. Her hair, *oh noooooo!* Some of it had dried in crinkles, some was still damp and stringy, and a section over her left ear looked like a furry earmuff. "Ooooaaaaahhhhhrrr," she said, and wearily laid her head on her arms on top of the dresser.

Maybe she'd just go back to bed and forget the whole thing. Maybe she'd just park in a chair all night and read her new library books. Maybe she'd just put a hat on and make a quick trip to the video store. Maybe she'd just run away from home.

Awww, the hell with it. One way or the other, she was going to have to get dressed.

She stood in the closet doorway and considered, grumpily. Finally she pulled out a gauzy full-skirted sundress with a pattern of pink and fuchsia flowers on a faded black background. She hadn't worn it since she couldn't remember when. It was way more than she usually got dressed up for band concerts, or for most other occasions for that matter, but maybe if she put on something a little higher up the sartorial ladder it would make her feel better. Maybe. She looked the dress over to make sure it wasn't too wrinkled and tossed it onto the bed. And then she dug out her wide-toothed comb, gritted her own teeth and got to work on her hair. After about five minutes of yanking and pulling and swearing she conceded defeat, bowed to the inevitable, filled the sink with warm water and dunked her head.

Wrapping the dripping mess up in a towel-turban, she glared at her reflection. Why she'd ever agreed to leave her nice apartment and her nice comfy chair and her nice library books to go to some miserable, stupid, boring old band concert...

Fifteen minutes later, dressed, hair damp but detangled and wrapped up in a bandana, munching on the last of a tuna sandwich, she looked out her front window at the center of the square. Everything was bathed in a warm golden glow from the western sky. Most of the benches were occupied already and there were plenty of blankets spread here and there on the grass. Some of the band members were setting up in the bandstand. She spotted a couple of friends making their way across the street. Well, maybe the evening wasn't going to be a total loss after all. Maybe.

She finished the sandwich, dealt with her hair, kicked into her sandals and got her Mexican embroidered shawl from the closet. Most of the band was beginning to honk and tootle as she made her way down the stairs.

A warm, faintly popcorn-scented breeze lifted her full skirt slightly as she crossed the street. There was a hum of conversation across the square, the occasional snap and hiss of a soft drink can being opened, and the tinny babble of portable radios and too-loud earbuds. Looking around for Eleanor, she spotted Jodi on a bench on the west side, sitting beside a huge black and white tote bag that took up more bench real estate than she did. And, unlike the casual t-shirt-and-sneakers masses, Jodi had chosen to wear a slinky hot pink jumpsuit that looked like it had been sprayed on. She'd also acquired a long red cigarette holder to wave in the air as she talked to a group of men standing beside her.

"Ruth! Ruth! Over here!" Eleanor waved both hands. She'd managed to snag one of the better benches, on the south side, not too close to the bandstand. Ruth waved back and hurried to join her. Eleanor's ten-year-old twins were not in evidence, although their jackets had been dumped on the bench next to their mother.

Ruth looked around. "Where's the kids?"

"Didn't you know? Once kids finish the fourth grade they follow the Official Kid Rules of Etiquette—don't go anywhere near your mom in public, but make sure she wears something you approve of even though you're not going to be caught dead in her vicinity. You should have heard those two when I put on this shirt." She brushed at the vivid picture of a tree frog on the front of her green t-shirt. "But I held to my principles, see?" She swung around to show off a yellow bandana holding her dark brown, waist-length hair in a ponytail. "A mom's gotta do what a mom's gotta do."

Ruth chuckled. "So are they hiding out or what?"

Eleanor waved a hand vaguely in the direction of the north side of the square. "They're over there somewhere—you'll probably hear them yelling when the music gets quiet. Hey, that dress looks great. I was starting to think you were going to chicken out." She leaned over to stuff the jackets under the bench next to a neatly folded blanket.

"Well, after I fell off the fire escape I almost did. But I figured you'd come looking for me."

Eleanor sat bolt upright. "You *what*? Fell off the *fire* escape? Are you all right?"

"I'm fine. I didn't really fall off—I locked myself out. That stupid screen latch broke or something and I couldn't get it open. I found out that the folding thingamajig on the stairs works, though."

"Honestly, leave you alone for a minute and..." She waved at someone behind Ruth. Kyle appeared, holding a large Kyle Feed & Seed paper bag.

"Hi ladies, got something here for ya." He dug into the bag and produced two smaller bags filled with hot popcorn. "Check this out and tell me what you think."

Ruth sampled, munched, smiled. "Wow, this is really good! Some special kind of popcorn?" It had a delicate, almost sweet taste and virtually no hull.

"Brand new in the store this week. I got some in for seed and I'm passing out free samples to help convince people to buy it."

Eleanor stopped munching long enough to laugh. "Oh really? You want Ruth to maybe plant some in the alley? It is tasty, though."

"For you ladies I'll make an exception on the planting. All you have to do is tell all your gardening friends to buy some, how's that?"

"Mmmm," said Ruth with her mouth full, "you got a deal. And if you have any more of just the popcorn for sale I'll buy some. This stuff is great."

"A man can't ask more than that."

Eleanor patted the bench. "Want to join us for the concert?"

"Maybe later, OK? I want to pass these around while they're still hot."

"Drat, and here we were hoping to get that bag all to ourselves..." Her voice trailed off as the conductor mounted the steps to the bandstand and the audience began to applaud. Kyle gave a quick thumbs-up and scooted off toward the east side of the square. Ruth hurried to sit down as Eleanor slid to the middle of the bench.

The band members made a great show of rustling papers, adjusting music stands, shuffling feet and ostentatiously getting themselves Ready to Perform. The conductor turned to the crowd and smiled, then blew into the microphone. He flipped the switch on and blew again. Windows rattled.

Ruth shot him an industrial strength glare and rubbed her ear. "Yeeeow. Can't he think of some other way to test that damn thing?"

"You'd rather he ask a trumpet player to come up and give us a blast?"

Oblivious to Ruth's disapproval, the conductor leaned in close to the microphone. His voice echoed off building fronts all around the square. "Ladies and gentlemen, good evening. Thank you all for coming tonight. I think we have a wonderful program picked out for to-night's concert and I'm sure you'll enjoy it."

He fumbled the switch off again, faced the podium and lifted his baton. "He says the same damn thing every week," Ruth grumped.

Eleanor poked her with an elbow. "If you're going to sit here and fuss I'm going to put the blanket over your head, I swear."

The musicians grew silent. The audience got some-what quieter, with only a few children's voices heard here and there. Ruth leaned back against the warm wood of the bench.

The baton came down with a mighty swing and the band launched into "The Light Horse Cavalry." A group of children sitting behind Ruth and Eleanor laughed delight-edly and began to sing along. Some of them galloped around the benches, shouting "Giddyup!" with each clash of the cymbals. A warm breeze ruffled Ruth's hair. She found herself nodding her head in time to the music. When the piece ended she joined agreeably in the ap-plause. Well, maybe this wasn't going to be so bad after all.

As the band members shuffled their sheet music El-eanor leaned over against Ruth's shoulder. "Did you see you-know-who over there?" She inclined her head in Jodi's direction. Ruth leaned forward slightly and looked past her friend at Jodi, whose group of admirers had now dwindled to two, both sitting on a blanket on the grass to her right.

Ruth laughed. "Yeah, I saw her when I was looking for you. I just wonder who she's saving that seat for—some poor sucker who wants two bags on a bench, right? ... Oh, I shouldn't be so catty. This is too nice a night."

"Uh huh. Get a load of that cig holder! Oh, *tres* vamp. She'll be lucky if she doesn't put someone's eye out with it or burn them right on the zipper." Eleanor chuckled. "That'd sure be worth the price of admission. Oh, here we go." The conductor lifted his baton again.

The next piece was Scott Joplin's "Entertainer," in an arrangement with plenty of oompahs. The two tuba players in the back row were having a wonderful time; the light winked off the rims of their instruments as they swung back and forth. More children began to run through the audience. Ruth tapped her foot in time to the music and watched the conductor, whose ornately decorated "Music Man" hat wiggled a bit with each flourish of the baton.

As the audience applauded the end of the piece, a large, long-haired, exceedingly frisky dog raced across the grass in front of Eleanor and Ruth and off toward the east side of the square with three children in hot pursuit. The two women turned to watch the chase and both spotted something far more interesting at the same time. Eleanor put her hand on Ruth's arm at the exact moment that Ruth whipped her head back to stare at the bandstand as though her life depended on it.

"Oh ho, here comes Big Deal Adam," murmured Eleanor, just as the band struck up "Hey, Look Me Over." "Are they playing his song, or what?"

To keep staring at the bandstand after she'd obviously seen him would look pretty stupid. Ruth turned reluctantly to wave hello. Adam wore body-hugging jeans and a faded short-sleeved blue chambray work shirt unbuttoned halfway down, with a black cotton crew-neck t-shirt underneath. Years ago she'd told him how good she thought that combination looked. It still did. A familiar, traitorous electric feeling rippled softly down her back. The band segued smoothly into another well-known show tune, but it might as well have been solid static for all Ruth could hear of it. Adam moved up close so he wouldn't have to shout over the music.

"Hello, Ruth. Hi, ah..." Adam's voice trailed off. Ruth smiled up at him and hoped she didn't look as phony as she felt.

Eleanor laughed. "Somehow I just *knew* you would-n't remember me, Adam. I should have hit you in the head with a rubber stopper when I had the chance back in chem class."

"Oh, that's right, you sat behind me. I remember now. I was usually in a fog in chem class anyway, Elea-nor... Eleanor Ward, wasn't it?"

"Still is."

"Uh, well, you know how it is, you just can't do too much thinking when the class is right after lunch and the teacher is as boring as old Whoozie-whoo... *Yaaah!*" Adam smacked the back of his left leg and then looked at his hand as Eleanor's daughter screeched to a halt in front of the bench. Her honey-blonde hair was coming loose from its ponytail and there was a suspicious-looking smear of something dark red across the front of her bright yellow t-shirt and down one leg of her jeans.

She stamped one shredded sneaker. "Mom! An-drew's got my squirt gun and he won't give it back!"

"Rachel, hush! People are trying to hear the music."

Her brother, armed with one green and one orange squirt gun, appeared from behind Adam. "Sorry mister, I wasn't aiming at you, I was aiming at *her* and she *moved*. Mom, she squirted me first!" He stuck out his tongue at his sister. A large wet patch in the middle of his matching yellow t-shirt proved his point.

"Andrew, you give me both guns, right now, and the two of you settle down." Eleanor held up a hand to stifle the stereo wail of protest. "And turn that hat around. The whole purpose of wearing a baseball cap is to have the brim in the front, and I don't care *what* the other boys are doing." She waited. Andrew glared at her, but even a fashion-conscious ten-year-old knew when appeasement was in order. He put up one grubby hand, lifted the cap off his damp hair and turned the brim to face front.

"Much better," said his mother, ignoring the glare. "Rachel, fix your hair." Her daughter reached back and pulled out on both sides of her ponytail so the scrunchie slid up toward the nape of her neck. "Now, you two go find something better to do. And I mean *now*!" The twins took off. As Andrew disappeared behind the bandstand his hand went up toward his cap.

Applause rippled as the band prepared to play the next number. Adam had moved a bit closer to Ruth's side of the bench during his investigation of the wet spot on the back of his pants; a trace of his aftershave came to Ruth on the breeze. What had the stuff been called, anyway? She'd given him a bottle of it for Christmas... Oh yes, "Canoe." Amazing that he was still wearing the same scent after all these years. Why hadn't she noticed it before? She glanced up at him, only to find that he'd stopped wiping at his pants leg and was looking over her head at something off to her left.

"Oh boy, you've done it now, Adam," Eleanor said in a mock-sarcastic tone. Ruth looked over to see Jodi standing up by her bench, dancing on her toes and waving.

"Guess I can't get away with pretending I didn't see her, can I." He gave Jodi a half-hearted wave. "I'll go see what she wants. Can I come back and join you two afterwards?"

The band struck up "Frankie and Johnny." "How appropriate," said Eleanor. "Oh sure, you can come back here if she lets you go in time, and if Kyle hasn't filled up the rest of the bench by then. Right, Ruth?"

Ruth made herself smile. "Right."

"I always did want to beat Kyle's time," Adam joked. "Back in a few." He sauntered off across the grass. The large dark splat and dribble-mark on the back of his left thigh showed up clearly.

"Twins one, sartorial elegance zero," said Eleanor in her best imitation Joan Rivers voice.

"Eleanorrrrrr..."

Eleanor knew Ruth didn't mean the fashion commentary. "Come on, Ruthie, you know she's not going to get her meathooks out of him before the concert's over. And he's probably safer over there than he would be here with the twins." She put the squirt guns under the bench. "Let the poor man hope."

"Yeah, you're right. She'll probably be sitting on his lap in a minute or two, and he'll never get off that bench alive." Ruth giggled. "Headline in tomorrow's paper: MAN PINNED TO PARK BENCH BY FACE-SUCKING BIMBO."

"Ruthie!" Eleanor gasped, laughing. "You're terrible!" She swatted Ruth playfully on the arm. The two women watched as Jodi sat back down, put her tote bag on the ground and patted the bench. "Five bucks says he sits."

"No bet."

Adam had stopped to talk to the men who sat by Jodi's bench and apparently had not noticed the invitation. Jodi leaned over and patted Adam on the leg, got his immediate attention and patted the bench again. He sat. She moved in closer. The band finished and the audience applauded.

"Awww, you should have bet."

"Not a chance," said Ruth. "I never bet on sure losers."

The band rustled music again, shifted in their chairs, cleaned their instruments and prepared for the next number. The conductor coughed, looking at the musicians till they settled down. Then he apparently felt safe in tapping his baton on the podium. With a huge flourish of the baton and a resounding crash, the band launched into one of its showpiece numbers, "The William Tell Overture." People whooped and whistled, and all around the square the children started running through the crowd, galloping in time to the music. Ruth and Eleanor leaned closer together and waved their hands, beating time.

The conductor was really giving it his all and his hat's position became ever more precarious. The twins whizzed by in a crowd of kids yelling "Hiyo Silver!" Ruth laughed out loud. Sometimes, just sometimes, life worked out right.

The street lights began to wink on around the square as the music crescendoed. Another group of kids galloped by. At the end of the piece there was thunderous applause, and the conductor gestured to the band members to stand up and take a bow. Then he bowed in turn and his hat finally fell off and rolled down the steps. The audience whooped as a small boy grabbed the hat and returned it to the conductor, who waved it in the air.

"Thank you, thank you everyone." His amplified voice echoed from the buildings again. "We're going to take a little intermission now, and we hope the second half of the concert will please you as much as the first."

Eleanor nudged Ruth in the ribs. "I wonder if he planned that hat thing?"

"Probably. I think that's his grandson who picked it up."

The band members put their instruments down. Some left the bandstand; some just stood and stretched a bit. Andrew and Rachel came racing up. "Mom, can we have some money for ice cream? Please? Can we, please? Everyone's going over to the drugstore for ice cream, can we go, please?"

"Calm down, you two. Let me see if I've got any money to give you." Eleanor dug under the bench for her purse. After a brief excavation inside it she came up with four bedraggled dollar bills. "This is all I've got, so it better be enough."

"Thanks mom! Thanks!" chorused the twins, grabbing the bills and racing off toward their friends.

"See what having kids does for you, Ruthie? Old and broke in one fell swoop."

Ruth laughed. "You're not old, Eleanor. And I bet I'm just as broke as you are, and I've got two years to go to catch up, and no kids to put the blame on."

"Well, I'll tell you something. If you ever get a craving for children, I know two used ten-year-olds who'd be available, cheap."

∞

Jodi hadn't left Adam any too much room on the bench and half of his backside was already sliding off. He shifted sideways so he could brace himself with his right foot. Which put him in even closer contact with Jodi—who immediately leaned in and patted him on the leg again. "So Adam, is this like you remembered it? A good old-fashioned Lyric band concert?"

"Seems to be pretty much the same. I'm surprised they haven't played any Sousa marches yet."

"Oh, they probably will. And if they don't this week, they will next week. Guess that means you'll have to keep coming to the concerts till you hear some, right?"

"Right. Can't live without old J. P. So, do you go to all the concerts, Jodi?" He shifted again, hoping he could find a way to move over just a bit and get comfortable without Jodi's getting the wrong idea.

"Oh, I guess. It's about the only social life there is in this hick town."

Adam made a noncommittal sound and looked around at the crowd in the square, trying to pick out familiar faces. Bits and pieces of old memories were beginning to come back to him. Still the same, but yet not the same...

"Hey, lucky you, I have exactly four bags of popcorn left." Kyle sat down on the other side of Jodi. "Here ya go, Adam, Frank, Carter, try this."

"Thanks, Kyle." Adam dug gratefully into the popcorn and passed two bags to the men on the grass. "Hey, this stuff's good. You selling it?"

"Mostly for planting. I tried to pass out a sample to every farmer and gardener on the square. Hey Jodi, how'bout you recycle this bag for me?"

148

She waved a hand at him, munching. He folded the bag and stuffed it into her tote.

The conversation on and around the bench lapsed as everyone chowed down on the popcorn. Kyle leaned back, stretched his legs out in front of him and closed his eyes. After a few minutes Jodi crumpled up her popcorn bag. "Well, why don't you guys talk about something?"

"Like what, Jodi?" said the man sitting beside Adam, brushing popcorn fragments off his chin. His companion got up, brushed the seat of his shorts with his hands and headed off in the direction of the water fountain.

"Oh geez, Frank, I don't know." She dropped the bag on the ground and made a great production out of digging a cigarette out of her tote and fitting it into her long red holder. "*You* decide." She waved the cigarette around expectantly and nudged Adam with her elbow as if by chance. He held up his hands and shrugged—no lighter. She cleared her throat and leaned over.

Frank produced a lighter, got up and lit the cigarette. As long as he was up, he stretched and took the opportunity to brush popcorn off his shirt. Jodi inhaled deeply and then exhaled with a sigh. "Well, come on, guys, there must be *something* we can talk about on a nice night like this, before the band starts making noise again."

Adam coughed. "Jodi, can you scoot over just a little bit? My butt is getting numb here." She laughed and scooted, all of about two inches. He re-settled, taking what he could get. "Actually, I can't stay here for the whole concert. There are a couple other people I promised to talk with tonight, and I see that some of them are here." Not really a fib; he looked over at where Ruth and Eleanor were sitting.

"Oh come on, you can catch them after the concert. Just stay here for a while and relax. Enjoy the social life of Bee-you-tee-ful Downtown Lyric. Besides, who on earth wants to talk business on a Saturday night?"

Adam grinned. "Well, Kyle just did. Of course he had the popcorn to distract people with."

"Works every time," said Kyle, opening his eyes and fanning at Jodi with one hand. "Jodi, do you have to suck on that thing?"

She glared at him. "As a matter of fact, yes I do."

"Well, in that case, I'm going to move along. I get enough air pollution making deliveries to pig farmers."

Jodi inhaled deeply and blew a cloud of smoke his way. "Buzz off, Kyle."

He was already on his way, waggling his fanny in her direction. Adam looked enviously at him as he headed toward where Ruth and Eleanor were sitting.

Jodi shifted over slightly toward the empty side of the bench, muttering. "Damn self-righteous..."

Adam turned quickly to his right. "So, Frank, what's the football season going to look like for L.H.S. this year?"

"Pretty good, actually..." and the men got started on an animated discussion of football prospects that left Jodi drumming her fingernails on the back of the bench in disgust.

Across the square, Jodi's irritation hadn't gone unnoticed. Eleanor watched the group around the bench with undisguised amusement and began a running commentary. Ruth did her best to pretend not to watch, but with Eleanor's animated and funny play-by-play description of the action it was difficult not to sneak a peek now and again. Eleanor's description of the cigarette-lighting maneuver made her laugh out loud. Kyle arrived, grinning.

"Join you happy ladies?"

"Oh, sure thing, Kyle. I see you got out while the getting was good." Eleanor patted the bench. Kyle sat, took an exaggerated deep breath and let it out with a huge sigh.

"Yeah, the air sure smells better over here." He chuckled. "I pity poor Adam, though. She's gonna smoke-bomb him right off that bench if he doesn't make a break for it soon."

The band members began to file back up onto the bandstand. The conductor strolled across the street, a cup of coffee still in his hand. He stopped to talk with someone in the audience as two tardy band members scurried up the steps and threaded their way through the chairs to their places.

Finally, with a few last-minute shuffles and shifts, the band took up its instruments and prepared to start the second half of the concert. The conductor looked up, hastily tossed his empty cup into a wastebasket and dashed back up the steps. After a quick head count he faced the audience, blew into the microphone, turned it on and announced that the band would begin with a medley of Strauss waltzes. The crowd quieted down as groups of wandering children found their seats again.

Not to be diverted by Strauss or anyone else, Eleanor and Kyle began a stage-whispered commentary on the group around Jodi's bench. "Oooh, Ruth," said Eleanor, patting Ruth on the arm, "she's moving in. She's got her arm on the bench behind his back. Hey Kyle, remember when you used to do that in the balcony at the movies? She's going to make her move any old time now."

"Who, me? I never made a move. Really I didn't. I'm innocent."

Eleanor swatted him lightly on the leg. "Oh sure. Innocent, my left rear foot! You probably taught Jodi everything she knows."

Kyle made a great show of gagging, wiping his mouth and holding his throat.

Ruth glared at her friends. "Hush, you two! I want to hear the music."

"Sure you do. Oh, now she's stepping on her cigarette. Can't make a move when you're sucking on one of those things. And now," said Eleanor *sotto voce* in her best sports-announcer voice, "ladies and gentlemen, she's moving in for the kill."

Ruth risked a look. Jodi had put her arm around Adam and was snuggled up against him, her cheek resting on his shoulder. Adam was sitting rather stiffly and looking straight at the bandstand. Ruth snorted and turned back to watch the band.

"She's *made* her move, ladies and gentlemen," Eleanor continued with whispered animation. "Yes, he's looking at *her* now, and, just a minute, sports fans, she's patting him on the leg! Is this the action we've all been waiting for?"

Ruth gritted her teeth. "Eleanor, for goodness sake, will you hush!"

"Why no, sports fans," Kyle joined in, "he must be wearing his hockey pads under those jeans because he's not moving an inch. That leg must be numb, ladies and gentlemen. We'll have to get an interview with Mr. Talbott after the game is over and find out the secret of his incredible stamina."

The band finished the waltz medley and there was a flurry of applause from the audience.

"Sports fans, my descriptive skills strain at the task of doing justice to this trip to the pre-bedroom ballet. You should watch for yourself; you'll see how funny it is." He leaned forward to look at Ruth, who was sitting stiffly, holding her shawl tightly around her. "Or maybe not."

Jodi took her pack of cigarettes out of her bag, tapped another one out and fitted it into the long red lacquered holder. No one seemed to notice. She waved the holder around and batted her eyelashes at her companions, neither of whom was looking in her direction. She shrugged, put the cigarette and holder down on the bench beside her and dug in the tote bag again, then leaned forward to speak to the man sitting on the blanket. There was a brief negotiation; he got up; she handed him something and he smiled and walked off in the direction of the coffee shop.

"She's sending out for reinforcements, Ruthie," Eleanor chuckled. The band began to play again, selections from *South Pacific*.

"Either that or getting rid of the competition. Poor Adam. I pity that guy." Kyle laughed. "What am I saying? I don't pity that sucker one little bit!" He let his head drop back and looked up at the rapidly darkening sky with a big grin.

Jodi leaned in closer to Adam, resting her head against his shoulder and her hand on his arm. Adam patted the hand absently and kept his eyes on the band.

Across the square the gesture hadn't gone unnoticed. As Adam shifted slightly on the bench he found himself looking right into Eleanor's eyes just as Jodi's pink fingernails made their way slowly up to his shirt collar. Eleanor gave him a wink and then ostentatiously looked away. He shrugged; Jodi looked up at him, curious. He smiled at her and turned his attention firmly back to the band.

After a minute or two, the music ended and the crowd applauded again. The sky was almost completely dark now and the breeze was noticeably cooler. The children were getting tired and returning to their parents; the noise level in the square was beginning to diminish.

"Well, whatever she sent him out for, he's back," said Eleanor as Jodi's companion returned with two large paper cups. He handed one to Jodi and then sat down on the bench beside her, apparently carrying on an animated discussion.

The conductor turned to the audience. "Ladies and gentlemen, for our final selection tonight we will feature a medley of love songs from great romantic movies from days gone by. I'm sure you'll recognize these beautiful tunes, and we all hope you enjoy them. Thank you for joining us here tonight." A wave of applause and whistles swept over the audience as he turned to face the band again. He lifted his baton; the musicians settled themselves. They struck up "Charade."

Ruth hummed along with the music. The song had been one of her favorites since junior high, when the chorus had sung it.

"Talk about charades, you should get a load of what's going on over there," said Eleanor, nudging her with an elbow.

"Eleanor, I am not going to waste my time looking at two people being silly." She was determined to enjoy the rest of the concert, come what might.

"Hmf. If you ask me, I'd say it was more than just *two* people being silly."

"Shhhh, I want to hear the music. And I *didn't* ask you."

"Mmmm, mmmm, mmmm," said Kyle. "She's draped all over him like Dracula's cape."

The band swung smoothly into "The Windmills of Your Mind." Ruth leaned forward a bit, telling herself that she was going to watch the band, no matter what. Her resolve lasted for all of about twenty seconds.

Jodi had picked up her cigarette and holder again, and the man on her left was flourishing a lighter. She inhaled deeply to get the flame going, then gave her benefactor a dazzling smile. Her other hand remained draped over Adam's shoulder. Adam appeared to be giving his full attention to the fingernails on his left hand. Ruth pressed her lips together and looked away. The band began to play the theme song from "Dr. Zhivago."

"She's really moving in now," said Eleanor. "Must be getting cold. Yeah, that's it."

"Uh huh," said Kyle. "There is just nothing like a big strong man on a cold Iowa summer night."

"Give me a *break*, guys," Ruth said tightly.

Eleanor turned to look at her friend. "Is this really bugging you? If so I'll stop."

Ruth sighed. "Of course you're not bugging me. It's all right. I've just had a long day, that's all, and..."

Her attention was caught by the animated, brightly glowing end of Jodi's cigarette. Jodi, attention deeply focused on Adam's left ear, flicked an absent-minded finger at the ashes and the cigarette fell out of its holder and landed in her lap.

"Uh oh."

"What? What'd she do?" Eleanor and Kyle turned to look.

"Dropped the cigarette right in her lap. That's going to do wonders for that cute little polyester outfit." The band was really putting its all into the performance now, as it finished with Russian love and swung into "If I Loved You."

A blood-curdling shriek rang out from across the square. Everyone's heads snapped around to see Jodi leaning back across the bench and batting frantically at her leg. Adam and the other man had jumped to their feet but were obviously completely at a loss as to what to do as Jodi wailed and wriggled. The conductor whipped around quickly to glare at the disturbance and promptly signaled to the band to crescendo. Finally the man who'd handed Jodi the paper cup got an inspiration and poured his own drink in Jodi's lap. "FRANK!" Jodi screamed, clearly audible over the music.

"Hey, what do you want from me? I put the fire out, didn't I?" Frank yelled back just as loudly. "Geez! Women!" And he threw his crumpled cup on the ground and stalked off.

"Frank, you asshole!" Jodi hopped up and down, trying to squeegee the remainder of the liquid off her leg with the side of one hand. "Aaaaaugh! Get *away* from me!" This to another man who had moved in with some kind of helpful intent.

Adam immediately made the most of his opportunity, left the others to deal with lemonade-basted fried leg and zipped across the grass toward Eleanor, Ruth, and Kyle, who were laughing hysterically and clinging to each other to keep from falling off the bench. Adam slid to a stop next to Ruth's side of the bench just as the band went into its grand finale, the theme from "Romeo and Juliet." He quickly seated himself on the grass beside Ruth and burst out laughing, leaning his left arm on the bench's seat for support. The two women giggled, sniffled, looked at each other and started laughing all over again. Kyle leaned his head back over the bench and roared.

The music came to a final, massive crescendo and the laughter died down to an occasional giggle. As the crowd whooped and applauded the band, Eleanor leaned over and said "Way to go, Adam. Always knew you were a knight in shining armor."

"More like a pawn in a rusty tin can," Adam laughed. "Now, you guys cover me so she doesn't find out where I went."

Kyle gave him a thumbs-up sign. "No problem, she already left. Whoo boy, you're in for it big time when she catches up with you."

"Guess you'll just have to cover yourself, Adam," Ruth added, wiping her eyes with the back of her hand. "Oh my, I haven't laughed that hard in years. What a show!"

Eleanor's children came racing around the bandstand, both yellow t-shirts now much the worse for wear—it was apparent that they'd had twin cravings for chocolate ice cream. Andrew had avoided another Cap War with his mom by taking the offending article completely off and stuffing it into the back pocket of his jeans.

"Hey Eleanor, how'bout I give you and the kids a ride home?"

"Oh... Thanks, Kyle. That's a great idea. I don't know if I could manage the walk after all that high class entertainment. My stomach hurts from laughing!" She laughed again and wiped her eyes with the side of her hand. "What a night! See, Ruthie? I told you you'd have fun."

"Best band concert ever, especially the unscheduled soprano," Ruth agreed.

As the twins wiggled into their jackets and their mother gathered up the blanket and squirt guns from under the bench, Adam spoke up. "May I walk you home, Ruth?"

Ruth was feeling wonderful. "Sure, if you don't think Jodi will try to run us down when we go across the street."

"I'll chance it." He grinned. "I think we'll be able to hear her coming a block away if she's still as mad as she looked."

Kyle, Eleanor and the kids waved goodnight and headed for the far south side of the square where Kyle had parked his truck. Ruth settled her shawl around her shoulders as she and Adam started strolling toward the north side. As they passed the bandstand she waved to a couple of her friends. "Great concert!"

They crossed the grass and stepped into the mid-block crosswalk, waiting for traffic to clear. It was obviously going to take a while. Adam looked around. "Beautiful evening, isn't it?"

"Yes, very nice." Even the small talk didn't sound strained.

He decided to take advantage of the moment. "Would you be interested in having a picnic lunch with me in the park tomorrow? I'll even bring the food."

"Picnic? Well... Whoa, here we go." The traffic cleared briefly and they dashed across the street and turned left toward Ruth's corner.

She considered the invitation. The park on Sunday would be safe enough. A picnic might even be fun. *Why not.* "Sure, a picnic in the park sounds good." They reached the bottom of the stairs. "I'll see you tomorrow, then." And Ruth quickly started up, leaving Adam standing on the sidewalk.

"Ruth?"

She stopped. "Yes Adam?" Even in her happy mood, she hoped he wasn't going to follow her up the stairs.

"We didn't decide on a time. How does this sound: I'll come pick you up at one, and like I said, I'll bring the food."

"That sounds great. I'll see you then. Goodnight." She waved and unlocked the door and stepped through into her warmly lit apartment, wondering if she'd just made the biggest mistake of her life.

At the bottom of the stairs, Adam clasped his hands together for a moment, looking up at the door. Then, whistling "Windmills of Your Mind," he strolled off in the direction of home.

Ants and Rain

Lydia juggled an untidy pile of folders from one arm to the other, wishing she'd taken the time to stuff them into her briefcase before she left the house. But Carl was annoyed enough with her for disrupting their Sunday morning with this trip to the office... The parking-garage elevator pinged and the doors slid open. As she crossed the lobby to the other bank of elevators the security guard greeted her. "Working on Sunday, Ms. Caldwell?"

What did he think she was doing, coming in for a dog grooming? But she knew he was just trying to make polite conversation. "Yes, Miguel, just this once. I shouldn't be too long, though." The guard got up from his station and scurried over to press the UP button for her, which made things quite a bit easier. She gave him a genuine smile.

On the eighteenth floor she juggled the folders from arm to arm again as she fished out her keys and unlocked the door to the Caldwell & Talbott suite. The answering machine on the receptionist's desk showed sixteen messages waiting. Could some be from Adam? Never mind. She'd be calling him anyway, and if she started playing messages now she'd never get out of here. She crossed the reception area and went into her office.

She flipped the switch on the surge protector on her desk and her computer system whirred to life. As it went through its start-up sequence she dumped the folders in a jumbled heap on top of the file cabinet, took off her jacket and threw it in a chair. Then it was a matter of only a moment to start the browser and pull up a list of sites. As the figures whizzed by she began to smile. Perfect, perfect! All the tension evaporated. She hummed happily as she took the folders one by one from the mess on top of the cabinet and arranged them in their proper spaces in the drawer.

The computer finished its business long before she did. Lydia hit a few more keys and her printer quietly began to spit pages as she sat down and picked up the phone. Adam's cell phone sent her straight to voicemail, but she didn't want to leave a message. The phone in the upstairs apartment rang and rang and rang. She drummed her fingernails on the desk and shifted the receiver from one ear to the other before dialing again. After four rings the answering machine in the Lyric office picked up. She slammed down the receiver and said something extremely unladylike.

She'd hoped to be able to get this business out of the way ahead of schedule, but obviously no dice. She'd just have to try him again at five, as they'd agreed. Carl was going to be royally irked if she didn't go home now. She scooped up the pages of printouts from the tray and locked them in her desk drawer, then shut the computer down. The whir of machinery faded away as she turned off the lights and went out.

CRBO

Ruth finished her breakfast and scowled out the window. The way the clouds were rolling in, she could well believe the radio's disgustingly cheerful prediction of a 70% chance of rain by that afternoon. "Plan a picnic and what do you get, ants and rain," she said, holding her hands out in an I-give-up gesture and looking up at the ceiling. "I guess I'd better not ask where the *ants* are."

She slipped into her pink sweatpants and a t-shirt and retrieved her bookkeeping supplies from the cabinet in the shop, to get an early start on the quarterly taxes. But first she had to buy groceries for the week. She looked out the window again. There might be just enough time to make it to the store and back before the deluge.

Not many people were in the small supermarket when she got there and it didn't take her long to stock up on what she needed. As she went through the checkout line the clerk greeted her with a smile.

"Heard there were fireworks at the band concert last night," he said.

"Fireworks?" Ruth looked blank.

"Yeah, my son told me Jodi Diamante put on quite a show."

Ruth laughed. "Oh, that. Yeah, she did kind of resemble a cherry bomb."

"Did Adam Talbott have something to do with it? I heard she was cussing like a sailor and threatening to kill him."

"Really? I hadn't heard that part. Adam was sitting by her but he took off when she started screaming."

"... Screaming?"

"She dropped a cigarette in her lap and didn't notice because she was climbing all over Adam at the time. She was wearing a real slinky outfit, and apparently the ash melted it and burned a hole in her leg."

"Oh, well, no wonder." The checker rang up the total. "Will this be all for you?"

Ruth looked at the amount and cringed. She dug in her wallet and discovered that she just had enough to cover it. "Yep, that's it. There's going to be moths in this wallet if I don't watch out. Or ants."

"Ants?"

"Private joke. I guess I'm just in one of those moods today."

"It must be the weather. People have been grouchy in here all morning. I wish it'd hurry up and rain and get it over with."

"Well, not before I get home, I hope," Ruth said as she fitted the grocery bags into her folding cart. "See you next week!"

As she bumped the cart up the last few stairs to her apartment she heard a louder rumble in the distance. She sighed and decided to call Adam and tell him to forget it. Directory Assistance gave her the number of Adam's apartment, but the phone rang and rang with no answer. Finally she gave up.

She was chewing on the end of her pencil, scowling at a particularly discouraging column of figures in the ledger, when she heard footsteps on the stairs. Footsteps? Who... She looked at the clock. *Damn!*

She slammed down the pencil and tried to smooth her hair. So much for changing clothes and tidying up before Adam arrived. She got to the door just a moment before he did. The brown paper bag in his arms was already water-spotted and now she could hear raindrops on the roof. Thunder came rolling across the square from the south.

"Plan a picnic and you get rain," he said with a smile.

Ruth pushed open the screen door. "Funny you should mention that, it's just what I was saying this morning. Or ants. You didn't bring ants, did you?"

Adam stepped inside and made a big show of looking into the bag. "I don't see any. I guess that's one point in my favor." A pause. "How are you today, Ruth?"

"Fine, I guess. Why don't you set the bag on the—oh, I've got the table covered. Put it in the kitchen, please. I guess I'd better close those windows."

She turned from closing the third living-room window to catch him standing by the table looking down at the papers. "Adam, *please* don't get into that stuff. Why don't you go see if the bathroom window is open. It's the door on your right in the back." He went.

Ruth closed her eyes for a moment and clenched her fists. Of all the people to go poking around in her ledger book... She quickly shut the book and shuffled everything onto the bookshelf in the corner. Adam came out of the bathroom.

"Should I close the bedroom window too?" He gestured at the closed door.

"No, I'll do it. The room is kind of a mess. Why don't you go sit down and I'll be back in a minute." Ruth slipped into the bedroom and closed the windows, then took a moment to comb her hair, scowling at her reflection. Quickly kicking off the sweatpants, she slipped into a faded pair of jeans.

Adam was still standing, looking out the front window at the rain. Lightning flashed, followed a few seconds later by an even louder thunderclap. "I'm sorry it turned out this way, Ruth. I was really looking forward to a sunny afternoon in the park. Wish I'd listened to the weather report before I suggested this. We could still go and sit under the shelter if you'd like. I parked the car out back, so we wouldn't get too wet on the way over."

"No, I don't think sitting in a soggy shelter is my idea of a good time today, thanks." She really didn't want to do this at all, but here he was, and she couldn't think of a good way to tell him to go on home. Suppressing a sigh, she said"We can eat lunch at the table, I guess, or... or put a blanket on the floor, if you really want to make it look like a picnic."

"The table will do fine." He paused. "I didn't mean to pry into your accounting, Ruth."

She shook her head irritably. "Never mind. It's all right. There wasn't much to look at anyway."

"No, I mean it, I didn't realize what the papers were. I'm sorry."

"It's all right," she repeated. There was an uncomfortable silence. Ruth shifted from one foot to the other, silently cursing the rain for placing them in such close proximity. "Um, are you hungry now, or do you want to wait a while to eat?"

"Whatever you'd like. If we don't want to eat right away, there's some stuff in the bag that ought to go into the refrigerator."

"Oh well, let's eat now. What kind of dishes should I get out?" Anything to keep moving, keep doing something, not have to sit down and look at him.

"Hey, I said I'd bring everything—and I did. I've got plates, glasses, plastic forks, you name it. Just sit down and relax and let me wait on you."

Ruth gave up. "All right, Adam, it's your show." Thunder boomed overhead and the rain beat down harder on the windows as Adam went into the kitchen.

"I even have a portable radio in the bag, but I bet your music collection would be more fun to listen to, not to mention having a lot less static. What kind of music do you like these days?" He crinkled plastic and rustled paper.

"Pretty much the same as always," Ruth said. "Do you want me to put on a CD?"

"That'd be great. Put on something cheerful to lighten up the day. Where do you keep the sharp knives?"

"Second drawer on the right." She sat cross-legged on the floor and turned her head sideways to look at CD cases. Something cheerful, but new enough not to be a reminder of the past. *Hmmmm....*

She put a John Fogerty disk in the player and turned the volume up a bit so the music was a little louder than the rain. Adam hurried out of the kitchen carrying two sagging paper plates. He quickly transferred them to the table and brushed off his hands. "Thought I was going to lose it there. They don't make paper plates like they used to. Would Madame care to join me for lunch?" He bowed with a flourish.

Ruth got up. "Just let me wash my hands."

"That's fine. It'll give me a chance to uncork the Soda Du Jour."

When Ruth returned from the bathroom Adam was pouring ginger ale into clear plastic cups on the table. The paper plates held thickly-layered pastrami sandwiches on rye bread, fat dill pickle spears and cheese-flavored corn chips.

"That looks good," Ruth said, sitting down at the table. "Where on earth did you get those sandwiches? Or did you make them yourself?"

"Oh, I do have my culinary talents, but making pastrami sandwiches isn't one of them. I spotted this neat little deli the last time I was in Blue River, so I zipped on over there this morning to pick this stuff up."

"Oh, so that's why..." Ruth stopped. No sense telling him she'd tried to call the whole thing off.

"That's why?"

Hastily, Ruth improvised. "Um, that's why I didn't recognize the sandwich maker. No deli in Lyric."

"I noticed. Maybe we can fix that." Adam pulled out the other chair and sat down.

"Oh, yet another in the continuing series of Caldwell and Talbott Rescue Attempts for Lyric?" She couldn't quite keep the sarcasm out of her voice.

"What? I was just thinking that a deli would be successful here, that's all. What's the problem?"

"I... oh, it's just that every time I turn around I hear another rumor about this, that, or the other thing that you two are going to do."

"I suspect most of it is..." He stopped. "Just gossip. Don't let it bother you."

"Gossip isn't always lies. And you two have given this town plenty to talk about lately." She tried very hard to keep her tone light.

"There's nothing I can do about that, really. If people want to talk, let them talk. They'll just look all the more stupid later on."

Stupid? Ruth started to snap at him, then made the supreme effort to let the incendiary word pass. Time out. If they got into a discussion it'd just mean he'd be here that much longer. She bit into her sandwich and chewed slowly, savoring the taste. Just the right amount of mustard, and caraway seeds in the rye. Delicious. Maybe a deli in town wasn't such a dumb idea after all. She swallowed the bite and cleared her throat. She still had to know.

"If you and Lydia do even half the things I've heard about, you'll just about wipe Lyric as we know it off the map."

He sighed and put his half-sandwich down. "Look, I promise you we have nothing like that planned. The longer I stay here, the more I get a sense that..."

"That the hicks here in Lyric don't want to be dragged kicking and screaming into the Space Age?" She tried to sound as if she were joking. It didn't quite work.

A pause. A bite of sandwich disappeared. He didn't look at her. "I didn't say that."

Ruth took a sip of her ginger ale and turned to look out the windows. This was getting her nowhere. She closed her eyes for a moment and counted to ten. "Right. Let's just eat. The sandwich is really good. Maybe we *should* have a deli."

He looked at her for a moment, then sighed. "I wanted this to be a pleasant lunch... a... a chance to get to know each other again. Why don't we find something else to talk about? Something like..."

A tremendous **CRACK!** sounded overhead and all the lights in the apartment went out. Breathlessly, Ruth said "Whoa, that was close!"

"Are you all right?"

"I'm fine. It just startled me, that's all." She got up. "I... let me get some candles." *Ruthie, what's the matter with you?* she thought. *It's not that dark in here.*

Adam rose quickly. "I'll get them, if you'll tell me where they are..." He turned toward the kitchen just as Ruth tried to brush past him.

"Oh!" She'd tripped over his foot, of all the stupid... Without conscious thought by either of them, he had caught her as she stumbled and was holding her gently in his arms. Ruth let herself be held for a moment, and then gasped as it dawned on her just where she was. She immediately pulled away and started backing toward the kitchen. "I, uh, it's easier for me just to get the candles than to try to explain where they are." In the kitchen she boosted her fanny onto the counter, stood up and took a small decorative tin from the back of the top shelf in one of the cupboards. When she turned to ease herself back down again, Adam was standing by the counter looking up at her.

He held up his arms. "May I help you get down?"

"No! ... I mean, no thank you, I can get down by myself."

He stepped back without a word. She sat down on the counter and then slipped to the floor, got some candlesticks from another cupboard and dug in a drawer for a box of matches. She carried everything to the table, carefully sidestepping so as not to make any further contact with Adam. It took only a moment to get the candles into their holders and casting a cheerful yellow light over the table. Ruth sat down again and picked up her sandwich. Adam was still standing near the kitchen, watching her. "Sit down, Adam, your lunch is getting stale." She forced herself to smile, then turned her attention to eating.

"Right." Adam watched Ruth's face in the candles' glow as he sat down and picked up his sandwich. He continued to watch her as he ate; she kept her eyes on her plate. Finally the silence was too much. He put the sandwich down. "I can go get the radio if you'd like."

"No, that's OK, it'd be nothing but static anyway."

"Ruth, am I making you uncomfortable?"

Was that the six million dollar question, or what? "Yes."

"Can you please believe me, that's the last thing I want to do? I was hoping we'd just have a nice lunch together, but if this is making you unhappy, I'll leave."

The lights came back on, the music started again and thunder rumbled outside, not so loudly as before. Ruth stared at her plate. She chewed her lower lip in indecision. If she followed her instincts and sent him away now it was likely that she'd never find out what he and Lydia had planned. And that was, after all, the whole reason she'd let him come here in the first place, wasn't it? Was it? She heard him push back his chair.

She looked up at him. She was going to have to tell him at least some of the truth to keep peace with herself. She chose her words carefully. "Adam, there's a lot of water under the bridge between us, if you'll forgive my saying that while it's pouring down rain outside." She brushed back her hair with both hands. "Finish your lunch. We'll just have to work things out one at a time."

He smiled and sat back down. "All right. So," he waved his hand over the table, "would you care to join me for a guaranteed non-personal, non-business, non-controversial lunch?"

Some of the tension evaporated. She smiled, picked up what was left of her sandwich and munched. "Best kind of lunch to have," she said with her mouth full.

"Now let's see if I can choose a suitably neutral subject for conversation. Um, what shall it be... how about 'You never told me who Eleanor married'?"

Ruth swallowed the bite of sandwich and took a sip of ginger ale. "That's probably because she didn't."

"Whoops. So much for non-controversial."

"Oh, it's not what you'd call controversial. She went through college on an accelerated course, graduated in three years and had the twins a few months later." Ruth looked thoughtful. "Lyric's changed, Adam. It's not like the old days. Not one person has ever said an unkind word. If anything, they've complimented her on her courage—and I mean to her face *and* behind her back."

"Um, if this isn't being too nosy, who's the twins' father?"

"I don't know. Nobody does. She's never told anyone, not even her own parents. And since the twins were born in November, uh, well, it could be someone we know or someone up in Ames. I won't lie to you, there was plenty of gossip at the time, but Eleanor didn't give a hoot what the gossips thought from the get-go. Like I said, things have changed." Silence fell again as the last of the sandwiches disappeared.

"Well," said Adam, licking mustard off his fingers, "now that we've disposed of non-controversial, how about non-business?"

Ruth chuckled. "But Adam, if you're not going to talk business all the time, can you call yourself a businessman? Maybe you should try for another profession... hmmm..." she tried to think of some totally implausible occupation for him. "I know, you could write scripts for soap operas."

He leaned back in his chair and laughed. "Nah. If I did that, everybody in Lyric would be sure I was writing about them. Who knows, they might be right." The wind blew the rain in sheets against the windowpanes and thunder rumbled outside. "On the other hand, if I wrote for soap operas, I could move to California where I wouldn't have to deal with" —he waved a hand at the window— "summer thunderstorms."

"Would you really want to do that? Move to California?"

There was a long pause as Adam looked past Ruth's shoulder to the window and the sheets of water sliding down. His brown eyes seemed almost black, so wide were the pupils. "To tell you the truth, no. The longer I stay in Lyric, the more it feels like home. I never really had a home town. This is about as close as it gets."

Surprised, Ruth groped for words. "I... never thought I'd hear you say anything like that, Adam."

He turned to look at her. "You know, up to the moment I said it I never thought I'd hear myself saying it either, but it's true." He looked down at his plate. "Even if I have to be the one to find someone to start a deli here." He looked quickly up at Ruth and held up a hand to still her automatic protest. "Just kidding, just kidding! Here, let me toss the plates and then you can show me the rest of your music collection."

സ്ദ

The thunder had faded away in the distance and the rain had diminished to an occasional flurry against the windowpanes. Adam sat cross-legged on the floor in front of the bookshelf and Ruth curled up in the overstuffed chair behind him, legs tucked under and her chin on her hand, her elbow on the chair arm.

Adam's fingers trailed over the spines of the CDs as he looked at the titles. A John Barrowman album was in the player and Ruth hummed softly along with one of her favorite tunes.

"You've got quite a collection here." Adam pulled a jewel case out of the shelf to look at it. "Oh, I remember this one." Ruth looked over his shoulder and pressed her hand to her mouth when she saw it. Julio Iglesias. Oh no. She looked away. That particular album held too many memories. *Put it back, please, Adam*, she thought, not daring to say it aloud. But he leaned the CD against the shelf, face out.

She cleared her throat and got up. "I'm going to get some more ginger ale. Would you like some?"

"Oh... sure," he said, leaning sideways to read disk titles. Ruth heard him pull another one out as she took the cups off the table and went into the kitchen. *Oh, please let him find ten other CDs to play before he got to that one, please.*

When she returned with the soda, Adam was holding up Judy Collins' "Who Knows Where the Time Goes" album. "I remember how mad you used to get when I sneered at Judy Collins. For the life of me I ouldn't understand what you saw in her. But you know, I've paid more attention in the last couple years, and I have to admit you were right."

"Well, of course I was right," Ruth said. "See what you could have learned if..." her voice trailed off and she handed him his drink.

"If I hadn't been such an idiot?" Adam smiled.

Ruth smiled back. "You said it, I didn't." She curled back up in the chair. "So when did your musical tastes change?"

He looked thoughtful. "Good question. Hard to say, really, but I'd guess probably about the time I started growing up. Mentally, I mean, not physically. A long time after I left Lyric, as you can tell."

Ruth sat silent, looking down at the floor. Adam ran a hand over the jewel case, gently brushing the singer's face.

"May I play this one?" He got up, set his cup on the shelf and ejected the John Barrowman CD without even waiting for her reply. As Judy Collins' beautiful voice filled the room, Adam stepped over to the rain-spattered window and looked out at the square. There was just a hint of blue sky visible over the roofs to the south. He put one bent arm on the window frame and leaned his head against it. His breath fogged the glass.

Ruth watched him as he idly traced a design on the breath-frosted pane. Who knows where the time goes, indeed. Wasn't it time, she suddenly thought, to listen to Eleanor and see the man and not the thoughtless boy?

As if he could hear her thoughts, he turned and silently held out his arms. This was too much, too soon. He waited, silent, eyes pleading.

Breathe, Ruth, she thought, *make your choice.* After a moment, she got up.

She seemed to fit right into the curve of his shoulder and the circle of his arms as if she'd never left them. He reached up to stroke her hair and made a very soft sound deep in his throat. Overwhelmed, she closed her eyes. This foolish deception wasn't going to be as simple as she'd planned.

After a moment he cupped her chin in his hand and gently turned her face up. She opened her eyes. He kissed her, even more gently. When he released her, she put a hand up and stroked his face.

"It's soft..."

An amused chuckle. "What did you expect, steel wool?"

Ruth was embarrassed. "It's just that I've never, um, never kissed a man with a mustache before."

"Ah," he said. "Well, for everything there's a first time. Now that the first time's been taken care of, would you like to try it again?" He didn't wait for a reply.

He's learned a few things since high school, Ruth thought. *But then, so have I.* Breathless, she ended the kiss and clung to him, her face nestled close under his chin, feeling his chest rise and fall, hearing the beating of his heart. After a long moment, he surprised her by asking "Do you think that chair will hold two of us?"

She looked at it. "I think it will, but why?"

"I'll show you." He let her go, then took her hand and led her to the chair, drawing her down on his lap as he sat.

Gingerly she leaned back just a bit, but she couldn't relax. How could she get out of *this* gracefully?

As if to answer her, the City Hall clock bonged out the three-quarter-hour chimes. "Has that stupid thing been ringing all this time?" Adam said. "I never heard it."

"Me neither," said Ruth, who was trying to pretend she enjoyed her present position.

Adam shifted a bit so he could look at his watch. "Oh, crap!"

"What is it?"

"It's 4:45, and I'm expecting an important call around 5."

"On a *Sunday*? You've got to be kidding!" Ruth sat up so that she could see his face.

"Hell of a time for me to do something so completely stupid, isn't it? But I really do have to take the call; it's very important. Would it be all right if I just run over to the office for as long as it takes and then come right back? I can pick up some groceries and cook supper if you'd like."

Oh, thank God, saved by the bell. "No, you go ahead. I never did get my bookkeeping finished, and I'd really like be done with it today." She smiled, got up and started clearing away the last remains of lunch.

"Well, at least let me come back and make supper. I'm actually a pretty good cook, and you won't want to have to mess around in the kitchen after all those facts and figures."

Ruth took the debris from the table into the kitchen and dropped it in the wastebasket. "No thanks. Maybe some other time, though—I'd like to see how you manage as a cook." Maybe some other time she'd be better prepared to play her part.

"All right. And I promise you will have my undivided attention for as long as you want it. No interruptions, no business talk." He picked up his jacket from the chair and looked at her, his dark brown eyes thoughtful. "You know, when I agreed to take this call..." he stopped and cleared his throat, "I... I was sure you'd want to head straight for home right after we ate our sandwiches. Or maybe even before. I didn't think you'd put up with me this long."

Ruth stood for a moment, carefully considering her answer. "I guess this has been a day full of surprises all around."

"Yes," he said, and held out his arms. Once again, she stood still for a moment.

They held each other in silence. Ruth finally relaxed and nestled against his shoulder again. He kissed the top of her head and let her go, looking down at her with those dark-brown eyes. "How about having lunch with me tomorrow?"

"I... I'll think about it. A lot depends on how much work I have to do." There was always plenty of work to do. And if she did decide to go, she'd pick some public place where dealing with him wouldn't be so tricky.

He took her hand and they walked to the door together. Hand on the doorknob, he turned and brushed the side of her face with gentle fingertips. "I'll call you at the shop in the morning, would that be OK?"

"Um... sure. I'll tell Chet not to snarl at you."

He laughed. "Ah, a good safety precaution." He opened the door. "Goodnight, Ruth."

"Goodnight, Adam."

She closed the door behind him and leaned up against it, eyes closed.

Across the street the engine in a battered green pickup truck parked diagonally at the curb roared to life as Adam emerged from the stairs. About flippin' *time* he got outta there. The driver waited, watching his rear-view mirror. As the silver Lexus turned out of the alley behind Ruth's building and went south, then west, the pickup pulled out of its parking space and followed, not too close. It zipped into the last parking space on the south side of the square and the driver leaped out, leaving the door open and the engine running. He stood on the corner and watched the Lexus turn into the alley behind the Caldwell & Talbott building, then he hopped back behind the wheel, slammed the door and gunned the engine again.

The pickup cruised slowly down the alley. The Lexus was parked and the light was on in the office. "Fifty bucks, man," the driver muttered, and opened his phone.

⊰⊱

Adam snapped out of his reverie in time to pick up the office phone on the third ring. "Caldwell and... Hi Lydia. What'd you find out?"

"Oh Adam, good news! I've got the tax records here, the assessments and a pretty good idea of who might be willing to sell. The list isn't complete yet, but there's enough here to get a real start on. This is turning out just like you said it would. It seems there are two more around the square than we originally thought, plus two by the college campus, an apartment building near the junior high, and believe it or not, that motel we stayed at. Wouldn't it be great to buy that fleabag place and fix it up?"

178

Adam's eyes had lost focus. Vaguely aware of a question, he snapped back to attention. More or less. "Oh... yeah, right, very good."

Lydia had barely paused. "And one or two of those so-called mansions near the park, and... Adam? Hello? Are you listening to me?"

Back to the present. "Of course I'm listening. Sounds like you and those investigators have done a super job, Lydia. Do you want to fax me that stuff or just send it along by overnight?"

"I'll send it. I left the printouts at the office. If I went back there, Carl would hit the ceiling. He's ticked enough at me for going in there today."

"Why'd you have to go to the office?"

"My laptop hasn't been working very well and I didn't want to trust it, so I thought I'd better use the office computer. I tried to call you before, but there was no answer anywhere. Where were you?"

"Am I supposed to be waiting for the phone all day?"

"Don't take that tone with me. Of course you're not. I could have given the information to you this morning if you'd been answering your phone, that's all."

"Yeah. I had some, uh, some errands to run."

Silence. Faint crackles on the phone line. "Adam? Is this a bad time to be calling? Is something wrong?"

"No, no, of course not. Not at all. I've just got a lot on my mind—what with these business deals getting rolling and all. I didn't realize my cell phone was off." He pulled it from his belt and looked at it. "The battery died. I'll charge it now."

Lydia chewed her lower lip. Why was he so distracted? She'd never known him to let his phone die before. "I can be back there on Friday if you need me."

"Oh, well, that's up to you. But it sounds to me like Carl wouldn't take too kindly to your traveling again so soon. I've got things under control here. Send me the information and I'll get moving on it as soon as it arrives."

She drummed her fingernails on the desk top, thinking. This was not like Adam at all. Was he getting cold feet now that they were nearly there? Surely not. If she only had a good reason to go back there and move things along for herself! But he did have a point, Carl would be furious. She pulled the phone mouthpiece up away from her face so he wouldn't hear her sigh. "All right," she said, moving the phone back in place, "I'll send everything along in the morning. And Adam?"

"Yes, Lydia?"

"Take care of yourself, won't you?"

He chuckled. "Now, when have you ever known me not to do that? Don't worry, I'll get going on this just as soon as I can."

But the sense of uncertainty still nagged at Lydia, long after she hung up the phone.

Adam put his feet up on the desk and his hands behind his head and leaned his chair back as far as it would go. His eyes lost focus again as he looked at the darkening sky through the slats of the venetian blinds.

Lyric, We Have a Problem

W e're fucked," he said, without preamble, as he got to the bottom of the stairs and found the owner mixing plant food into a watering can on a table in the back.

"Oh for fuck's sake, what now?" The fluorescent lights at the back of the room were flickering, and the usual smell of something burnt was a lot more pronounced. He set the box of plant food down on the counter and put his hands on his hips.

"This kid I work with has been doing a real unsubtle job of hinting he'd like to help distribute the weed."

"Which you know nothing about."

"The hell d'you take me for? Which I know *absolutely* nothing about, *but* this is the mayor's kid we're talking about."

"Fuck. Aaron Porter. That kid's got shit for brains—it means that goddamn Duane Haldeman put him up to it."

"Or his old man did, and we're totally hosed here."

"I really doubt Aaron's old man doesn't know his precious baby is a total fuckup. He'd never send an idiot like that to go ask questions."

"I don't know the kid except to work with him. How can you be so sure it's not his old man behind this?"

"His mom's my old girlfriend. Trust me, I know."

"OK, if you say so. Now what?"

"Let me think about it. Right now we need to finish feeding the plants and start the dryer."

"Why do you only run the dryer at night? My wife's getting on my case about 'going out with the boys' so often."

"Damn thing plays hell with the phone and the radio when it's on, nothing but static. It was driving me crazy. Come on, let's get this done."

"Do you think that fucker Aaron will rat me out if I keep playing dumb?"

"I doubt it, but I'll start checking around, try to find out how much that dickwad Duane knows." He smacked a hand on the counter. "Just one fucking thing after another."

಄಄

All Monday morning Ruth was distracted and off kilter. Despite her best efforts to Think Of Something Else, she kept replaying Sunday afternoon in her mind, wondering what she could have done to have kept it all on much more neutral ground.

It was warm in the shop when she opened up, it got warmer as the morning wore on, and the rain had left the air completely soggy. The floor fan was going full blast but it didn't do much more than push sticky air around. Ruth set a plastic spray bottle on the bench, and every now and again she'd mist herself and lean over into the path of the breeze from the fan. The evaporation would help for a short time, but then it was back to the same old sweat. Her pink tank top had turned a deep rose color before the second hour was past. The shop was beginning to smell of hot wire insulation, wet cardboard and a very faint tinge of old garbage. She wrinkled her nose and wrote herself a note to buy an air freshener or maybe some potpourri to put on the counter. Just what she needed, to have the customers think their appliances were molding away in the back.

And to make things worse, Chet came to work grumpy and stayed that way. Nothing seemed to satisfy him; he groused and swore and banged things around and rattled his tools until Ruth had to get up and go sweep the sidewalk out front again to get away from the commotion in the back. The thermometer at the bank said ninety degrees already and it wasn't even noon. She came back inside wilted and warmer than ever.

Despite the heat and distractions, she did manage to finish fixing Mrs. Lewis' Roosevelt radio, and felt she'd really accomplished something when it worked when she turned it on. But Mrs. Lewis was out, or wasn't answering her phone that morning. After the third fruitless phone call Ruth picked up the heavy wooden case and set it in a place of honor alongside the old Victrola in the front window. "Might as well get some use out of it while we wait, right Charlie?" she said, scratching him behind his ear. Charlie purred and curled the tip of his long, soft tail. "Wish I had your outlook on life today, cat," she said, with a final ruffle of his fur. "How you can stand this heat in that fur coat, I will never understand."

She'd hardly set foot inside the workshop when the explosion came. "This dad-blasted..." Chet snarled and flung a pair of short-handled wire cutters at the wall.

Wham! A chip of brick flew off and spun away into the space behind his shelves. The wire cutters rebounded, skittered across the top of the bench and crashed to the floor.

"Chet! For Heaven's sake! I can't afford to buy you new tools! What's the matter with you?"

"Never you mind! I'll buy my own doggone tools! You stay out of it!" He slammed both fists down on the bench hard enough to make all the small items on it jump. Ruth stood frozen, absolutely speechless. She'd never heard an outburst like this from Chet for as long as she'd known him.

There was a long pause; Ruth dared not move or speak. Finally, Chet took a deep breath and let it out with a shaky sigh. His shoulders slumped. "I'm sorry, Ruthie. I shouldn't take this all out on you. It's just that I got a notice from my landlady on Saturday that the rent's going up next month, and I been fretting for two days on how I'm going to manage. I'm pushed to the limit as it is, with bills, and Eddie, and..." His mouth twisted and he looked away. "I mean, I just wanted to keep the boy out of trouble..." He took another shaky breath. "My pension from the city don't go as far as it used to..." He looked back at her. "Now see, I've gone and done just what I swore I wouldn't do. I didn't want to worry you with any of this mess. You're doing the absolute best you can with the place. It's not your fault I don't know how to budget." He tried to laugh, but it came out harsh.

Tears welled up in Ruth's eyes. "Oh, Chet..."

He got up hastily. "That was just wrong of me, I shouldn't-a done it. Don't know why I let myself get all worked up. It's not your fault, not a bit of it. I'll manage, don't you worry now."

Ruth wiped her eyes with a corner of her shop apron. Chet patted her awkwardly on the back. "Don't you worry, Ruthie. I'm just an old coot who's making mountains out of molehills. Don't know why you keep such a cranky old geezer around the place, I really don't." Ruth sniffed and tried to smile.

The bell over the front door chimed. Ruth looked at the curtain. Chet quickly said "You go wash your face now, I'll take care of that. Go on now." He patted her again and slipped through the curtain into the front. Ruth went into the small washroom, turned on the tap full blast in the vain hope the water would get cold, doused a paper towel under the stream and tried to pat away the redness around her eyes. It didn't help much. She gave up, turned off the water and dried her face as best she could. As she walked back to her bench she heard Chet say "What in tarnation did you do to it?"

Adam's voice came clearly through the curtain, and Ruth had to close her eyes for a moment and take a deep breath. "Dropped it on the bathroom floor," he said. Ruth brushed her hair back from her face, wiped her hands on her apron and pushed through the curtain. Adam and Chet were looking down at the remains of Adam's small portable radio. "Hi Ruth," said Adam. "Look what I did to my radio this morning. Dropped it on a tile floor. I'm hoping you or Chet can fix it for me."

"I dunno, sonny, you really mashed it." Chet picked up the radio and a corner of the plastic case fell off. "You'd do better to buy yourself a new radio. This'n couldn't have cost that much."

"It, um, it has sentimental value. I'd rather have the old radio fixed than get a new one, if you can. I'll pay you whatever it costs to fix it."

"I'll try, but I'm no miracle worker. Ruth can tell you that. Still think you'd be happier with a new one." Chet reached under the counter for a small paper bag and put the pieces of the radio in it. He handed Adam a work order form to fill out, looked at Ruth and took the bag of radio parts back into the workshop. Ruth stood by the counter, looking down at her hands.

Adam was busy writing on the work order. "Darn stupid thing for me to do. My hands were wet and it just dropped..." He finished with the form and handed it to her. "Ruth, is something wrong?"

"I... uh, no, no, nothing's wrong. I'm fine." She took the form from him without looking up at his face. "Excuse me just a minute while I give this to Chet." She turned and zipped into the workshop and held out the form. Chet was brushing brick dust off the back of the bench. He took the paper from her without a word. Ruth squared her shoulders and returned to the front of the shop. Adam was leaning over the curtain rod in the front window, petting the cat.

He turned as he heard her come through the doorway. "I'm sorry, I know I said I'd call this morning, but it's been just one thing after another. Are you busy? Would you like to come have lunch with me now? I thought maybe we could walk over to the hot dog place and sit at one of the picnic tables. I've been wanting to do that ever since I got here." He waved at the brilliant summer sunshine outside. "Looks like the perfect day for it. What'dya say?"

Ruth looked up at the clock. 11:30 already. She thought about it for a moment. Maybe it would help everyone if she went out and left Chet alone for a while. "All right. Just let me clean up my bench and get rid of this apron and we can go." She eyed his short-sleeved white shirt and striped silk tie skeptically. "But if you're dressed like that on a day like this, are you going to want to be seen with me?"

He laughed as he quickly stripped off the tie, stuffed it in his pocket and unbuttoned three buttons on his shirt. "Satisfied?"

"Oh yeah. Now you look like you're going slumming. I guess I'll consider being seen in public with you."

"Well, that's good," he chuckled as she disappeared through the drapes. "Do they still serve chili dogs with the works?"

"You bet," Ruth called back as she rustled her tools into their carrier and hung her apron on the swing-armed lamp. She looked down at her tank top, pulled the neckline away from her skin and sighed. A Chanel exclusive it wasn't. But it was going to have to do. "Chet, I'm going to..."

"I heard you. You run along now. Chili dog might just be the best thing for you."

"Will you be all right?"

"Ruthie, I can take care of myself, you should know that by now," Chet said with a smile. "Run along and chow down."

⋅⋅⋅⋅⋅⋅⋅

Adam carried a tray laden with chili dogs, fries and two large paper cups of root beer to the picnic table under the trees. Ruth had shed her shoes and socks and was blissfully wiggling her toes in the grass. The breeze had already evaporated most of the morning's sweat and her tank top was almost back to its original color. "Worst thing about my job," she told him as he sat down, "is having to wear real shoes all day in the summertime."

"Worst thing about my job is that every day seems to be pretty much the same. At least when we were in school the seasons made some kind of difference." Adam passed Ruth's lunch over to her. "You know what we ought to do? We should have a big end of summer party just for the people our age. Why should the kids have all the fun?"

Ruth took a bite of chili dog, chewed, swallowed, and licked errant drips of chili off her wrist. She'd forgotten just how good a loaded hot dog with plenty of mustard and onions could taste. "Funny you should mention that. Some of us have been trying to get together some kind of reunion for our class and it's one big fizzle. Nobody wants to take on the job of coordinating everything there is to do. We were thinking, school starts the first week in September, so if anyone can get their act together we could have a party or a dance the weekend before, and we could invite everyone who was in school the same time we were."

"Wouldn't it be great if we could get the Veterans' Hall, just like the old days? Are Darlene and the band still playing?"

"No, they broke up years ago, but I bet we could find someone."

Adam took a huge, drippy bite of chili dog and was momentarily silenced. He swallowed, took a sip of his drink and sighed. "Ooooh boy, that tastes even better than I remembered it. How on earth did I survive away from Lyric so long?"

"Most of us find our way back here sometime, one way or another, and with good reason." She paused for a moment, considering what she wanted to say. "That's why people are so curious about why you've come back after all these years."

There was a long silence as Adam deliberately munched his chili dog, chewed thoroughly and swallowed. Ruth waited. He took a sip of his drink, swallowed again and looked down at the cup in his hands.

"Did I have a good reason, you mean? I think I did. There are some things I've wanted to do for a long time, Ruth. And now I have the... uh, well, now I can do them. You may not believe it, but I've been thinking about coming back to Lyric for ages."

"Why now? And why all the hush-hush? I asked Lydia if you two were going to buy up the whole square, and she said 'No, just the...' and then shut up like a clam. Just the what? Or *do* you have some crazy notion of buying up the square? Every time I hear a story they've got you buying this, that, or the other kind of business. But as far as I know, the square isn't for sale."

Adam sighed and set the cup down. "Ruth, really, we're not going to do anything like that. Look, I can't help what people think, and I certainly can't answer for every rumor that goes around." He wiped beads of sweat off his forehead with a paper napkin. "I'll tell you something, though—I refuse to worry about what some old biddy tells her neighbor over the back fence. I just haven't got time to waste on gossip control."

"Haven't got..." She was warmer than ever, even with the shade and the breeze. "Well, just what do you have planned, Adam? I'm no 'old biddy,' but I'd sure like to have some idea if what people are saying is true."

"Look... I know this is going to sound like an evasion, and it's probably going to tick you off even more, but

I can't talk about our plans till I've worked a few more things out. Can you understand why that has to be?"

Ruth set the remains of her chili dog down and wiped her hands with a napkin. "Oh, all of a sudden no more talk about buried treasure? Well, well, well. Why am I not surprised? Did you do a 'study' to see if we'd blab that stuff all over town?"

"Of course not," he said, just a little too quickly.

Ruth snorted. "Adam, Lydia acted as though she was all set to tell me exactly what you two were up to, that day in the coffee shop. But she ended up stomping out before she said much of anything. That made me very uneasy. It still does. Every time I hear someone else talking about this, that, or the other that you two supposedly plan to do, I wonder if it's just another one of your stories coming home to roost. I can't help wondering if the two of you started all this gossip yourselves, just to see what would happen."

He turned slightly on the bench and looked away. After a moment, he sighed and turned back to face her. "I can see I'm going to have to speak to Lydia this afternoon."

"Damage control? Rumor control? What?" Had the temperature risen so many degrees so quickly? Ruth felt a bead of sweat beginning a slow run down the middle of her back.

"Look, I said I'd talk with her, and I'll straighten things out. I..." He stopped. "Believe it or not, I don't want to see you angry or upset."

"You keep saying that, but you know what? I'm not sure either one of us really believes it. If you'd like to settle me down, how about telling me honestly what did bring you back to Lyric after all these years? If it's a good story, then maybe I can go talk to a few old biddies myself."

He put both hands flat on the green, scarred, initial-carved wood of the picnic table. "You don't really mean that."

"Oh, don't I?" She looked him right in the eye. He was the first to look away. "What is it, Adam? What's going on?"

He swung back to her. "I can't tell you now. But I will. When the time is right. Trust me, Ruth."

"Trust you? Isn't that one of those statements like 'the check is in the mail'?" Ruth got up from the table. "You know what? I'm not very hungry and it's really too hot to be outside. I think maybe I'd better go on back to work." She grabbed her shoes and socks off the grass, whirled and marched away.

"Ruth! Wait!" Adam struggled to unfold his legs from under the picnic table. As he stood up, the table tilted and he lost his balance and sat down hard. Ruth's abandoned cup of root beer tipped over and poured into his lap. *"Shit!"* By the time he untangled himself from the table Ruth was halfway down the block, moving surprisingly smoothly for having bare feet on a hot sidewalk. He kicked the dirt in utter frustration and then began mopping root beer off his pants with a handful of napkins.

Across the street, two pairs of eyes watching through the window of the auto parts store crinkled in amusement.

⚭

It was a very subdued Adam Talbott who showed up at the store the next day carrying a small bouquet of daisies. Chet, putting down the receiver of the old pay phone, greeted him with "She ain't here."

"Will you tell me she's here if I tell you I'm going to try real hard not to make her mad at me today?"

Chet looked the younger man up and down and snorted. "Uh huh. Sure. Oh, by the way, I don't think I'm gonna be able to fix that radio of yours. It's just in too many pieces. You want me to keep trying, or you want to go get another one?"

"Give it a try, Chet. If it can be fixed at all, I'd really like to have it back. Charge me whatever it's worth to you. I've had that radio for a long time. It was a present from..." he cleared his throat. "From someone who mattered to me."

"Oh, a lady friend, uh huh. Well, all right, I'll see what I can do, but I won't give you no guarantees."

Nettled, Adam began, "It wasn't..." but stopped as Ruth came through from the back. Her hair was gathered up haphazardly into a floppy ponytail on the very top of her head and a few damp tendrils stuck to the back of her neck. The tank top visible under the stained green strings of her shop apron was yellow today. A fine film of sweat made her skin shine softly in the sunlight reflected off the dusty floor, but the dark circles under her eyes were no trick of sunlight and shadow. He held out the bouquet. "Would you be willing to risk another chili dog?"

"Not today." Her voice was tired.

"Well, how about Mexican food? Or burgers? Or maybe a pizza?"

"No, really. Not today. I look like the bottom of a birdcage and I'm not in the mood. Thanks anyway."

Adam's shoulders drooped. "OK, I understand. Would you like some flowers to brighten up the shop?"

"Um... sure. Thanks. Now Chet and I really do need to get back to work."

୦ଞ୦

Eddie stuffed another quarter into the pay phone and punched buttons. The phone on the other end rang and rang and then the answering machine picked up. He shifted from one foot to the other, muttering "Yeah, yeah" while the message played.

"Look, I know you told me not to leave messages, but I've had it. This is stupid. Ain't nothing going on and it's like a hundred degrees out here. You wanna watch 'em, *you* watch 'em. I got better things to do. Bad enough sitting on my ass in that damn place every day with no air conditioning. You want this to go any farther, it's gonna cost you. And don't call me at my place no more, my mom's getting pissed. Call me at Duane's tonight."

He slammed down the receiver and wiped sweat off his forehead with the back of his hand. Fuck those two, he was going to head over to the bowling alley where the air conditioning was working and the waitress wasn't too picky about serving him a nice cold beer. He scrubbed his face with the sticky lower portion of his sweaty t-shirt. Oh well, maybe someone he knew would come along and give him a ride. He smacked the side of the plastic pay-phone enclosure with his hand and turned and ambled south.

Half a block behind him, Adam emerged into the sunshine and headed for the coffee shop, alone.

୦ଞ୦

At about 4:00 that afternoon the door bell jangled. Before Ruth could peel her sweaty fanny off the stool she heard Eleanor call "Hi Ruthie, it's me!"

"Come on back, Eleanor, I'm stuck to my seat back here."

Her friend pushed through the curtain. "Phew, don't you guys know it's summer out there? What did you do, Chet, turn on the furnace?" Chet, whose faded blue chambray shirt had darkened nearly to its original color, turned slowly around, glared at Eleanor, and went back to work without a word.

"Nice to see you too, Chet. Someday you really ought to fix that fan." She watched for a reaction that never came. Then she grinned and shrugged. "Can't stay long, Ruthie—I'm on my way to pick up the kids at the pool. I just wanted to drop by and see how you were doing."

"And ask about what else?" Ruth said, doing her best to smile back.

Eleanor laughed. "Caught me. So what is it with you and you know who?"

"I might have known," Ruth sighed. "We had one and a half lunches. That's it."

"One and... what happened?"

"Nothing."

"Bring Ruthie flowers, nothing?" Eleanor pointed to the daisies in their jar of water on top of the file cabinet.

"How do you know I didn't buy those myself?"

"Because I've never seen you buy a daisy in your life. Come on."

Ruth wiped her forehead with the back of her arm and sighed. "Can we just drop the subject for now? I really don't want to talk about it."

Eleanor gave her friend a quick hug. "No problem. Want to come over tonight and enjoy my air conditioning and my cooking? We can elbow the kids away from the video collection after supper."

Ruth gave a weary smile. "How'bout I let you know when we close up for the night?"

"Sounds like a plan."

CRO

Adam stopped by the shop every few days, ostensibly to see if his radio was fixed. "Damn it, sonny, I will *call* you when it's done!" snapped Chet after the third such visit.

"Sorry, Chet. I won't bug you any more about it, I promise."

"Hah. We both know that ain't why you're here."

Adam started to say something, then just hung his head. "You're right. Is Ruth here?"

"No, she ain't. She went out to lunch and I ain't saying where. Run along now."

As it happened, Ruth was sitting on an old beach towel, peacefully eating a sandwich under one of the trees in the center of the square. She looked up as Adam approached, sighed wearily and set the sandwich down. Adam sat on the grass beside her, heedless of what that might do to his slacks. "Can we just talk for a minute?"

"I'm not the one you need to talk with. Did you ever call Lydia?"

"Call Lydia? Yes, I call her a couple times a week... oh. No, we've only talked business, Ruth, sorry."

"I might have known."

"Ruth, I really don't think she spread rumors around, and I'll be honest with you, I'd feel pretty silly asking her about something like that."

Ruth was silent for a moment, and then she shrugged. "So you lied." She leaned over to pick up her shoes and socks.

"Ruth, don't run off again, please. If you really want me to give Lydia the third degree..."

"That's not what I wanted and you know it, Adam." She heaved a deep sigh. "I thought my question was entirely reasonable and I can see you don't, so there's not much more to be said. I have to get back to work."

"What do you want from me? Isn't my word good enough?"

Ruth's temper flared. How *dare* he play the wounded innocent? She jumped to her feet. "What I want from you, Adam, is just one simple thing—the truth! Nothing more than that. God, how stupid could I be? Here I thought maybe you'd changed, but I was so, so wrong! You're just the same old Adam, doing what *Adam* wants to do and to hell with anyone else. I've had it! I'm not interested in associating with someone who's going to... to... God, who knows, tear down my business and throw me out of my home!"

"Would you associate with me if I wasn't going to do any such thing?"

She looked at him, mouth open in disbelief. "You've got a lot of nerve." Tossing her shoes and the remains of her lunch into the beach towel, she scooped it up and walked away.

Adam smacked the ground with his palm, hard, and closed his eyes, willing his breathing to return to normal.

When it did, he got up, dusted off his pants and walked back to his office.

Ruth returned to the shop to find Chet standing by his bench, arms folded, waiting for her.

"Where the heck you been? I ain't got time to run this place and do my work while you're out gallivanting around."

"I was only gone for 45 minutes, Chet. What's the problem?"

"That numbskull Duane Haldeman came in while I was trying to get that DVD player back together. Barged right into the back here when I didn't hop to it out front as fast as he wanted. Had some cheap walkie-talkies with him and wanted to know if I could fix them so they had a longer range. Told him I couldn't and he got all huffy. Told him he'd oughta get a radio license so he could use real walkie-talkies and he about threw a fit. Said I was a hopeless retard and he'd take the walkie-talkies to some place where they had some real technicians. Told him any 'real technician' would tell him the same, but he was out of here in a huff. I got better things to do than put up with that kind of folderol."

Ruth held her hands out, palms up. "I don't know that I could have handled him any better, Chet. I'll bet if I'd told him the same thing he'd have demanded to talk with you and you would have had to go through the whole scene with him anyway." She shook her head and sighed. "I just don't understand some people."

"Well, you best get to work. Been a bunch of things come in here while you were out to lunch. I guess I got worried about the rent too soon—now what I got to worry about is getting home at all."

"You're right, Chet. I'll get to work." Funny, a bunch of things coming in while she was in the square with Adam. Oh yes, so so funny. She sat down at her bench and picked up an old Tamagotchi that probably hadn't been used in ten years, wondering if its owner would even bother to turn it on once he got it back.

༜

Adam approached the back door just as Ruth and Chet were locking up at noon on Saturday. "Hi Chet, hi Ruth." Chet gave Adam a look fit to blister the pavement, grumbled and walked off in the direction of home. "What's with him?"

"Nothing. Lots of work in a brick oven. All of a sudden we've got broken appliances up the wazoo." Ruth pulled her t-shirt away from her sweaty chest and wiped her face with the side of her hand. "I wish he wasn't so darn stubborn about fixing that ceiling fan."

"Want to get a quick lunch and then take in a movie? I don't care what's playing. Sitting in the air conditioning all afternoon would improve the quality of anything."

Ruth looked at him in disbelief. "I thought I made myself pretty clear a couple days ago."

He hung his head. "You did. And I've felt terrible ever since. What I did was unforgivable, but I'm still asking you to forgive me."

Ruth scowled. "Don't push your luck," she finally said.

"OK. I know I'm on very shaky ground. *Broiling* shaky ground," he said, wiping his face with an already soggy handkerchief. "Could I at least try to make amends by taking you someplace air conditioned for lunch?"

Ruth considered the cooling situation in her apartment, where she'd been headed before Adam appeared. Was the principle of the thing that important? Yes, but on the other hand..."I suppose an air-conditioned lunch would be OK," she said, reluctantly. Everything around them was shimmering in the heat. The clock on the bank blinked the unwelcome news that it was already 102°.

Adam wiped his face again. "Wish I'd brought the car."

"We wouldn't be in it long enough for the air conditioning to even kick in. Why don't we just go to the coffee shop and have some ice cream first?"

"Eat dessert first because you might not be hungry for it later?"

Despite herself, she smiled. "Something like that."

As they waited for their sundaes and sandwiches to arrive, Adam tried again. "I was trying to think where else might be cooler this afternoon. The pool will probably have half the town in it by now. I don't suppose I could convince you to come over and watch a DVD at my place?" He didn't even wait for her to finish shaking her head. "Well, my car has really good air conditioning. Maybe we could take a drive through Chautauqua Park?"

Ruth thought that over. The simple relief of sitting somewhere cool for the first time in days was improving her outlook on life in general. A drive through the park with the air conditioner blasting might actually be nice.

As Adam pulled his car out of the alley behind the Caldwell & Talbott office building, Ruth leaned over to adjust the air-conditioning vents and caught a glimpse of a familiar figure walking down the library steps. "There's Jodi," she said, with some surprise. "I had no idea she even had a library card. I've never seen her in the library."

"Uh-huh." Adam wasn't really interested. "Why don't you take my iPod out of that case on the floor there and plug it into the stereo?"

"You left an iPod in the car in this weather?"

"Not on purpose. I did some driving yesterday, got home after dark and forgot the case was in here. I think it'll still work. If not, maybe you can fix it." The iPod was definitely hot to the touch, but it did work. "Well, at least I'm not going to be giving Chet any more reasons to yell at me by bringing that in to the shop."

"He'll be very disappointed," said Ruth. "I think he likes yelling at you."

"I do my best to keep Chet happy, can't you tell?"

As they drove slowly through the park, cool air washing over them, soft music playing, Adam said "Hey, how about I make dinner tonight? I'm beginning to think you think I can't cook."

"I told Eleanor I'd babysit for her kids tonight."

He chuckled. "OK, I know when I'm getting the brushoff."

Ruth smiled. "Believe it or not, I really am going to babysit for Eleanor tonight. She's working on a quilt for someone's anniversary next weekend, her mother's meeting friends for dinner at the Elks Club and the twins only think they're old enough to be left on their own."

"All right then, dinner tomorrow? Or should we try for that picnic in the park we never got to have?"

Well, crap. That's what she got for throwing the principle of the thing out the window for a breath of cool air, right? She considered her reply and finally settled for "Depends on the weather. If it's like this again tomorrow, I don't think a picnic would be much fun."

"OK, at least you didn't say no. That's progress. Look, I have a few things to take care of in the early afternoon, so why don't I stop by around four tomorrow and we'll take it from there?"

Ruth turned to look out the window for a moment. *What an arrogant...* "No, I don't think so. Today was nice, but I don't want to make a habit of it."

"Habit?" He blinked. His fingers tightened on the steering wheel, and then he eased the car off the road and onto the grass, parking and letting it idle so the air conditioner kept running. "Ruth, I said I was sorry."

"You said a lot of other things, too, and you lied."

He looked straight ahead for a moment, hands still clenched on the wheel. She could see his jaw muscles working. She was prepared to wait. Finally, he put his hands in his lap. "You're right. I said a lot of things. I... I guess I've gotten into the habit of telling people what I think they want to hear."

"Uh huh. But when I made it quite clear I wanted to hear the truth, you turned around and told me everything but."

He looked away. "I did. I'm sorry for that, too."

She waited.

Finally he turned to her. "It's like you said. There's a lot of water under the bridge between us, and I'm still learning how to swim. We aren't the people we used to be."

"What does that have to do with anything?" She shifted on the seat and got into a more comfortable position to see him as he spoke.

"It means that I've been away for a long time and whether I like it or not, we're closer to being strangers than to being friends after all these years. I don't just instinctively know how to talk with you like I used to."

Ruth raised an eyebrow and considered this for a minute. "You're right," she said, finally.

"Could we please just spend a little more time together, so I can maybe get back on track?"

She looked out the side window, thinking this over. Finally she sighed. "All right, Adam, four tomorrow it is. But let's both make an effort to be honest with each other from now on. Would you take me home, please?"

He gave her a shaky smile. "Of course."

C380

The man finished carefully laying the bunches of leaves on the screen he'd fitted inside the dryer, then turned the big knob on the wall ever so slightly. The dryer started moving, slowly. The fluorescent lights started flickering again. He set the timer for an hour, then went briskly up the stairs, flipped the lights off and went out.

Picnic Al Not So Fresco

Adam looked at the web page that Lydia had linked to in her latest email. He was beginning to get a headache from having peered at his computer screen for so long. He took his hand off the mouse and stretched both arms over his head, leaning back as far as his chair would recline and putting his feet up on the desk. He told himself that he'd just have to quit being so vain about getting computer glasses, because this was getting ridiculous. As he rolled his head around to get the cricks out of his neck he saw the wall clock.

"Oh shit!" The chair teetered on the brink of catastrophe. "*Whooooa..!*" His feet came up off the desk as he lurched forward, and after one long unbalanced moment the chair's front casters crashed back down on the floor. Three o'clock already and he hadn't even thought of shopping for the supplies for dinner. "*Shit!*"

Quickly shutting down the computer, he switched on the answering machine and made a dash for the back door, which balked, as usual. He yanked it closed and ran upstairs to shower and change. Fifteen minutes later, dressed in shorts, a soft knit pullover shirt and leather sandals, he hurried back down the stairs and headed for the supermarket. He'd figure out what he was going to cook when he saw what was on sale.

⋘⋙

Ruth rubbed her damp hair listlessly with a towel as she listened to the weather report on the radio. A hundred and four for the high today. No way, no *way* was she stirring outside of this apartment for picnic, park or full-fledged circus parade. The place was just, just bearable with all the shades drawn and fans going full blast. Even after a half hour under a cool shower she was sweaty and miserably sticky. The thought of having to put more clothes on was depressing in the extreme. But she supposed she couldn't greet Adam in nothing more than a thin cotton tank top and underpants, to say nothing of what she'd do if someone else happened to come to the door. She sighed and went to look for the scented powder.

Half an hour later, well powdered, having decided on a slightly less ratty tank top and faded denim shorts, she stood by the bedroom mirror and fastened her silver barrettes in her hair above each ear. She had to pull the hair up off her neck somehow, and the usual I-don't-care ponytail on top of her head just wasn't going to cut it. She twisted the hair in the back into a loose knot and stuck a lacquered chopstick through it to keep it in place.

There was a knock on the door. Was he here already?

Adam stood on the landing holding two brown paper bags. He stepped back so that she could push the screen door open for him.

"Well, Madame, zee chef is here, and he would twirl his mustache for you if he didn't have his arms full." He dropped the bags on the dining room table. "What do you think, is it too hot to picnic? At least it's not a hundred and four any more."

Ruth pushed the shade aside so she could look out the front window and waited for the thermometer at the bank to blink the temperature. "Oh, right. It's a hundred and two. It's too hot to move. Why don't you just put that stuff in the fridge and we can sit here in front of the fans for a while."

"Hey, my place is air conditioned. Why don't we go over there for dinner instead?"

"No thanks, I don't even want to think about going anywhere." Especially not his apartment, but that was beside the point. She flopped into one of her living room chairs, facing a fan, and tried to get comfortable.

Adam stood for a moment and then smacked himself on the forehead. "God, you know what? I just realized that I am the world's worst landlord. Tomorrow I'll buy some air conditioners for this place, how's that?"

"Everybody and their dog is buying air conditioners in this weather, but I would definitely appreciate it if you'd try."

"I'm sorry it never occurred to me before now. I should do something about cooling the shop, too."

"I think that'd take more than just a window unit."

"I'll look into it anyway. Can't believe I never thought of it before. God, I'm dumb."

He began extracting packages from the bags and ferrying them into the kitchen. "How does Chinese chicken salad, grapes, bread sticks and sparkling apple juice sound to you?"

At this point and in this mood, even cordon bleu dining would have sounded like dog food to Ruth, but she did her best. "Uh, sounds delicious." She paused. "I don't know about you, but I'm not really hungry right now. Something about being baked alive does a number on my appetite."

Adam came back into the living room and flopped down in the other chair. "No kidding. I didn't realize how bad it was till I went to get the groceries. People who work in air-conditioned offices get spoiled. And I'm really sorry I didn't do anything about the building. I just wasn't thinking."

Ruth sighed and changed positions in the chair again. "I can't even get Chet to help me fix the ceiling fan. He's still griping that I spent money on 'something that ridiculous' even though it's been months since I bought it. Oh well, I bet by the end of summer he'll come around. It's either that or melt."

"I'll do my best to get that place cooled for you, fan or no fan. Oh, hey, speaking of 'end of summer,' do you still think we should have a dance?"

"It's too hot to think about it. Ask me again in a month or two."

"Can I at least ask you now if you'll go with me?"

"Ask me that again in a month too."

Adam smiled. "All right." He paused. "Maybe... maybe that will help make up for that other dance?"

Ruth said nothing for a moment. Then she rose. "I'm... kind of thirsty. Can I get you something cold to drink? I have a couple of bottles of beer left over from the last time I had friends over."

"Uh, no, no thanks. Got any soda? If not, I'll take plain ice water."

"Ginger ale OK?"

"Sounds great. I'd forgotten how much you liked ginger ale."

She quickly grabbed two cans from the refrigerator and turned to get some glasses. His voice from behind her made her jump.

"Ruth, did I say something that upset you?"

"No. No. Everything's fine," she said crossly. "It's just the heat, that's all." She set the glasses on the counter and started pouring the soda.

There was a pause. "Ruth, we did agree to be honest, and I'm doing my best. Can't I at least try to make up for having been such a jerk after I left here?"

Ruth stood still for a moment. "I suppose eventually we would have had to deal with that." She sighed and squared her shoulders as she faced him. "All right. Honesty. Heck of a seventeenth birthday present you sent, Adam, that bracelet. I wish I knew how many years it took me to figure out that you didn't do it on purpose."

"Birthday... is that when it got there? Oh, shit." He wiped his forehead with his arm. "Look," he said, holding out his hands in mute appeal, "how can I possibly explain it? I was a selfish, stupid kid who was just too wrapped up in himself and his own little world to think about what he might do to anyone else. Or about the calendar, or about how long it might take a letter to travel. The honest truth is that I just didn't think at all." He dropped his hands, looked down at the floor again, then up at her. "Ruth... I'm... I'm sure it doesn't help anything now to say I'm sorry, but I am. So very sorry. I was a total jackass and there's no excuse."

Ruth turned away. In all these years she'd so often imagined Adam Talbott coming back to her and saying he was sorry, and how she'd make him grovel and show him the door. But she'd never imagined it like this. Now what? She heard his footsteps. She tensed, wary. He stood behind her, close enough for her to feel the warmth of his body but not quite touching her. Too warm, too hot, too close.

And then he put his arms around her, pulling her back gently against him. She stiffened and pulled slightly away, not wanting to be touched. But oh, she thought, how good it did feel to be back in his arms again. Tears slid down her face. And finally she relaxed, nestling against his shoulder as he laid his cheek on her hair. The pressing, pulsing heat of the kitchen seemed to fade. He tightened his hold on her a bit and they stood there in silence, listening to the sounds of their own hearts.

Finally she left his embrace, wiping her eyes with one hand. She found that she couldn't quite face those dark-brown eyes when she turned toward him. "Look, Adam," she said in a shaky voice, "I... we can't change our history in a minute, can we? I mean... I... I need a little more time to adjust. If we could just... just talk about something else for a while... just... do something else..." her voice trailed off.

"I... Sure." His voice was none too steady either. "Whatever you need. But just... look, I don't know if I can put this properly, so bear with me, OK? It's like I tried to say yesterday—those two kids, Adam and Ruth, from way back when—they don't exist any more. Can we try to let that other Adam and Ruth go and start again as the people we are now?"

She looked at the floor, considering. Then, determined to clear the air all at once, she said "But what about Lydia?"

"Lydia? What about Lydia?"

"If we... uh, I mean, won't you and she..." Ruth's voice trailed off in embarrassment.

"Wh... You think Lydia and I are having an affair, is that it?"

Blushing, Ruth nodded. Adam burst out laughing.

"Is that what everyone thinks? Well, no *wonder*... No, Lydia and I are not having an affair. Believe it or not, she's a very happily married woman, and the last thing she'd ever do is get involved with me. Or I with her, for that matter. Lydia is my partner and my friend, but it's never going to go beyond that." Another pause. "Why did you think something was going on between us?"

"Never mind. Why don't you... uh, why don't you put some ice in the ginger ale while I go wash my face? I must look like a scarecrow by now."

"Never, Ruth. Not you."

When she came back, feeling much refreshed, Adam was busy dicing a chunk of cooked chicken. He looked up, put down the knife, wiped his hands and held out his arms. She hesitated. Was that what she really wanted? How to know until she tried? She stepped forward into the embrace.

After a moment's careful thought she turned her face up to be kissed.

What started as a light, friendly greeting changed slowly, deliciously, as she let the kiss continue. *I should stop this*, she thought, but without conviction. Adam tightened his arms around her and pressed her more firmly against him; amazed, she found her body responding electrically to the feel of his muscles through his thin shirt, the feel of his warm bare legs against hers. He brought up one hand behind her head and pulled her lips harder against his. She gasped and clung to him, feeling her nipples hardening against his chest.

Time seemed to stand still as they held each other. But then, overwhelmed, she pulled away, ending the kiss softly and nestling into the hollow of his shoulder as he stroked her hair, unable to speak. Their breathing seemed to be the only sound in the room. She closed her eyes.

"Well," he said, finally, smiling, "That's a start. Now I guess I'd better earn my keep by finishing supper."

The spell was broken. She stepped back, also smiling. "Guess so. Wouldn't want anyone to think you were totally useless. I'll go put on some music to flip burgers by."

"Burgers! Hey, I told you, Chinese chicken salad. Burgers, indeed," he said, mock-indignantly. "Besides, I never know how long to boil the buns." They both laughed.

Ruth put on the John Barrowman CD and rejoined Adam in the kitchen, taking plates and wineglasses from the cupboard and setting them on the table. "Does zee chef want zee tablecloth to go with zis?"

"Zee chef will be lucky to get zee supper on zee dishes at zis rate."

⋙⋘

Afterwards, sipping the last of her apple juice, Ruth had to admit that Adam was a good chef. As he stacked the dishes and took them to the kitchen she watched the play of muscles under his shirt and smiled. He looked up to find her watching him and smiled back. Outside, the street lights were beginning to flicker on around the square and the sky glowed purple and red. It felt cooler inside the apartment; the heat of the day was broken. Adam ran water in the sink and began to rinse the plates. Ruth went into the living room, opened the windows and moved the fans to pull in the cooler air from outside. Charlie appeared from his usual haunts in her bedroom and meowed to be fed. Adam filled Charlie's dish and was rewarded with a purr.

Ruth looked out the window for a moment, watching the play of colors in the sky and the slow traffic around the square. Finally she turned away, switched on a lamp and went to curl up in her favorite chair.

A few minutes later Adam put the last dish into the drainer and came in to settle down cross-legged on the floor in front of Ruth's CD collection. "I'll get you a dishwasher, too," he said with a smile.

"Oh really? Washing dishes for two was such a hard job?"

"Men are lazy, you know that. Besides, as a landlord I definitely need to make up for lost time." He selected some disks, took one out of its jewel case and put it in the player. "Would you like to dance?"

Ruth thought about it, and was about to decline. Even with the cooler breeze coming through the fans it was still too warm for prolonged close contact. But then, hearing the beginning song on her Julio Iglesias album, she sat up straight and bit her lip. Misunderstanding her motion, Adam stood beside the chair and held out his hand. After a moment, she took it. They danced slowly across the floor, nestled together, following the slow rhythm of the music. "Do you suppose we should pull the shades again?" Adam murmured.

Ruth smiled. "To keep down the gossip, you mean?"

"Wouldn't want them saying you were in cahoots with the destroyer." The song ended and they looked at each other. "Seriously, Ruth, do you think we should?"

"No. If someone's looking, which I doubt, that would just make them even more suspicious. You've been in the big city too long."

Wordlessly, he gathered her back into his arms. *This is all wrong,* Ruth thought. *I shouldn't be doing this. It's too much, too soon.* But she couldn't bring herself to pull away.

After a moment Adam said, "You probably won't believe this, but the first night I saw you again I was trying to remember that old college girlfriend's name and I couldn't do it. Still can't. I don't think we dated for more than a month, after all that. Not coming back for that Homecoming was probably the dumbest thing I've ever done."

Ruth bit her lip again. She wasn't ready to discuss it. Adam leaned his cheek on her hair.

"Did you ever think about me?" he asked. "I mean, besides thinking about running over me with a tank or dropping a piano on my head or something?"

Ruth took a breath. "Um, once in a while."

"Ah," he said, "that's good to know." He tightened his arms around her a bit and they danced in silence for a few moments more. The song ended. Ruth stepped back, not looking at Adam.

"It's still a little warm for dancing," she said, her voice a bit shaky. "Can we sit the next couple out?"

"Sure." He took her hand and drew her over to the chair, sitting down and pulling her onto his lap. She felt stiff and awkward, not sure whether she wanted to stay. He reached up to caress the side of her face gently with his fingertips. Then he pulled her closer to him, snuggling her into the curve of his shoulder and holding her gently. She relaxed. He stroked her hair. They sat in silence for a long time, listening to the music. Charlie hopped up and snuggled in.

The disk ended. Ruth thought about getting up to find another one, but she didn't feel much like moving. Neither, apparently, did Adam.

"Does that thing have a remote control?" he said softly.

"Fat chance. Someone decided not to claim it after I fixed it, so I kept it. Too cheap for a remote. Both me and the player."

Adam laughed and hugged her tightly. "Oh Ruthie, this feels so good. I wish I hadn't been so unforgivably stupid. I would have tried to make things up with you a long time ago."

Ruth was thoughtful. "I don't know whether that would have worked or not, Adam. I was really angry with you for years."

"Quite rightly so."

She nestled back against his shoulder again and they sat for a moment, petting the cat, completely at peace.

The phone rang, making Ruth jump. Charlie hissed. She sat up, and Adam pulled her back. "Let the machine get it," he said.

"I don't turn the machine on when I'm home."

"Ewww," he said with a grin. "Then just let it ring. They'll call back."

"No, I think I'd better answer it." She scooped up a very disgruntled cat and got to her feet. Adam shook his head but let her go. She went into the kitchen and picked up the receiver just in time to hear a click. "Typical," she said. "They hung up."

"If it was important, they'll call back. Well, as long as you're off my lap, let me pick another CD."

Whatever he was about to say next was drowned out by a horrible crash of broken glass from below, followed by the shrill ringing of the shop alarm and running footsteps.

"What the...!" Ruth gasped.

Charlie, panicked, struggled out of her arms and disappeared into the bedroom at top speed. Ruth ran to the front window. She pushed her head hard against the screen, trying to see the sidewalk. Tires squealed from the side street as Adam ran out the door. He was already at the bottom of the stairs by the time Ruth stepped out on the landing.

"No lights on the truck and it was too far away when I got here," he called up to her. "You better go put some shoes on before you come down. There's glass all over the place."

"Shoes... oh!" Ruth dashed into the bedroom to slip on her sneakers. By the time she joined Adam in front of the shattered shop window quite a few people had gathered. Broken glass littered the sidewalk. She stared at the destruction in shock. "Oh, my God..." There wasn't much of the plate glass left intact. A rusty old car wheel lay in the window area next to the Victrola. Mrs. Lewis's antique radio was gone.

Adam was taking action. "Any of you see what happened? Anyone recognize who did it or get the license number on that truck?" No one had been near enough to see clearly, apparently. They shook their heads, murmuring among themselves. One of the bystanders spoke up.

"It was at least three people, I saw that much—two of them jumped into the back of the truck. Looked like men. Must have been, to pitch that wheel through the window. But they were wearing jackets and baseball caps. I couldn't see who they were."

"Ruth?" Adam took her elbow. "Does the alarm ring the police, or should I call them? Ruth?"

She shook her head and turned away from the window. "Alarm... oh... Yes, it rings the police. They should be here any minute." She started toward the remains of the window.

"No, don't touch anything till they get here." He pulled her back.

"Adam, my window! And the radio! We're insured, but..."

"Don't worry about any of that. Where are your keys?"

"Um, upstairs, on the table by the door." A police car came wheeling around the far corner of the square, siren blaring and lights flashing. By this time quite a crowd had gathered. The car stopped and two officers got out.

"Ruth, what happened here? Is anything missing from the store?" one of them asked.

"I... I don't know. I heard a crash and ran down. I didn't see who did it. Oh... A radio was stolen from the window."

"Did any of you see anything?" the officer asked the people milling around. The man who had spoken up earlier stepped forward to tell his story again and the cop began to take notes. Adam returned with Ruth's keys and handed them to her.

"Adam?" said the other officer, turning back from the window, "Were you here when this happened?"

"Yes, but about all I saw was a light-colored pickup truck heading off in that direction," Adam said, pointing up the street behind him. "It had no lights on and I didn't get a good look at it."

"OK," said the officer, "Ruth, why don't you give me the keys and I'll open up and see if there's anything inside and shut off the alarm while I'm in there."

Ruth handed over the keys without a word, still numbly staring at the remains of her shattered window.

ℭℛℬ

Much later, the police report finished, and having seen to getting the shop window boarded up, Adam tucked Ruth into bed and kissed her gently on the forehead. Charlie was already curled at the end of the bed, purring. "Don't worry about anything. If the insurance doesn't cover the window, I will."

"But what about the radio?" she said, for what seemed like the hundredth time that night. "It wasn't worth anything much to anyone but Mrs. Lewis..."

Adam stroked her hair. "Time enough to worry about that in the morning. I bet Mrs. Lewis will just be glad that you're all right."

Ruth tried to smile. "Yes, I guess she will. I'll sleep now. Thanks for everything."

He turned out the light on her bedside table. "I'll latch the door on my way out. And don't worry about anything, please. I'll come by in the morning and we'll get this whole mess straightened out."

216

"Thank you, Adam." She held his hand tightly for a moment and then let it go.

As Adam pulled his car into the parking space behind his building, he blinked. *What the hell?* Leaving his headlights on, he turned off the engine and got out to take a look. He swore once, sharply. The office door stood slightly open.

 C380

At four o'clock in the morning Adam cradled the phone against his shoulder, leaned back in his chair and stretched, wearily stifling another yawn. "I can't tell if they took anything or not. I ran out of here in a hurry yesterday so the door probably didn't shut right, and I left the copier on. So they could have come in here and copied anything they wanted. Nothing looks disturbed, but I just can't tell. If it's any help, the police can't tell either." He listened for a moment and sighed. "No, I didn't check the counter on the copier. It was only the two of us using it. I have no idea how many copies have been made."

Lydia's voice came tinnily down the line and he shifted the receiver a bit closer to his ear. "I'll be there just as soon as I can," she said. "In the meantime, give the place a thorough going-over and see if you can find anything missing or disturbed. I'm sure I don't have to tell you how important that is."

"You don't have to, but you'll tell me anyway, right?" he snapped. Silence on the other end of the line. "I'm sorry, Lydia, but I've been up all night. I'm so tired right now, I couldn't tell if a herd of elephants went through this place. I'm going to lock up and get some sleep. I've got a guy coming first thing in the morning to fix that back door. That's about the best I can do right now." He looked at his watch for what felt like the fiftieth time since he'd dialed the phone. He stretched again and this time he let himself yawn, not caring if it went directly into Lydia's ear.

It must have. "You go ahead and get some rest and I'll talk with you after I get to New Orleans tomorrow. Goodbye, Adam." The line went dead. *Oh brother,* he thought, *now she's pissed at me. Well, she's just going to have to be pissed for a while.* He got wearily to his feet and looked around the office, still seeing nothing out of place except traces of fingerprint powder here and there. He switched on the answering machine, slammed the back door shut and made sure it latched behind him before he trudged up the stairs.

It was already beginning to get light outside. In the apartment he paused only long enough to kick off his shoes, flip on the air conditioner and turn off all his phones before he lay face-down on the bed and fell asleep.

CฦBO

Papers were strewn all over the carpet. Two young men lounged in the chairs, nodding, dozing, heads snapping awake now and again. The woman on the floor pawed through sheet after sheet.

"Geez, I'm glad I'm not paying you guys by the page," she muttered. "Where did all this shit come from?"

"I told you already. Buncha folders in his desk drawer, mostly. Wasn't too much worth looking at in the file cabinets."

"I can't make heads nor tails out of most of this... Heyyy, wait a minute!" She held a sheet of paper closer to the light. "Where's the rest of this, now..." She ruffled through the pages on the floor again. "Here, and here, and... Oh yeah, this is it, this has gotta be it!"

"You still ain't told us what we were after. You about done now? We gotta get going, I know my old lady'll kill me if I'm gone when she gets up."

She waved a hand absently. "In a minute. Don't be so flippin' anxious."

"Anxious my ass, I want my money!"

"Yeah," the other young man chimed in. "Me too. And we gotta get going."

"All right, all right, all right! Hand me my purse, it's on the floor by your chair." He tossed it over; she opened it up and took several bills out of her wallet. "Here, I'll even throw in an extra twenty each as a bonus. Now get going, and I'll call you later if I need you."

The young men got up and took the money and headed for the door. She barely heard the slam as they went out. Oh, this was prime stuff all right. Now she had him, right in the palm of her hand.

Jodi squeezed the stack of papers against her chest and laughed and laughed and laughed.

Broken Glass

At 11:15 the next morning Ruth stepped cautiously over the window display area's curtain rod and onto the seat of a rickety wooden chair inside the shop. The heavy dustpan full of broken glass wobbled in her hand and she had to grab quickly to steady it. The last thing she needed was more glass on the floor. The chair creaked. She swayed, got her balance with an effort and hopped down to dump the last load of debris into a fiberboard barrel.

After setting the dustpan and whisk broom safely on the counter, she wiped her face with the corner of her apron and sighed. This was the first time all morning she'd been left alone long enough to make any headway in the window. It felt like everyone in town had come in to check up on her. The shelves in the back were stacked with enough old broken appliances to stock a thrift store for a year. Well, at least they'd all tried to help out.

With the plywood covering what was left of the front window, the room was depressingly dark. The fluorescent light was on overhead but it just wasn't the same. And even with one of her box fans from upstairs humming away on the counter the heat was oppressive. She pulled one of Chet's old bandanas out of her back pocket and wiped her face and neck. In ten seconds she was sweaty all over again.

The Victrola was on the counter. She looked at it and picked one last sliver of glass out of the horn. "You wouldn't think that one lousy window could break into so many pieces," she said sadly.

The bell jangled a warning as Mrs. Lewis came hurrying through the door. "Oh, my dear, this is terrible! The police just got ahold of me. I'd been visiting my sister and I'd forgotten all about that radio. Are you all right, Ruth?"

"I'm fine, Mrs. Lewis, but I... I guess the police told you that they took your radio. I... I think my insurance will cover it, but it will be a while before I can pay you what it was worth."

"Oh, heavens, dearie, don't you worry about that. I didn't mean terrible that the radio was gone, I meant terrible that this happened to you! I just came down here to tell you not to worry about that old thing. It probably isn't worth two cents. I only kept it because my father gave it to us as a wedding present. I've been trying to call you all morning, but your line was busy. I got worried about you so I just came on down to see what was the matter. Honestly, this town. You go months without anything happening and then all of a sudden the police are all over the place. Here and over to that Talbott boy's office. And I used to think this was such a peaceful place to live." The elderly lady shook her head.

"Over to... The police were at Adam's office? Did something happen there too?"

"Oh, hadn't you heard? They think someone broke in there. Just pushed the back door open and walked right in. Regular crime wave." She took a handkerchief out of her purse and patted her face. "To go along with the heat wave."

"I... yes, regular crime wave." Ruth chewed her lower lip. "Well, if we ever get the radio back I promise I'll call you first thing. I did manage to get it working, and I just had it here in the window because I thought it looked good with the Victrola. I never dreamed someone would want to steal it."

"Well, I'm just glad to hear you're all right, Ruth. Don't you worry about the radio. It'll turn up. And even if it doesn't it's no great loss. Are you going to be able to get that window fixed?"

"Yes, but the glass company didn't have that size plate glass in stock so it'll probably be a day or two."

"Oh, well, then that's not so bad. I was going to say that maybe you could make the best of it by having a fire sale, but in this heat I don't know that people would get the joke."

⋘⋙

Ruth pulled the long cord of the workshop phone behind her as she paced nervously back and forth in the cluttered space between the two benches. She'd left a message on Adam's office answering machine and was trying his apartment number. No answer. She let the phone ring about twenty times and finally hung up. Chet came through the back door with two large bags from the hardware store and dumped them on top of an old dead console TV. "Where'd that fool cat get to?"

"Cat..." Ruth shook her head, trying to get her mind back on track. "Oh, I left him upstairs. He'd be way too spooked down here. He'd probably try to make a break for it out the door before his paws hit the ground. I guess we should call someone to come fix the screen while they're fixing everything else."

"I'll fix the screen. Been meaning to for a while now. That's part of what's in the bags." He gestured toward the front of the shop. "Insurance gonna cover it?"

"Yes, they say it's covered, but it looks like the premium is going to go up." She sighed.

"Look, you been fretting over this thing all morning. Why don't you take a break? Get out of here and go do something nice for yourself. I can handle the counter for a while. I think everyone who's gonna come in here has already been."

Ruth looked at the overburdened shelves. "Yeah, I wouldn't know where to start on all that junk even if I felt like it. All right, I guess I'll go take a walk. If anyone calls, I'll be back in about half an hour, OK?"

"Take your time. You've done all you can in here for now."

A few minutes later she wandered down the sidewalk past the high school, wishing she'd gone swimming instead. The air around her shimmered. Seeking shade, she turned and crossed the street. It was only marginally cooler under the trees. She trudged along for half a block, then turned to go back. But then it occurred to her that the Veterans' Club offices were just a bit farther down the block. As long as she was out, she thought, she might as well check into getting the Veterans' Hall for the end-of-summer dance.

The air conditioning in the office was blessedly cool. The secretary greeted Ruth cheerfully, checked the calendar and found that renting the hall for the Saturday night before school started was possible. "There's a hundred dollar deposit to reserve it."

"Oh dear, I forgot my purse." Well, she thought, that much was true. No need to mention that there wasn't any money in it anyway. "Look, would you pencil us in for that night and I'll bring you the money later? What with the window being broken and all I really haven't got my act together today."

"Oh, of course. I heard about that. Are you all right? Was anything stolen?"

"Just an old radio out of the window. I don't know what I would have done if they'd taken more than that."

"I can't believe they'd try something like that when people were still walking around in the square. Didn't any-one see who did it?"

Ruth sighed. "No, nobody was close enough. I guess whoever did it must have just sat and waited for the right moment."

"Honestly, if a person's not safe on the square... Well, anyway, don't worry about the deposit. You can get it to me any time before the end of the month. The dance sounds like a lot of fun. If you need help planning let me know, OK?"

By the time she got back to the shop she felt more wilted than ever. Chet had the floor fan going but the breeze did little good. They sat at their benches listlessly, the occasional sound of a tool being dropped breaking the silence. Finally, Ruth heaved a sigh and stood up. "Look, Chet, let's just close the place down for the day. We're not going to get anything done and we haven't got any space left for more stuff to fix. No use our sitting here and melt-ing. I'm going to head on over to the library for the rest of the afternoon."

"Yeah," Chet said wearily, "I guess you're right. I think I'll go spend some time down at the tavern, check out their cooling system. Can't be much worse there than it is here. I might just take a walk around town later on."

"What for?"

"I got to thinking about all these supposedly busted gizmos that work fine once I get 'em on the bench. I got an idea about what might be causing the problem."

"Really? What?"

"Well, not sure about it yet, but seems to me they're all coming from houses in the same area. Wonder if there's something wrong with the power in that neighborhood that the electric company hasn't gotten around to fixing."

"I wouldn't put it past those guys, they'll wait till something blows up before they'll agree it might need to be looked at. Good idea, Chet. Just don't fry yourself looking at power lines if you don't have to."

"I can see sparks spitting a lot easier in the dark," said Chet with a smile. "Now go on, you, git."

⁂

Ruth stood in the relentless heat on the sidewalk in front of the library and looked at Adam's building across the street. The curtains in the office were drawn and the lights appeared to be off. An air conditioner rattled away in one of the front windows upstairs.

She shifted from one foot to the other, trying to decide whether she should go over and check on Adam. Finally she crossed the street and tried the office door. It was locked. Oh well, he was probably asleep upstairs. As she turned to cross back to the library she heard the phone ring inside. Curious, she pressed an ear against the glass.

The answering machine picked up and she could just make out the sound of Adam's voice on the answering message. Then the beep, and what sounded like laughter. Ruth pressed her ear harder against the glass, but she couldn't quite catch what the caller—a woman—was saying, nor whose voice it might be. The caller hung up and Ruth shrugged, wiped sweat off her face with her hand and crossed the street.

Oh, the blessed coolness of the inside of the library. For once the beleaguered maintenance crew seemed to have gotten the air conditioning working right. Ruth said as much to Karleen at the circulation desk.

"Wait till you've been in here a while and you may not be so sure. It just feels good because you've come in from outside."

"I don't care. I'm going to go get a long novel and plop myself in a chair for the rest of the afternoon. If the Queen of England calls for me, take a message, ok?" Ruth waved and walked off into the stacks to look for something suitably long and non-demanding to occupy the afternoon. As she passed the reference aisle it occurred to her that she might look for a book that would show her how to fix the ceiling fan. As she browsed through home-improvement books, none of which looked particularly promising, she gradually became aware of a whispered argument between two young men in the next aisle.

"... not here, they're at City Hall."

"You gotta be nuts. We can't just go in there and ask for them. There's gotta be something like that around here."

"No, you moron, I been telling you. They keep that stuff at City Hall. Or at the courthouse."

"Shhhhh! We're just gonna have to do the best we can here. Come on, let's try the computer again."

Ruth tried to peer through the shelves, but whoever it was had already started walking away. She glanced to her left as they passed the far end of the aisle and saw two guys with baseball caps pulled down over their eyes. Duane? Eddie? Surely not. There was a muffled exclamation and their whispers faded away under the sound of the air conditioning. She went back to her search for "fan fixit" instructions and the two young men were quickly forgotten.

⊂⊃

The hand on her shoulder was insistent. "Ruth? Ruth?"

Her eyes snapped open. In a fog, she shook her head and looked around. Wh... where was she?

"Ruth? I'm sorry to wake you, but we're closing in twenty minutes."

Ruth's vision gradually cleared and it dawned on her that she'd fallen asleep in one of the library's comfortable reading chairs. Karleen stood over her.

"Oh... Thanks, Karleen. It must have been a longer night than I thought."

She sat up and took her feet down off the low table in front of her. Her leg muscles protested. She stretched, trying to bring life back into her stiff body. It was an effort. Finally she gathered up her books and headed for the checkout counter and then for home. The heat outside hit her like a furnace blast. The clock on the bank said that it was 5:45 PM and 98 degrees.

Her apartment was still like an oven even though she'd had the windows closed, the shades drawn and two box fans going all afternoon. Charlie was flaked out on the wooden floor in the bedroom, panting. "I know how you feel, cat," she said as she changed into short cutoffs, a sports bra and a loose-fitting t-shirt. "I bet you wish you could shed that fur coat." She petted Charlie, who gave her a brief "mrow" in return and put his head down on the floor. "We'll have air conditioning soon. I hope."

She was standing in front of the open refrigerator door, trying halfheartedly to decide what to eat, when the phone rang.

"Hi," said Adam, "I just woke up. Would you like to go get some supper and then take in a movie? It doesn't matter what's playing as long as the air conditioning works."

"They've got some teenybop flick again this week and not even air conditioning would make it worth sitting through that. But I'd love to go have some supper. I've been standing in front of the refrigerator for five minutes and all that's done is chill my feet. Pretty expensive way to cool off," she said with a laugh.

"Well, look, we can decide on what to do when I get there. Give me about half an hour to shower and I'll come get you. Pick wherever you want to have supper. I'll even take you out of town if you don't want to be seen in Lyric with me."

"I don't feel like driving. Maybe I'll just put a bag over your head so they won't know who I'm with." They both laughed. After a short pause, Ruth hesitantly asked "Adam, did someone break into your place last night?"

She heard him sigh. "Yeah, it looks like they did, but I can't tell if they took anything. Nothing is obviously disturbed. That old back door never did latch right and I guess someone took advantage of it." He sighed again. "Well, we can talk about that when I get there. Right now I need to go scrub myself off and wake up a bit more. I'll see you in a little while."

"I'll change into something a bit more suitable to being seen in public myself."

An hour later they sat at a table in La Cocina Mexicana, dipping freshly made tortilla chips in salsa and sipping cold iced tea. Ruth's friend Grace came over to say hello. "I was real sorry to hear about the break-in, Ruth."

Ruth thanked her and quickly changed the subject. "Hey, did I mention we're thinking about having an end-of-summer dance just for us grownup types, the Saturday before school starts? Want to help plan it?"

"What a great idea! I haven't been dancing in what feels like forever. Sure I'll help. Which band are you going to get to play?

"I have no idea. Do you know anyone who might be available that weekend? Or a DJ who'll play records if we can't find a band?"

"No, but I'll check around. It's not like the local bands are on nationwide tour or anything. Of course, most of them are too punk for us old folks." She grinned, then looked up as the restaurant door opened and a group of people came in. "Uh oh, I'll talk with you later! Great idea!"

Ruth turned to Adam. "That reminds me, the Veterans' Club needs a hundred dollars for the deposit on the hall. Can you take care of that? I told Jennie at the office that I'd bring it in when I could."

"Oh sure, no problem. And I mean it; I want you to let me know what the new window will cost."

She looked away. "Don't worry about that. The insurance will cover it." Why was she so reluctant to let him help? She focused her attention on a large bullfight poster on the wall and bit her lip. There was a brief silence. Then Adam reached across the table and patted her hand.

"Are you... oh, hi!"

What? Ruth turned to see two more classmates greeting Adam.

"So Ruth, what's this Grace was saying about a dance? She said to come ask you two."

"Yeah, end of summer dance. Wanna help? We're taking names for the planning committee."

"Oh, well, I don't know about planning..."

Reprieved, Ruth continued the discussion about the dance and the window was quickly forgotten.

After supper they strolled slowly around the square in the direction of the movie theater. The sun had set and the air was a little cooler. The breeze swirled little bits of paper around in curlicues on the sidewalk. "Looks like the dance idea is a big hit." Ruth was feeling happy for the first time all day.

Adam looked at her and smiled. Ruth leaned her cheek against his arm. A warm glow spread through her, and it had nothing to do with the weather.

They reached the movie theater, which was indeed showing the Grade-Z teenybop movie. "Oh brother," said Adam, "you were right. Well, how about we get my car and go check out some of the drive-ins? Surely there must be a few of them still operating."

"A few of them are still open, but I'm not sure any of them would have anything better than this. Why don't we just take a drive out to the lake instead, get some ice cream or something? It's not that hot out any more."

"Ice cream sounds like a great idea."

They sat at a battered metal picnic table beside the soft-serve ice cream stand near the lake and licked swirled cones, watching clouds of bugs coalesce around the lights. Adam wiped a dribble of white off the corner of his mustache and grinned. "This stuff tastes just like it always did."

Ruth smiled. "See what you've been missing, staying away so long?"

"All the comforts of home... huh, that's weird."

"What?"

He turned his head slightly and watched a hopped-up car cruise down the dirt road, turn the corner and disappear. "I could swear that's the third time that car has been past here in the last few minutes. It's got rocks in one of its hubcaps or something."

"It's a good night for cruising. Don't you remember spending all those summer nights just riding around?"

"Yeah, but it usually took us longer to drive around here than that. I wonder what's going on?"

"You're just jumpy because of last night. It's some kids with nothing better to do."

"Yeah, I guess you're right... wait, here it comes again the other way." Adam turned and stared at the car. Reflections of the ice-cream stand's neon sign in the windshield made it impossible to see the driver clearly. Suddenly the car accelerated, raised a cloud of dust and took off.

"There, see?" said Ruth. "Kids. Eat your ice cream before it all ends up in your lap."

"Yeah..." His voiced trailed off as he looked down the road after the car.

മാ

Chet strolled down the sidewalk, checking a short list of addresses on a grubby piece of paper. What, he wondered, did these places have in common besides being within a block or two of each other? He looked up at the power lines and saw nothing obviously wrong. No signs of sparking or burning or squirrel damage or anything that might cause trouble. There was only one transformer in the area and it looked OK. He paused at a corner and wiped his face with a bandana. Well, so much for that idea. But then, as he turned to head for home, on the opposite corner he saw one of the few commercial buildings in the area, and stopped dead. Could it be something in there? He vaguely remembered having repaired something from that place. He took a pen out of his pocket and added a note to the list. Chet crossed the street and walked along the two sides of the building facing the sidewalk. Then he pulled the earphone from an old transistor radio out of his pocket and stuck it in his ear. Even with the radio barely turned on, the blast of static made him yank the earphone right out. He chewed on the end of his pen for a moment, thinking. And then he put the pen back in his pocket and headed for home.

മാ

As Adam and Ruth went up the stairs to Ruth's apartment, her phone began to ring. She hurried up the last few stairs, unlocked the door and went into the bedroom to pick up the extension before the answering machine kicked in. But by the time she got the receiver to her ear, whoever was calling had hung up. She shrugged. Adam stood in the doorway, stroking the side of his face absently with the backs of his fingers.

"They hung up?" She nodded. He thought for a moment. "Something weird is going on around here. I'm getting a real bad feeling about all this."

"What, because of that phone call? Come on, Adam, this is Lyric. No grand conspiracies here."

"I guess not. I must just be suffering fallout from the office break-in. Lydia busted my chops about it. It just seems so weird that they broke in and didn't take anything."

"Are you sure you didn't leave the door open by mistake?"

"Pretty sure. That back door never did shut right. But I'm almost positive I pulled it all the way closed when I left."

"Well, if nothing's obviously missing, maybe whoever it was got scared off before they could get into anything."

"That's what I'm hoping."

She opened the refrigerator door. "What would you like to drink? Eleanor brought over a bottle of wine and there's some left."

"Ginger ale will be fine, or ice water."

She turned her head to one side, thinking. "You don't drink alcohol, do you."

He ran his hands through his hair. "Uh, no. No, I don't. Is that a problem?" He sounded ever so faintly uneasy.

"Why would it be a problem? I just wondered. Now I'll know not to offer you wine, that's all."

He looked at her for a long moment. It seemed to her as though he were debating about what to say next. But when he finally spoke, it was only a mild "Why would anyone want to ruin good grape juice, anyway?"

"Oh, it's not as vile as it sounds. But on a night like tonight ginger ale is probably a better idea."

When she came out of the kitchen with two brimming glasses on a tray he was sitting in front of the stereo browsing CDs again. She set the tray down on the floor beside him as he put *Switched-On Bach* in the player.

"My gosh, I haven't heard that one in ages. Good choice."

He settled into an armchair and took a long drink. The glass was half empty when he set it down on the bookshelf beside him, reached to switch off the lamp and held out his arms. She took one final sip of her own drink and hesitantly sat.

A deep chuckle. "I won't bite. Unless of course you want me to."

"That's... uh, that's good to know." She tried to smile.

He pulled her gently toward him, letting her nestle into the curve of his shoulder. She put one arm around his waist with a sigh. After a moment she relaxed completely. He reached up and gently stroked her hair.

For Ruth, time seemed to stand still. Adam shifted in the chair, turned her gently to face him, put his hand on the side of her face and waited till her eyes looked into his. Finding the answer he sought, he leaned forward to kiss her. Slowly, deliciously, he tasted her lips with his tongue. She closed her eyes and drew a shaky breath, feeling a deeply erotic electricity coursing through her body. Tentatively, then with growing passion, her tongue answered his. She felt him gasp. *I should stop this,* she thought. *This is wrong. It's too much, too soon. I should stop...* the thought trailed off as he brought one warm hand up under her shirt, gentle fingertips tracing trails up her back. *Oh,* she thought, *but it feels so right.*

He shifted position slightly, turning to bring his hand around to the front. He stopped, released her slightly so he could look into her eyes again. The silent question was asked and answered.

As gentle fingers caressed her breast, tracing circles around the nipple, that electric feeling coursing through her again, Ruth closed her eyes and let her head drop back slightly. Adam leaned forward and kissed her at the base of her throat, his whiskers very slightly scratchy against her skin. She was helplessly lost, overwhelmed.

After a moment, breathing heavily, he stopped. She opened her eyes, looked up at him with a question.

"I need to catch my breath for a moment. Oh, Ruth..."

She brought one hand up to brush the side of his neck with her fingertips. He kissed the top of her head. His hand began to move again, ever so softly. She gasped, shifted position on his lap, buried her head in the crook of his neck.

The music faded out. He stroked her hair, then brought gentle fingers around to lift her chin. She resisted for a moment, then raised her head, expecting a kiss. But instead he looked first into her eyes, then toward the bedroom door. Ruth smiled, got to her feet, held out her hand. They walked together toward the door, but they'd taken no more than ten steps when Adam suddenly stopped. "Uh, just a sec..." He let go her hand. "I... I, uh, I forgot something. I'll be right back." He dashed out the door and down the stairs, leaving Ruth standing in absolute, open-mouthed astonishment.

"What the..." *Dumped at the bedroom door? Of all the... Now what?* She shut her mouth with an audible snap. She heard his car door open, then slam. But instead of the sound of an engine starting, she heard the thump of footsteps as he took the stairs two at a time coming back. And then he reappeared, breathless, looking exceedingly sheepish and holding a small, crumpled white paper bag with a drugstore logo on the side.

Ruth's mouth dropped open again and she put her hands on her hips. "Well! You were awfully damn sure of yourself, weren't you?"

Adam's face flushed red. "Ruth, I... uh..." He looked down at the bag. "I've been thinking about you ever since..." He cleared his throat. "What I mean is, I hoped that... Uh, I didn't want to be unprepared... I mean..." His voice trailed off and his face blazed. Ruth leaned against the bedroom door frame, folded her arms across her chest and tapped her foot on the floor, speechless.

Adam came over to her, took her hand, his face still bright red. "I drove two counties over to buy those. This is one time I *did* care what people might say."

Ruth made a strangled sound and Adam dropped her hand. He looked at her in abject misery. She covered her face with her hands and her shoulders shook. He stepped back, unsure of what to do next. Suddenly Ruth dropped her hands and whooped with laughter. Helpless, weak-kneed, she leaned against the door frame and laughed until she choked, waving a helplessly limp hand in his direction.

It was Adam's turn to stare in absolute astonishment. This was hardly the reaction he'd expected. Finally the laughter trailed off into a chuckle and a misty-eyed sniff. Ruth wiped the tears from her eyes, took his hand again, drew him into the bedroom and snuggled into his arms. He breathed a silent sigh of relief. They cuddled for a moment. Then he released her and stepped back. "Shouldn't I close the front door, now that I don't have any more reason to escape?"

Ruth chuckled. "I suppose you'd better. I'd hate to have you run away like that again."

"I guess this is something I'll be able to laugh about in ten years or so." She could see his grin in the dim illumination from the street lights outside. "I'll go lock myself in."

She circled the end of the bed and stood in front of the window fan, letting the gentle breeze blow her shirt up and away from her skin as she stepped out of her sandals. In a moment he was back, arms around her waist, head bent down to nestle on her shoulder. Except for the hum of the fan, the room was very still.

"After all this time," he said softly, "I'm almost afraid to begin. I've spent so many hours imagining how it would be."

"Who was it that said that it's always best to begin at the beginning?" Ruth reached up to brush his cheek gently with her fingertips. "Although I never imagined you with a mustache."

"I could shave it off, but that would take some time," he chuckled.

"Oh... no, I didn't mean that!" She caressed his face again. "It's... It feels..." Whatever she was about to say was lost against his lips. He kissed her gently, lovingly, and she responded with passion, using her tongue to trace the curve of his lower lip. She felt his sharp intake of breath as his arms slid down her back and up under her shirt. She stepped back and let him pull it over her head. He kissed the curve of her neck as he slid the shirt and then the bra over her bare arms. He looked at her for a moment, his pupils dilated so widely in the dimly lit room that his eyes looked black. He cupped her face in both his hands.

"God, you're beautiful. I... I thought about you so often, but I could never have imagined this," he whispered. She reached to pull his shirt free, and then ran her hands up underneath it and over his smooth bare chest. His skin was warm and soft and as she pressed her fingertips against it she could feel the beating of his heart. He pulled the shirt over his head and dropped it, not caring where it fell. They looked at each other, breathing rapidly. Then Ruth stepped back, untied the belt of her skirt and let it unwrap itself in a graceful circle to the floor, her eyes never leaving his. She stood for a moment, gathering courage, then slipped out of her panties and tossed them away. "Beautiful..." he whispered again.

"Your turn." She smiled. He sat down on the bed, slipped off his sandals and stood up. And in a moment he too stood unclothed, looking, Ruth thought, like a bronzed Greek statue. She had a brief, devilish flash of humor thinking *Hercules with a hard-on*, and smiled as she turned back the covers and wordlessly invited him in. As they slid beneath the cool single sheet he suddenly chuckled.

"What is it?" she whispered.

"No parked car." And they both laughed.

"Did you ever want to do it in a parked car, Adam? I'll bet it worked a lot better in the days before bucket seats were invented."

He snorted in amusement. "Tried it once. Never again." He leaned over and kissed her quickly. "And never, never with you. I couldn't do you justice."

They lay on their sides, facing each other. He put a gentle hand on her hip and then slid it down behind her, pulling her closer to him so he could bend and kiss her throat. His mustache tickled and she squirmed gently. She brought a hand up to caress his ear and he made a soft sound deep in his throat.

"Do you like that?" she whispered.

"Mmmm. How did you know?"

"Oh... call it intuition." She smiled. Her hand ran down and around the back of his neck, circling gently, and she felt him arch back. "That too?"

His answer was not in words. He rolled toward her and over her and his mouth met hers, fiercely, passionately. Her arms went up and tightened around his back. She brought her fingertips down his back and around his sides, making him squirm again. She could feel his arousal, hard between their bodies. Oh yes, this was the way she'd imagined it. He pulled away, panting, raised up on his arms to look down at her.

"Do you... does your... intuition..."

"Do I know? Let me try, and we'll see." She moved sideways and he rolled to his back. She could see the faint sheen of sweat on his skin in the light shining in through the window fan. She nestled onto his shoulder and ran her fingertips slowly down from his collarbone, circling his nipple with the backs of her fingernails ever so gently. He caught his breath and his arm tightened around her. She rose up on her elbow and leaned over to retrace her fingers' path with her tongue. "Mmmmm... I'm glad you're not..." she looked up just as she reached the nipple, "... furry."

His chuckle turned to a gasp as she sucked, hard. His head arched back. "Oh God..."

Her hand traced its gentle way downward, drawing the backs of the fingernails lightly over his skin. His muscles fluttered and she could feel his whole body go tense. She made circles around his navel, down his flanks, finally caressing her way down his leg as far as she could reach, and then back up again, slowly. He arched to meet her hand, but she wouldn't touch him there, not yet. Her tongue made circles around and around and around the nipple. His breathing was ragged. His hand came up behind her head and pressed her against him. She bit him, very, very softly and he made a deep animal sound and writhed on the bed. Her hand came in contact with his erection and she stroked downward, gently, cupping him in her palm.

"Oh my God... Ruth... yes, you know..." He took a deep breath. "Was it... intuition... or imagination?"

She looked up, smiled. "I'll... never tell."

He pressed her shoulder, rolled her over on her back. "Let me show you... how I imagined it would be..." and his mouth descended on hers again. And then on her throat, her collarbone, her breastbone. He pulled away from her, slid down the bed. Her navel. The inside of her thigh. A soft bite. She ran her fingers through his hair. He slid back up again. His face was surprisingly soft against her stomach, her breast. He ran his tongue around the darkness of the areola and it was her turn to gasp. He pulled the nipple into his mouth and she arched against him, her fingers pulling his head closer, closer. His hand slid downwards, circling, caressing damp curls. And then she arched again and the hand slid between her legs, finding her almost painfully aroused. *He knew.* Two gentle fingers circled, circled, circled, circled, circled...

The speed and fury of the climax astonished her. She rose up off the bed with a gasp, a moan, pressing into his hand, fingers clenched tight in his hair. Circled, circled, circled... the ripples crescendoed once more and then faded away, leaving her limp and covered with sweat. Her breath came in ragged pants. He looked up at her. Her hand dropped to the bed. He kissed her gently, turned to pick up the small paper bag from the floor. She closed her eyes. Time seemed to fade away until suddenly he was over her, pressing her legs gently apart, leaning forward, finding his way.

He entered; an electric thrill. She arched against him, wrapped her arms around him, welcomed him in. Imaginary lovers, she thought, always turn out to be smaller than the real thing...

They moved in rhythm, rocking, arching, pulling apart, sliding together. She urged him faster.

"Ruth... I can't... It won't last..."

"I know..." She slid her hands down, pressed against the small of his back, pulling him deeper. "I know..." Would she make it, one more time? Would she? Would she? Oh yes, oh yes. Her fingers splayed out, beyond her control. The rhythm changed, faster, deeper, out of sync...

He gasped, shuddered, thrust again, again, again... And then was still.

附

Much later, she lay with her head in the hollow of his shoulder, her leg thrown across his, listening to the slow beating of his heart. His cheek was pressed against her head and he stroked her hair softly, but he hadn't yet said a word. The ancient town clock rattled, clanked, and bonged out the three-quarter-hour chimes. He turned lazily and looked at the clock on the nightstand. "Hmmm, 1:45 already. I suppose I'd better think about getting home before the gossips catch me."

Ruth stretched and then rose up on one elbow. "Yes, I suppose you'd better." She rolled over onto her back, then sat up and put her feet on the floor. She didn't look at him. Was that all he had to say? Was that it, just a comment on the time? No endearments, no acknowledgement of what they'd shared after all this time? *Oh God*, she thought, *what have I done?* She cleared her throat. "Adam?"

"Yes?"

"Um... do you want the light on so you can find your clothes?"

He looked at her, silhouetted against the soft glow from the window. There was a brief silence. "No, I think I can manage." He rolled onto his side and sat up, then leaned over and kissed her lightly on the shoulder. She said nothing. After a moment, he got up, found his clothes where he'd dropped them. When he went into the bathroom Ruth pressed a hand over her mouth. What had she done?

When Adam emerged, dressed, Ruth was out in the dimly lit living room putting things away, wearing a knee-length nightshirt. He walked up behind her and drew her back into his arms. His thoughts were obviously miles away. After what seemed like an eternity, he spoke. "I'd like to stay here all night, but I don't think that would be a good idea. The biddies must be on overload by now."

Ruth laughed and hoped it sounded natural. "Oh, no overloaded biddies allowed. Yes, go get some rest." He laid his head on her hair. There was another long silence. Finally he kissed her and let her go.

"I'm probably going to be very busy over the next couple days, getting things cleared up in the office and dealing with Lydia. So if I don't come by, I hope you'll understand. Even if I can't oversee it myself I'll send someone to install the air conditioners up here as fast as I can get them to do it."

"Sure, first things first." Her insides were tied up in knots. But he smiled and caressed her cheek with the back of his hand.

"It's just till I get everything straightened away. That shouldn't take too long."

"Right." No talk of anything romantic, just business, just landlord.

As she watched him walk down the stairs, she had to bite firmly on her hand to keep from crying.

CঃৎO

Across town, another phone rang. "He just left," the caller said. "Want me to follow him?"

"Just check to see if he goes home. If he does, leave him. But if he goes somewhere else let me know."

"You got it. Find anything more?"

"Lots of stuff. But I'm not sure what to make of it. When I get it figured out I'll let you know. I'm going to make a bunch more copies and spread them around."

A chuckle on the other end of the line. "So much for the big-shot businessman, huh?"

A laugh. "Yeah. He's going to get his."

The Widening Gyre

The glaziers—one on a ladder and one not—were busy washing the last few fingerprints off the new front window. A small group of mostly elderly sidewalk supervisors stood behind them, watching and pointing, making sure no smudges remained. Ruth came through the curtain from the back, put a blender on the pickup shelf and smiled. Oh, how nice it was to have sunshine in the shop front again. Especially since the original estimate of the time needed to get the new glass had proved overly optimistic.

The workmen gave one last flourish of their squeegees, waved at Ruth through the window, put their tools back in their truck and drove away. The sidewalk supervisors went on about their business around the square.

Ruth stood and looked out the window for quite a while, chewing on a thumbnail, pensive. The sunshine was lovely, but she'd seen what the bill was going to be and only hoped that the glass company wouldn't send it to her till after the first of the month. The insurance company would pay for most of it once she finished filling out all the paperwork. But she still had to come up with the money for the deductible and the agent had told her that the premium would be going up. There went a big chunk of the profits they'd make from fixing the huge stack of broken appliances in the back. And with the higher premiums every month...

Oh well, no use standing around sighing over broken glass. She pushed through the curtain into the back. Chet looked up from the scrambled innards of a Japanese pachinko pinball game. "Darndest thing I've ever seen," he said. "Somebody musta been desperate for something to bring in to be fixed, that's all I can say."

Ruth laughed. "No kidding. Let's just hope people didn't bring in all the broken electronic doodads in town this week."

Chet scowled. "Uh-huh. But what happens if they did? Once we get done fixing this load of junk we'll really be done."

"Oh Chet, don't be such a sourpuss. This couldn't possibly be all of it. Just concentrate on how nice people have been, bringing this much stuff in to help us out." But deep inside, Ruth had to admit she didn't feel as optimistic as she sounded.

"I dunno, Ruthie, I been hearing rumors. Seems your old boyfriend and his partner might just have plans for this town and we ain't part of 'em."

A chill ran down Ruth's spine. "Plans? What are you talking about?"

"Well, leastways what I've picked up, so far it seems like everyone's heard something different. But what the stories boil down to is that they've got something up their sleeves and they're gonna try to make some big changes."

Uh oh. "Well, if every story is different, it's undoubtedly all just gossip."

"That's what I thought at the beginning, but you know as well as I do that gossip doesn't have to be all lies. You know, where there's smoke there's fire. They did buy this building—do you s'poze they bought some of the others too?"

"But wouldn't we have heard if they'd bought more buildings? Eleanor would have told me."

"She didn't tell you about this building getting bought."

"That's because Mr. and Mrs. Shapiro sold it privately and didn't go through the real estate office."

"Right. And if they did it once, they could do it again."

Ruth chewed a thumbnail thoughtfully. "But the only other building we know they bought, they did go through the real estate office."

"That was just to throw us all off the track, I bet."

"Oh come on, Chet. Now you're really getting paranoid."

He huffed and ran a hand through his hair, making it stand straight up on end. "All right, you b'lieve what you want. But I think you ain't paying attention to how serious this could be. That Talbott's gone and pulled the wool over your eyes."

Her indignant reply was cut off by the chime of the bell on the front door. She gave him a glare fit to melt quartz. "I'll be right back," was all she said, but the implication was quite clear that then he'd catch it but good. *But he just might be right. And then what kind of idiot am I?*

CRBD

As her customer paid for his newly repaired toaster oven, he asked, by way of conversation, "Is there any truth to the rumor that we're going to get a new supermarket, do you know?"

"Supermarket? No, I hadn't heard anything about that. Where's it going to be?"

"Well, that's the thing. Nobody seems to know. Heard it was going to be on the square, but that's impossible. I was just wondering if you knew anything about it."

"No," said Ruth, thoughtfully, "I haven't heard anything."

"Oh well, just another one of those urban legends, I guess." He thanked Ruth and walked off across the square, the oven a bulky shape under his arm.

Chet came through from the back. "Now, see, that's what I've been talking about. All of a sudden there's a lot of extra gossip and I'm wondering where it's all coming from. Just like I said, where there's smoke, there's fire. If that Talbott boy is involved in any shady stuff, you better watch your step."

"A supermarket? That's shady?"

"You know what I meant. The point is that all of a sudden there's all these stories going round town about some kind of big business moving in. Now who on earth would be behind something like that but your buddy Adam?"

"Chet," she flared, "it's just gossip! And do you mean to tell me you can't think of anyone else in town who might just be interested in improving the place? Bringing in some kind of business that hasn't already been here for ten gazillion years?" She thought for a moment. "Or, for that matter, spreading lies deliberately to make Adam look bad?"

"All right, all right. I've said my say and I'll shut up." He ran his hands through his hair again. "I just... it's just that I don't want you getting so involved with that boy that you get hurt if something bad does happen."

Ruth looked away. "I'm doing the best I can, Chet."

"I know that, but I'm just asking you to be careful." He shifted from one foot to the other and cleared his throat. "I don't want anything bad to happen to you, Ruth."

Ruth was touched. "Thank you, Chet. I'll do my best to listen to your advice and I will be careful. I'm glad I've got someone like you watching out for me." Chet looked down, embarrassed. Ruth quickly covered by saying "Well, now I think we'd both better get back to work and let the gossip take care of itself. Oh, by the way, did you ever figure out what's wrong with all that stuff that turned out not to be broken?"

"Yeah, there's definitely something funny going on in that part of town. I'm just trying to figure out how I can get a look at the place I think is causing the problem without them seeing me first."

"That sounds like it might be dangerous, Chet."

"Nah. I just don't want them catching me poking around, especially if this is what I think it might be. I'll keep looking. Now I gotta tackle that fool pinball gadget. What on earth possessed them...?" He walked off, muttering.

But after Ruth sat down at her bench she couldn't seem to concentrate on her work. Like it or not, Chet did have a point. Why this sudden surge in the gossip? Could there be something shady going on? She shook her head. Back to work, and no more distractions!

Just before noon, Adam called to say that he would be tied up in a meeting and couldn't join her for lunch as they'd planned, and that he'd been having no luck finding the size air conditioners he wanted, but he was going to keep trying. Ruth ended the conversation pleasantly enough, but after she heard the click on the other end of the line she banged the receiver of the old pay phone harder than she needed to.

"Talbott not buying lunch today?" Chet's voice startled her. He'd pushed through the curtain without her hearing him.

"Guess not. Guess I'll have to go upstairs and make myself a sandwich."

"Your digestion will be better anyway, not having to look at that guy while you're eating."

"True." *Very true.* She marched to the front door, put up the OUT TO LUNCH sign, turned the latch and went out.

As she moodily munched the last of her sandwich, it occurred to her that time for planning the end-of-summer dance was running out. Might as well get a start on it; anything to take her mind off the gossip and her own worries. She got out a pad and pencil and sat staring into space, tapping her teeth absently with the eraser. Who would be best to help get things organized? She scribbled some names with possible jobs. Now, who would be call-able at this time of day...?

With each call she felt brighter. People were enthusiastic about the idea, eager to help, and she was amazed at how easy it was to get the jobs all taken. By the time she hung up the phone half an hour later she had volunteers to find a band, look after getting the refreshments, email as many Lyric expatriates as possible and decorate the hall. And she was pleasantly surprised to find that Adam had taken care of the deposit as he'd promised, and also promised to pay any expenses the admission didn't cover. She was feeling a lot more chipper as she went back down to the shop.

She walked in the back door and found Chet standing in the middle of the workshop floor, eyeing the ceiling fan. "Y'know," he said, "I bet fixing that sucker wouldn't be so doggone tough."

"I don't believe my ears." She made a great show of fanning herself with one hand and collapsing onto her stool. "Do you feel all right, Chet? You do realize you just volunteered to fix that fan, you know that, don't you?"

He scowled at her. "Now don't you be getting your hopes up. I got this dad-blasted pinball thingie to deal with first. That might take days. And that thing" —he waved a hand at the fan— "is still a piece of junk."

"Right. Absolutely. Piece of junk. But pretty soon it's going to be a piece of junk that works, right?"

"I told you, don't get your hopes up. I'm just gonna take a look at it is all."

Well, well, well. Things are looking up all over, she thought with a smile as she got back to work at her bench.

෴

Ruth was just getting ready to close out the cash register for the day when the door bell jangled and Adam came in, tie untied, rumpled white shirt unbuttoned and his suit jacket slung over his shoulder. He looked like someone had taken him through the car wash with the top down.

"Want to go get a pizza or something? I've been driving all over creation and I'm beat. I could use some pleasant company for a change today." He pulled a crumpled handkerchief out of his back pocket, scrubbed his forehead and gave her a weary smile.

Ruth blinked. "I... Well, if you consider someone in a filthy t-shirt and ripped jeans pleasant company, sure. But I don't know that I'd want to be seen with me this evening."

"It's not your clothes I'm interested in." He winked.

She laughed. "Now, don't start leering at me. I won't be decently leer-able till I've at least had a bath."

He leaned on the counter and gently touched the tip of her nose with a fingertip. "To me you're leer-able no matter what."

She looked directly into his eyes for a moment, then, flustered, busied herself with the cash register. "Um, let's just say that after an hour spent cleaning twenty years of dust balls out of someone's old TV I don't feel very attractive. Did you really want pizza for dinner?"

"I don't really care where I eat dinner as long as it's with you, how does that sound?"

Was this the same man who'd walked out of her apartment with barely a word? She chewed her lip. "Look, I have a few more things to finish here and then I really do want to get cleaned up. Why don't you go get rid of that suit and tie and meet me over here in about an hour? Then we can decide where we want to go for dinner."

"Sounds like a plan to me. I'm through with the business and looking forward to the pleasure."

Ruth grinned. "I'll have you know I'm not that kind of girl."

"Mmmm," he said, touching her nose again, "well, we'll have to see about that, won't we?"

And left her standing flat-footed behind the counter.

Two hours later, Ruth wiped the last traces of a chocolate sundae off her chin and smiled. "This was such a good idea. I'm glad I thought of it."

"Oh you did, did you? Well, in that case, yes, I'm glad you thought of it too." Adam took several bills out of his wallet and put them on the small brown plastic tray under the check. "And now what would you think of a stroll through the courthouse park on the way home?"

"I think that sounds like a great idea." She tucked her hand into the crook of his elbow as they walked beneath the trees in deep twilight. The birds trilled and caroled overhead and they could hear children laughing as they played on the swings and merry-go-round. The lights in the park, old-fashioned ones with large glass globes atop cast-iron poles, glowed warmly around them. Someone was barbecuing chicken not too far away and the aromatic smoke filtered through the air. It was very nearly a perfect evening, Ruth thought.

They reached a wooden bench beside the path and sat. She leaned her cheek against his shoulder and slid her hand down into his. He reached up with his other hand to stroke her hair. After a long, companionable silence she whispered, "Beautiful, isn't it?"

"Mmmm. This is one of those nights you wish could go on forever."

She smiled. "Every time I get to thinking that the time has finally come for me to move on, something like this reminds me of just how great the old home town can be."

He was quiet for a moment. When he spoke, Ruth heard a very faint quiver in his voice. "I wish," he said softly, "that I had a home town."

She pulled back so that she could look at him. "But wouldn't Atlanta be your home town? Didn't you grow up there?"

He was staring off at something in the middle distance. "No, not really. We only lived there for eight years. Before that we lived in Pennsylvania. I never told you much about my childhood, did I? I will, someday." He rubbed his chin. "But not tonight. I wonder what makes a town a home town?"

"Well... I don't really know. I suppose it's just that you think of it that way. I know you guys only lived here a few years, but couldn't you think of Lyric as a home town?"

"No. No, I... just... no. I wish I could." She felt his hand tighten on hers. The other hand was a fist on his knee.

She waited for him to go on. He didn't. "I'm sorry you feel that way. I've never lived anyplace else, except for college, so I guess I don't have a choice. Maybe your home town is... is someplace yet to come," she finished lamely.

He sighed. "Yes, maybe that's it." He uncurled the fist, spread his palm out on his thigh. "You know what I really wish I could do this beautiful evening?"

"No, what?"

"Take you home with me and..." he looked around, dropped his voice to a husky whisper, "make love with you all night long."

"You do? I mean... I thought... I mean, after the last time..."

"What was wrong with the last time?"

Ruth could feel her face blazing red and hoped it was dark enough that he couldn't see. "Oh... I... it's just that you were so quiet."

"Afterwards, you mean? I had a lot on my mind. I'm sorry if I seemed cold. That wasn't what I'd intended at all."

Relief flooded through Ruth like silver rain. She leaned back against the bench and closed her eyes.

He patted her hand. "The next time will be even better. But next time I want to have the whole night together."

"And we can't do that tonight?"

A deep, resonant chuckle. "Well, even if we don't take the gossip factor into account, no, I'm afraid not. I have to get up at the crack of dawn and drive to Chicago. And if I don't want to end up in a ditch in Dixon I'll have to get a good night's sleep."

She opened her eyes and sat up straight. "Leave? Tomorrow?"

"Only for a week. I have to go back to Chicago and then to Des Moines on business."

She sighed. "Well, I suppose if you have to, you have to."

"I don't want to go, believe me. But I just can't put this off."

"Huh. Running off again. I should make you grovel on the floor before I'll take you back." She winked at him.

He grinned. "Grovel? Now that's kinky. I'll think about it." He angled his watch face so he could see it in the light of the park lamps. "Want to stroll a little longer, and then I'll escort you home?"

"I guess so. Might as well enjoy the night while we have it."

"We'll have many more, when I get back. I promise you that."

It wasn't till long after he'd kissed her goodnight and walked down the wooden stairs alone that she remembered all the questions she'd been meaning to ask.

∞

The back door of the building was in shadows, but not so dark as to be completely invisible in the light of the three-quarters moon. Someone dressed all in black opened it slowly and peered out. Seeing nothing alarming, he stepped out onto the concrete steps and looked around. Then he walked down to stand beside the car and look again. "OK," he said softly, and beckoned toward the door. Two other dark shapes emerged, carrying several large bags apiece. The trunk lid popped open and the light inside flashed on. There was a muffled exclamation. One man darted forward to put his hand over the bulb, but not quickly enough. There was a whispered altercation that quickly settled down.

Across the street, deep in the shadow cast by a large tree, someone else was watching. Chet pressed the binoculars a bit more firmly against his glasses and took a close look, nodding as his suspicions were confirmed. After the trunk lid was closed and the men had gotten into the car and driven away, Chet waited a few minutes, then walked briskly back the way he had come.

❦

As the long hot days dragged on, Ruth began to think she knew how that old Greek guy with the boulder must have felt. The unsettled, tornado-watch weather didn't help anyone's disposition much. Two people she'd been counting on to do most of the dance organization got into a major fight and each called her in righteous indignation to announce they weren't speaking to each other, not now, not ever. It took all her powers of persuasion and the last of her patience to get them to quit fussing and start working again.

It took most of a week for the air conditioners for the apartment to arrive, and the process of getting them installed and secured worked Chet into a lather, since he was convinced the workmen hadn't braced them properly in the second-floor windows—and said so, which halted work for half an hour while the matter was discussed. The first test of the bedroom unit blew a circuit breaker and everything had to come to a halt while an electrician was summoned. After that, though, it seemed like smooth sailing. The installers had instructions to tell Ruth that her rent included utilities and that included the air conditioners, so run them all she wanted. She did.

Despite what he'd promised that night in the park, when Adam returned he was busy and distracted. Their only time alone together was one quick lunch in his apartment, cut short by a long-distance call from Lydia. Ruth quietly left rather than appear to be eavesdropping.

Ruth and Chet kept pecking away at the pile of post-window appliances, but it began to look as though Chet's gloomiest prediction was at least partly true. Everyday business in the shop was very slow indeed.

But for all its fits and starts and fights and setbacks, the dance was slowly beginning to take shape. A band had been found and Grace had persuaded her father to help provide the refreshments. Several more people had volunteered to help with decorations and one of Ruth's classmates had used his computer to design some very attractive flyers. Word had gotten around town and even those who couldn't actively help with the dance were eager to attend.

As she closed up the shop on Friday evening, heat lightning rippled through the sky. The dark clouds overhead were swirling ominously and the wind was picking up. The radio reported a tornado watch for neighboring counties, speculated that it could be extended to include Lyric, and mentioned a seventy percent chance of rain later that night. Ruth was tired, frazzled and more than a little peeved at Adam, from whom she'd heard nothing all day. As she trudged up the stairs to her apartment she decided to make herself an especially nice supper and then spend the evening relaxing and watching television, and to hell with Adam Talbott. The apartment was cool, at least. But with a storm coming in, she decided to turn the air conditioners off and open the windows. No sense tempting more blown fuses. Charlie greeted her with a friendly meow and rubbed against her legs. "We'll just watch the boob tube till the power goes out, right, cat?" She took his answering meow as agreement and laughed, feeling a bit better.

She'd just finished washing her supper dishes and was lifting her small portable television up onto the table in the living room when Adam appeared at the door. He handed her a bright yellow ceramic planter filled with a bouquet of multicolored silk flowers and kissed her.

"I'm sorry I've been so out of it this week, Ruth. It's just been one thing after another, and Lydia's constant bitching about what someone might have gotten into in the office hasn't helped any. I'm going to have to head back to Chicago tomorrow for a few days to get things straightened out."

Ruth's shoulders sagged in disappointment. She turned and carried his gift over to the dining room table. "Oh, well, that's business," she said, trying to keep her tone light.

Adam followed her and gently turned her to face him. "I'm so sorry, Ruth. The last thing I want to do is leave you right now, but I really don't have much choice. Lydia's been traveling, and she finally got back to the home office today and she and I have a lot of things that need to be worked out. I'll be back as soon as I can." He kissed her forehead, the end of her nose, then put his hand under her chin and brought her mouth up to his. After a long, gentle, loving kiss he whispered "I really don't want to leave you again."

Ruth closed her eyes and nestled into his shoulder. He stroked her hair gently. After a moment's silence she took a deep breath and let it out with a sigh. He held her a bit tighter and kissed the top of her head. Finally she stepped back, smiling, trying to lighten the mood. "Have you had supper? I just finished, but I'd be glad to make you something to eat."

"I'm not hungry—I had a late lunch. But thanks anyway. I'm getting really tired of all this restaurant food," he said with a grimace. "When I get back you'll have to cook dinner for me for a change."

"You got a deal. Can't have you wasting away on junk food forever."

He laughed. "Would you like to go catch a movie or something? I don't even know what's playing, but surely it can't be as bad as what they had the last time."

"No, actually I just planned to sit here and watch television tonight, and with the weather like this I don't really feel like going out. Would you like to join me for an evening of mindless entertainment?" She gestured toward the living room chairs. "We can order a pizza later if television isn't exciting enough."

He gathered her back into his arms. "I'll tell you what's exciting, and it hasn't got anything to do with television."

"Mmmmm," she said, but whatever comment she'd planned to make was cut off by her sigh of pleasure as he bent down, brushed her hair aside and kissed the nape of her neck. The slightly scratchy texture of his whiskers sent tingles racing all the way down her spine and she clung to him. He kissed her shoulder, the base of her throat, and then gently brought his lips up to meet hers. There was nothing gentle in the way her body responded to the kiss. She parted her lips and brushed his mouth with her tongue, feeling his instant reaction to that as his tongue caressed hers in return. His arms tightened around her and his arousal was very plain.

Suddenly something soft brushed against her bare leg and she gasped and jumped back. Charlie looked up at them and meowed, curling the tip of his long, fluffy tail in the air. Ruth burst out laughing. "Are we neglecting you, you dopey cat?" She picked Charlie up and scratched him behind the ears. Charlie closed his eyes and purred.

"I'd purr too if you'd do that to me," Adam said with a smile.

"I'll bet you would." The mood was broken, for the moment. She handed the cat to Adam. "Here, you hold this beast and I'll go warm up the TV. We can, um, continue the other discussion a little later." She winked. Adam burst out laughing.

"I know when I've been relegated to second place," he said. "C'mon, Charlie, us guys gotta stick together." He sat down on the couch and settled the cat on his lap. Charlie immediately curled up, closed his eyes and started purring loudly, kneading on Adam's leg.

Ruth looked through the television listings in the newspaper. To her delight, "Casablanca" would be starting in ten minutes on the one movie channel the local cable company offered without extra cost. She switched on the television and waited for it to warm up.

"What, no color TV?"

"What we're going to be watching is in black and white anyway," she said, slightly nettled. "And besides, I don't watch TV often enough to care about color."

"You're right. Listen, if you ever do want a color TV I'll buy you one, OK? You haven't lived till you've seen the commercials in old black-and-white movies in living color."

"Hmph," she said, but she could see he was grinning. He moved the cat to a perch on his shoulder and patted his lap in invitation. "I should make you buy me a whole entertainment center and pay for all the movie channels too," Ruth said as she sat down.

"You're right," he said, wrapping his arms around her and pulling her down to be kissed, "you should. But I'll have you know I'm very easily entertained by other things." The last phrase tickled his whiskers against her lips and she giggled. The kiss was just beginning to get interesting when the phone rang.

"Drat," Ruth whispered. "I should have turned on the answering machine."

"Don't answer it. They'll call back." He pulled her back and kissed her again. The phone continued to ring and ring and ring.

"Whoever it is, sounds like they mean business," Ruth sighed. "I'd better go answer it and get it over with."

"Hurry back," he said as she got reluctantly to her feet and picked up the phone.

"Hello? Eleanor? What..."

Eleanor interrupted her. "Ruth, is Adam there?"

"Yes, but..."

"Don't talk, just listen. There's a bunch of people standing down in front of the shop right now and they're getting really ugly. I was just stopping by the bakery and saw them down there so I ran over to see what was going on. That little punk Duane Haldeman was telling everyone they've got copies of some stuff from Adam's office that will 'knock their eyes out' and that they were just waiting for a couple more people to get there before they charge upstairs and 'get some answers.' They know Adam is up there. I had to run around the corner to call you without being heard, so they may be heading up the stairs any time now. You better lock your door and call the cops."

"How... how did they get stuff from Adam's office?" Ruth was still trying to take it all in. "What else did he say?"

"Never mind that, just get to your door and lock it! Then call the cops and make sure Adam stays out of sight till they get there. No—let me call the cops. And you ask them to find out where these guys got the stuff from Adam's office when they get there. Go do it, Ruthie!" The phone went dead.

Ruth held the receiver in her hand, momentarily stunned.

"What is it?" Adam set the indignant cat down on the floor and got up. Ruth shook her head and put down the phone. Now she could hear the sound of voices buzzing from downstairs.

"Eleanor says there's a crowd downstairs and they've got stuff from your office. She says they're getting nasty and they're going to come up here and get some answers. You go... go lock yourself in the bathroom for right now. I need to lock the front door. Eleanor's calling the cops."

Adam swore. "I'm not going to... Ruth, is there another way out of here?"

"Yes, there's that folding fire escape in the back, but... Adam, you're not going to run out, are you? You can't do that!" Ruth stared at him in absolute disbelief. "Just go stay in the bathroom till they're gone. You can't leave!"

"Look, I know this looks bad but I just don't have time to explain everything. You lock the door and when they all get to the top of the stairs I'll go down the fire escape." Heavy footsteps sounded on the wooden stairs. "Run, Ruth! Lock the door!" He made a dash past her and into the bedroom. Ruth darted over to her wooden door,

263

slammed and locked it, still not believing what was happening. She looked into the bedroom to see Adam undoing the latch on the screen. Her mouth dropped open.

"I don't believe this! You can't just run out and leave me to face this... this mob!" Someone pounded on the door. "Adam, no! At the very least, stay in the bedroom and wait till they're gone! That thing makes a horrendous noise and they'll know it's you!"

"I don't have time to discuss it, Ruth. Goodbye..." and he slipped through the screen and out onto the fire escape. Ruth took two steps toward the bedroom and stopped, speechless with rage as the screen swung shut. He was really going to run away! She clenched both hands into fists and ground her teeth together till she thought her jaw would break. A red-hot flush ran all the way to the roots of her hair and left her staggered and dizzy. "You lousy, cold-hearted, sneaky, slimy, stinking *bastard!*" she shrieked, and burst into tears. The pounding on her door continued and she could hear people shouting to her to open it. Her whole body shook; she leaned against the wall for support, fighting to get herself under control again. With the utmost effort, gasping for breath, her body rigid and shaking, she forced the tears to stop. After a moment, panting, she wiped the streaks from her face. And then, head held high, she took a deep breath and went to open the door. Let them do whatever they wanted to do; she no longer cared what happened to her or to Adam Talbott.

Jodi Diamante stood on the landing, backed by a crowd of angry-looking people. "Where's Adam? We know he's in here and we want some answers now!"

"He's *not* here, Jodi. If you don't believe it, you can come in and look for yourself." Ruth looked her adversary squarely in the eye.

"Don't give me that. I've got people who saw him come in." Jodi pushed back against the people behind her till she had just enough room to open the screen door, slipped into the room and looked around while the crowd pushed up onto the landing, trying to see what was happening. Jodi waved a sheaf of papers at Ruth. "He's got a lot to answer for and we're going to make him answer."

"I don't think you or anyone else can make Adam do anything," Ruth said bitterly.

At that moment there was a horrible screech of metal from the back of the building. It took a few seconds to register and then Jodi shouted "He's getting away down the fire escape! Some of you guys go after him!" She ran back to the doorway. But the crowd on the stairs was so thick that people couldn't move quickly. Two men elbowed their way off the stairs, but the sounds of a car starting up came from the alley long before they got to the bottom.

After a moment Ruth heard someone shout "He got away!" from the sidewalk. She no longer cared. Her whole inside felt like it was on fire.

"Doesn't matter," Jodi called, "we've got people watching his place too. They'll nail him when he gets there."

In a daze, Ruth watched Jodi turn from the door and wave her papers again.

"Real hero, that Adam. Boy, I just love how he stuck around to face the music, don't you? Want to see what kind of guy you were sleeping with? Take a look at these," Jodi sneered.

Ruth shook her head to clear it and took several deep breaths, trying to get her emotions under control. Jodi thrust the papers out and waggled them, waiting for a reaction. Finally, without touching the papers, Ruth came to a decision. She squared her shoulders and said "Look, why don't you all come in here and say what you're going to say and then get out of my house. Someone has already called the cops, so you can just talk fast and leave." There was an angry rumble from the crowd. "Come on in here, the lot of you. And believe me, I'll remember who you all are."

People squeezed their way in through the door and stood behind Jodi, nearly filling Ruth's small living room. Ruth sent up a silent prayer that Eleanor really had called the police. "You better say your say and get out unless you want to be arrested."

"We're not going to be arrested. You invited us in here, remember? And the cops aren't going to help your precious boyfriend either," Jodi retorted as dozens of feet shuffled behind her and people milled around. "Look here. He's got files on just about every building on the square. He's got tax records. He's got lists of property values. We've got copies of letters between him and some private investigator he hired to dig up who knows what. How long do you think he's going to let that pitiful little shop of yours last before he tears your building down, Ruth?"

She shuffled papers. "Here, here's some more letters between that slut partner of his," the crowd's muttering grew louder, "and the president of a construction company in Chicago. And here's one from the corporate headquarters of Biggest Discount Stores saying that some 'proposal is extremely interesting' and they'll discuss it further when they see her. What do you think of that?" There were grumbles of assent from the crowd. The people pressed forward; the room seemed to Ruth like a sea of angry faces.

She took the papers, looking down at them without seeing. There was something wrong in what Jodi was saying, but she couldn't put it together. Something... something didn't add up... Everything around her seemed to be lost in a white haze. *That bastard*, was all she could think, over and over again. Tears began to trickle down her face again.

"Yeah, I'd cry too if I were you," said one of the men behind Jodi. "That..." he looked around and changed the language he was going to use, "that jackass sold us out. He's had people here counting cars and doing studies of traffic patterns around the square and down the highway. He's written letters to get bids on some kind of major project. He's even got guys coming in from half the towns around here, asking them to invest in whatever this project is. It looks like he's been asking everyone but the people here in town to go in with him on this! And you've been going along with him all this time. So what's *your* cut of the deal?"

"I... I didn't... I didn't know..." Ruth's voice trailed off. Sneers from the crowd drowned her out. She hung her head. Thunder rumbled outside and the first big raindrops splashed against the front windows.

Footsteps pounded up the stairs and a uniformed police officer appeared at the door. Three more quickly reached the top of the stairs behind him. "What's going on in here?" He stepped inside, one hand on his holster, the other holding his radio at the ready. The crowd in the apartment shuffled feet, cleared throats and moved away from the door. Two of the other officers stepped inside.

Jodi quickly snatched the papers out of Ruth's hand and crammed them into her bag. "Nothing, Officer. Ruth asked us in here. We were just leaving."

"Is that true, Ruth? Did you ask these people in?"

Numbly, Ruth nodded.

"She may have asked you in," said the officer, "but I'm telling you all to get out. *Now!*" People started shuffling toward the door.

Jodi turned to Ruth with a triumphant smile. "When your boyfriend calls from jail or wherever he ends up, Ruth, you tell him he'd better get his little yellow ass out of this town for good. How nice of him to just run away like that. If by any chance he managed to get away, you be sure you tell him to just keep on running."

"Didn't I hear you say you were leaving, Jodi? Then I suggest you move along. *Now.*" The third officer stepped inside. "And don't any of you hang around the square, either. Go home where you belong and stay there, and we'll be watching to see that you do. Never thought I'd see the day when we'd have something like this in Lyric. You all ought to be ashamed of yourselves."

Ruth stood, seeing nothing, hearing nothing, staring fixedly at the floor while the crowd filed slowly out. The officers watched them go down the stairs, then one turned to Ruth. "Are you all right? Did these folks do any damage? Ruth?"

Consciousness dawned for a moment. "Huh? Oh... no, no damage, no harm. I'm fine. I'll be all right." The words came out automatically; she was having trouble even thinking straight.

"Well, if you're sure you're all right, I'll say goodnight. You be sure to lock your door, though, and call us right away if those folks come back. We'll run a few extra patrols by here tonight just to make sure. Do you want me to call someone to come stay with you?"

"Oh... right, I'll do that. I'll be fine. Thank you. Goodnight." She watched the officer pull the door closed through vision that seemed like wavering glass. After a few moments of silence Charlie poked his nose out of the bathroom and meowed long and loud. Ruth looked at him, not seeing. The whole world seemed to be whirling around her.

Tears welled up in her eyes. Charlie meowed again, rubbing against her legs, and she absently bent down to stroke his soft fur. A wave of dizziness washed over her. She ran for the bathroom and threw up again and again till her stomach was empty and she was in pain. But the pain in her stomach was no match for the pain in her soul. Finally the spasms subsided and she sat on the cool tile floor and cried, her heartbroken sobs echoing in the tiny room.

At last, when no more tears would come, she staggered to her feet, washed her hands and face with cool water and went out into the living room. Rain streaked the front windows and "Casablanca" was still playing on the television. Numb with grief, she snapped it off. As she turned away, she saw Adam's gift sitting on the table. "Never leave me again, will you, you double-dealing, sneaky, lying..." The red flame swept through her body again; she grabbed the planter from the table and smashed it on the floor.

Circle in the Square

The old City Hall clock bonged out the three-quarter-hour notes. Ruth opened her eyes and turned to check her bedside clock. Oh say can you see by the dawn's early light—5:45. She kicked and thrashed herself free of the sweaty tangle of sheets. She'd slept for maybe two hours. If that. But she could tell it was no use trying to sleep any more.

Now what? Too restless to rest and too worn out to face the day, she rolled wearily out of bed, pulled off her rumpled sleep shirt and dragged herself into the bathroom.

Breakfast was a miserable effort to choke down soggy cold cereal as she listlessly flipped pages in the newspaper. No mention of the mob scene last night, but she could just imagine what today's prime topic of conversation was going to be all over town. Lyric might as well not bother with a local paper, she thought, because the news was always stale by the time it was printed. As she stirred half-and-half into her second cup of coffee the phone rang. Her first reaction was to let it ring till whoever was on the other end gave up. But after the fifteenth ring she got wearily to her feet and answered. It was Eleanor.

"Ruth! Are you all right? I was just about to come check on you!"

"Good question. I don't know."

"Oh Lord, Ruthie, I tried to get up there to be with you last night but I couldn't get through the mob, and I got scared and ran back to call the cops again, and then the cops chased everyone away and I couldn't argue my way past them. And on top of everything else I left the twins alone in the house and I had to run back when the thunderstorm came through. The cops did say you were all right, but I felt so bad about leaving! Are you all right? Tell me!"

Dead silence. "Ruth? Are you still there? What's the matter?"

"I... Nothing. Everything's... everything's fine..." Her voice broke and she turned her face away from the phone.

"Ruth, what's wrong? What's happened? Should I come over? Can I help?"

Ruth's chin quivered. She pressed her lips firmly together. "I'll be all right. I will. Really. I... I just need some time. I... Thanks, El, but don't come over right now, OK? I have to go down and open up the store."

"Ruth, it's not even eight o'clock yet. You're not due to open the store for at least another hour. Do you want to talk for a while? Tell me. Shall I stop by for lunch? I can take the day off work if you need me."

"I don't know. Maybe. Maybe later in the week. I'm so tired I can't even think straight."

Eleanor hesitated. "Look, why don't you just have Chet open up today and you stay home and get some rest?"

"It wouldn't work. I can't sleep. I'd be up here looking at the walls and going nuts. At least in the store I'll have something to keep me busy."

"If you go to work in this condition you're not going to do yourself or anyone else any good. Hey, how about you and I go for a long drive? You can sleep in the back of the Jeep if you want. I can just keep driving around, how's that sound?"

Ruth rubbed her forehead and pressed her chin into her chest to loosen up her neck muscles. "I don't know, El. I think I need to be doing something."

Her friend was silent for a moment. She'd run out of ideas. "Um, look, I don't want to pry, but I'd really like to hear what happened last night when you feel like talking about it. You know I'm here for you, Ruthie."

Will I ever want to talk about it? "I'll let you know when I'm ready, El. Look, call me later at the shop and maybe I'll be a little less foggy by then, OK? I really have to go now. I'm glad you called." She put down the phone and stared blankly into space for a long time.

⊂ঙ৮ও

When she went downstairs Chet was waiting outside the back door. "Ruth! I was just gonna come up and check on you! I was over at the newsstand and heard what happened. You all right? I heard that no-good son..." he cleared his throat, "that no-good Talbott snuck out the back. I'm gonna give that boy a piece of my mind, and maybe a knuckle sandwich!" Chet shook his fist. "He better be glad my ma always told me to pick on people my own size, that's all I can say."

Tears welled up in Ruth's eyes and she bit her lip and looked away. Chet sized up the situation, took out his keys and opened the door. The telephone started ringing and he went to answer it while Ruth took her shop apron down from its peg and wiped her eyes.

"No, she ain't here. She'll talk to you later. I got a phone call to make now. Goodbye." He slammed down the phone, then took it off the hook before it could ring again and turned to Ruth. "Annie at the newspaper. Three guesses what she wants." He turned back to the phone and dialed Directory Assistance. "I want the number for Adam Talbott. You better give me all the numbers you can find." He pulled a pencil stub out of his shirt pocket and wrote two phone numbers on the wall. "Thanks." Ruth stood silently by her bench, looking at the floor. Chet punched the phone buttons viciously with his thumb. He listened for an answer, tapping his foot on the floor. "Just you wait, boy. You got some talking to do."

After a long pause Chet snorted and said "No answer at his place and sounds like no machine. Prob'ly hiding out in the office trying to cover his sneaking tracks." He pushed down the hook, dialed again. Another long pause. "Yeah, you bet I got a message for you, Talbott. This is Chet Walker, *Mister* Walker to you. I bet you're in there just a-hiding on the floor! I'm tellin' you now, you better have eyes in the back of your head, and you better stay away from Ruth, you yellow little..." Chet snapped his mouth shut. "That's all." He slammed down the phone again.

"Stupid no-good answering machines, never did like the... Ruth? Don't you worry now. Nothing's gonna happen to you if I got anything to say about it." He stood awkwardly for a moment, then grabbed a tissue box off his bench and held it out to her. "Don't you worry now," he repeated, patting her gently on the back as she wiped her eyes and blew her nose.

"Thanks, Chet. I'm so glad I have you looking out for me." She managed a smile.

"Well, you'll see. There's some fight in the old dog yet," he said gruffly. "Now, we best get to work. Take your mind off things."

"I doubt that very much, Chet, but I'll give it a try."

"I may have some interesting news of my own in a couple days. I think I figured out where the problem with those pesky appliances is coming from, and I'm pretty sure I know why. Just want to be sure I'm on the right track."

Ruth smiled, a real smile. "I'm glad you're on the case, Chet. There is no problem in this town you can't solve, I'm sure of it."

"Aww, g'wan." But she could see the corners of his mouth twitch as he turned to his bench.

Ten minutes after the shop opened, a small bouquet of flowers was delivered for Ruth. "They're from all of us," said the delivery-truck driver. "And Larry said to tell you that if you need anything, anything at all, just give him a call and he'll take care of it. We're awfully sorry about what happened, Ruth. We just wanted you to know that not everyone in town was in that crowd of morons last night."

Ruth bit her lip and bent down to smell the flowers—carnations, her favorite. "Thank you, Cheryl." Her voice quivered. "I... this really means a lot. And thank Larry and

Chris, too." She blinked several times. "These are beautiful. I'll just put them right here on the counter."

"You take care of yourself, OK? And don't forget to call us if you need anything. Larry really meant it. And so do Chris and I."

"I know that. Thank you. I will. I... will you excuse me now, Cheryl? I have some things to do in the back." And she fled. As she ducked through the curtain, the phone rang. Chet was there to pick it up before the second ring.

"Elect... No, she's busy right now, can't come to the phone... Uh huh... Uh huh... No, she's fine, she's here at work all right but she's real busy. Got a big project to work on... Uh huh... Yep, I'll let her know. Got to go now. G'bye." He cradled the phone. "Marco at the drugstore. Just wanted to know if you were OK, didn't want to bother you by barging in here. Said to tell you if you need anything just call him or Lou."

Before Ruth could say anything the phone rang again. Chet grabbed the receiver. "Electronic Wizardry... No, she can't come to the phone right now, she's with a customer out front... Yes, she's here and she's just fine, don't you worry none... Really, she's just fine, I'll tell her you called. I got to get back to work now. I'll give her the message. G'bye." He dropped the receiver again and ran his hands through his hair. "Mrs. Lewis. Just heard the news, wanted to see if you were all right. I expect the old biddy will be over here this morning checking up on you."

Ruth put her face into her hands and put both elbows on the bench and drew a long, slow breath and let it out. "I expect everyone in town will be checking up on me, one way or another. Why is it that when a person feels least like talking there's the most people wanting to talk?"

"You want me to call the phone company and get Caller ID for this phone? Or just turn on the machine for the day?"

"No, that wouldn't do any good, they'd just come in if they can't get ahold of us on the phone. I guess we're going to have to live with it." She raised her head. "I'll just work on something that doesn't take much in the way of brains. Hand me one of those clock radios over there."

The door bell jangled and Chet went through the curtain to the front.

By noon there were two bouquets and three plants sitting on the counter out front, and a huge basket of silk ivy covering the top of the Captain Kangaroo TV. Chet had started keeping a log of messages in an old spiral notebook and had filled four pages with notes. A few people stopped by to offer support, most saying that they would have called first but the line had been busy all morning.

Right before lunch the manager from the supermarket arrived with a paper bag overflowing with groceries. It was only because she indicated that some of the food would have to be refrigerated that Chet grumpily went back to ask Ruth to go to the counter and deal with it.

"Ruth, I stopped by here first because I didn't want to go barging in upstairs if you weren't at work today. I know this is an interruption, but... well, all of us felt real bad about what happened and... uh, well, we thought this might help. It's not much, I know, but..." She slid the bag across the counter. "Some of that stuff should go in the refrigerator. I just... we're all sorry."

The bag held canned goods, half a spiral sliced ham, fresh vegetables, some gourmet frozen dinners and five assorted flavors of Ben & Jerry's ice cream. Ruth looked up with a wavery smile. "Thanks, LeeAnn. I guess by now you all know what I like."

"Of course we do. And listen, if you want more ice cream it's on the house."

"I... this is so nice of you all... Excuse me, I'd better run these up to the refrigerator." She almost made it through the curtain before the tears overflowed.

Upstairs the answering machine indicated that she'd gotten eighteen messages already. The phone rang again as she put the last carton of ice cream in the freezer. She snapped down the switch on the side that silenced the bell and slid the volume control on the answering machine as low as it would go. She'd have to listen to all the messages sometime. But not now. She put the perishables away, sat down in her favorite chair, leaned back and closed her eyes. Just for a minute.

When she opened them again the light was golden and the sun had already slipped behind the buildings on the west side of the square. Her mouth was dry and her eyes felt sandy and it took a minute before she could get all her joints working properly again. Six forty-five. She got up and stretched, reaching for the ceiling and listening to all her vertebrae go off like firecrackers down her back. The answering machine said twenty-three messages. Sometime tonight she'd have to listen to them all. If she could manage to get to them before the memory got used up.

CRANK

Ruth went through the next few days in a fog. She declined to be interviewed by the newspaper and Chet chased an inquisitive reporter away with a broom. A few of Jodi's group tried to "demand answers," but Chet put a quick stop to that. "You better tell the rest of your pack of hyenas that I'm takin' names. Next one of you comes in here or calls here botherin' Ruth, the whole list goes to the cops to start checking. Bet one of you was responsible for breakin' the window."

Jodi herself strolled by one morning and looked in the front window with a triumphant smile while Ruth was dusting the countertop, but when Chet pulled open the shop door and demanded that she state her business, she gave him the finger and left. Chet told Ruth he'd be stepping out for a few minutes, was gone half an hour, and didn't want to talk about the reason for his errand when he got back. Ruth just shrugged and went back to work.

The biggest surprise of the whole week was that Eddie was unusually quiet and cooperative. He even began coming in a bit earlier every day. Chet explained that he couldn't afford to pay for the extra time and was astonished to hear Eddie say that he didn't want any extra money; he just wanted to help out.

While Chet was at the front counter dealing with a customer, Eddie looked up from the vacuum cleaner he was putting back together. "Ruth?" he said softly.

"Yes, Eddie?"

"I..." he looked down again, fidgeted, bit his lip. "Nothing. Just... I'm sorry."

"About what?" She raised an eyebrow.

"Nothing." And he turned back to his work. Ruth waited, but he never said anything more.

There was another small flurry of "bring in anything you've got that might possibly need repair." Ruth laughed when she looked at the overflowing shelves in the back.

"It'll take a town twice the size of Lyric to use up all these clock radios once we get them fixed. People gotta be cleaning out their attics and cellars by now." It was the first thing that had made her feel really cheerful since that awful night. The laughter felt good. As long as she didn't do too much thinking or too much remembering; as long as she dealt strictly with the present, she could tell herself that she was going to be all right.

Eddie and Chet seemed to enjoy working on old clock radios together, so Ruth spent most of her time rearranging things in the shop and answering the occasional phone call. That didn't take much mental effort. She seemed to be able to concentrate on more taxing tasks only in short bursts. People still stopped by now and again to check up on her, make sure she was all right, but word had apparently gotten around town that she was going to be OK. Whether that was true or not, Ruth didn't care to speculate. She could pretend.

As Eddie picked up skills and could be left to do more repairs on his own, Chet finally got around to disconnecting the ceiling fan. After that he made an elaborate show of taking it apart. Ruth looked at its innards and still couldn't see anything wrong, but she decided to say nothing and leave the whole production number to Chet. There was no word on whether there would be an air conditioner installed in the shop.

The occasional small gift kept arriving now and again, too. Ruth passed around a box of cream-centered chocolates late one afternoon. "Better eat 'em up, guys, they'll be a big brown puddle if you don't. It must be a hundred and five in here." She wiped her face with her apron. "I hate to nag, Chet, but... any progress on the fan?"

"I can't see one darn thing wrong with that stupid fan. Soon's I get a free minute I'll hook it back up. But I ain't got time to do it today."

"Want me to try it, Uncle Chet?" That was the first peep out of Eddie all day, other than a muffled thanks when he'd taken some of the chocolates.

Chet regarded his nephew with mild suspicion. "No thanks, Eddie, I've started it so I'll finish it. Nice of you to offer, though."

Eddie ducked his head and went back to the latest cobwebby clock radio. Chet wiped his face with his apron and then stood watching Eddie's diligent back with a frown. But in the end he said nothing and went back to his own work-in-progress.

CRED

Late that week, Ruth was sitting at her bench staring off into the distance and idly flipping the handles on a hemostat back and forth when the phone rang. With a muffled curse, Chet got up to answer it.

"You want to talk with Eleanor?"

"Sure. Thanks, Chet." She took the phone and pulled the receiver on its long cord over to her bench so she could sit down again. "Hi Eleanor, what's up?"

"Just your old nosy friend checking in to see if you're all right. Want to go get some lunch? I'm buying."

Ruth sighed. "I don't really feel like going out. Even if people aren't looking at me I still think they are. Silly of me, I know."

"Well, how about I get something to go and come over and we'll just brown bag it together? I'll bring an extra bag for my head if that'll make you feel better."

Ruth chuckled. "Might want to bring a few extras for me and Chet."

"I'm glad to hear you can still laugh. I'll be over in about half an hour or so."

Ruth gave in. "All right, see you then."

It actually took closer to an hour before her friend could get free and they could escape to Ruth's apartment. True to her word, Eleanor had brought sandwiches, marinated vegetables, chips and cans of soda. The two friends munched in companionable silence at the table, enjoying the air conditioning. Ruth was hungrier than she'd thought. The lunch was gone in what seemed like no time at all.

Eleanor mixed mocha flavored coffee powder with boiling water in the coffeemaker carafe, then poured the milky brown liquid over ice in two tall glasses. She looked at Ruth, who was sitting at the table idly tracing a finger around the rim of a crumb-filled plate. "Here. It's just sugar and chemicals, but it's *good* sugar and chemicals."

Ruth laughed. "Good old American food technology."

There was a pause. Finally Eleanor said, carefully, "They haven't found Adam yet, have they?"

Ruth stirred her iced coffee for a moment before replying. "No, apparently not. His car's gone and I guess his answering machine finally quit taking messages. Chet even got the number of the office in Chicago and got an answering machine there too. I pity whoever has to listen to the message he left." She smiled. "The one nice thing about all this is finding out who my real friends are."

Eleanor patted her hand. "We're all your friends, Ruthie. Some of us just had to be reminded."

"Yeah... it must be tough for people who don't have a home town." She looked off into the distance again. "I pity the ones who never find a home," she whispered, so softly that her friend didn't catch it.

But before Eleanor could ask her what she'd said, the phone rang once, stopped, then rang again. Ruth had long since arranged that code with the people she didn't mind talking with. She got up to answer, talked briefly, sat down again. "That was Grace. She said the refreshment committee has finally gotten its act together and we'll have all kinds of munchies for the dance."

"I wish you'd change your mind about going to the dance. I know at least five guys who'd love to take you."

"I know. Three of them have already asked me," she grinned. "But I really don't feel like going. I'll work on the decorations and maybe eat a few goodies while they're setting up the tables, but after that I'm going to head on home. I just don't think I could handle it."

Eleanor sighed. "I could just kill that jackass Adam. And I feel even worse that I wanted you two to get back together in the first place."

"Don't. I had my own reasons. And... you know, it was better that he acted like the dirtbag he is now, before... before I really got involved with him." She looked away. "It hurts, I'd be a flaming liar if I said it didn't... but I'm better off this way, really. Like ripping a bandage off your skin all at once, you know?"

"Yes, Ruthie, I really do know."

Ruth wiped her face with a paper napkin. "Oh... Of course you do." She squeezed Eleanor's hand again. "I guess we all think our own little problems are the worst... are you ever going to talk about the twins' father?"

Her friend smiled. "Someday, maybe. I guess I just didn't get the bandages that let go without a fight."

ೣೠ

Ruth was replacing the back on a cordless phone base station when Chet came through from the front carrying the day's mail. The ceiling fan whirred quietly overhead and the breeze was heavenly. After all that fuss it had turned out that there hadn't been a problem with the fan after all; Chet had discovered that the circuit she'd so carefully wired it into had been disconnected at the fuse box.

She smiled. "I can't see anything wrong with this phone, Chet. Maybe you can take a look at it..." her voice trailed off and the smile faded as she looked through the pile of envelopes Chet had handed her. Finally she sighed. "Oh boy, more bills." She took a small pocketknife from a drawer and began slitting envelopes open. Chet picked up the phone and went over to his bench, but when he sat down he put the phone on the bench and turned to watch Ruth.

Ruth unfolded several bills, looked at the amounts due, carefully refolded the papers and put them back in their envelopes, her motions growing slower and slower. Finally she dropped the pile of bills on the bench and put her head in her hands.

"Ruth? You all right?"

It took a moment before she could reply. "I'm all right. It's just that I'm tired of the same old, same old, you know?"

Chet chewed his lower lip. "We got problems with the bills this month?"

She looked up at him in surprise. "Oh no, actually we're doing pretty well. All this extra work has put us ahead for a change. It isn't that. It's just that it seems like nothing ever changes around here. Same old bills, same old customers, same old junk to repair. I feel like a hamster in a wheel sometimes."

"Well, as soon as I'm up to speed on fixing computers maybe that'll make a difference."

She shook her head. "No, it'd still be the same old same old, just with different junk. I dunno, Chet, lately I've been thinking about just turning the shop over to you and taking a real vacation."

Chet considered that. "Well, whatever you want to do, Ruthie. Take some time if you need it. I can keep the place going for you and you can take over when you've had enough of fun in the sun."

Ruth smiled. "Thanks, Chet. I just don't know what I'd do without you."

"Prob'ly have had that ceiling fan going a lot sooner, that's what."

"No kidding, you stubborn old coot." They both laughed. "Well," she said, "I haven't come to any decisions yet. I'll at least wait till after the dance and then take a real hard look at all my options. And you be thinking about what's right for you, too."

"Us old coots are easy to please. Don't you worry about me."

"You know something, Chet? Sometimes I think you're the best friend I ever had."

"Awww..." Chet's eyes glistened and he quickly turned away. He cleared his throat noisily and picked up the broken phone.

∞

The long hot August days dragged on toward the end. Ruth began to feel that coordinating the dance was the only thing that preserved her sanity. Keeping all the various committee members from killing each other gave her little time to brood on her own troubles. Despite all the annoyances, things were looking good. A surprising number of people who'd long since moved away from Lyric had said they'd be coming back for the dance. The motel manager called to thank Ruth for having such good ideas.

A sheriff's deputy stopped by one afternoon to ask some questions about the break-in at her shop. She went through the story again, knowing that she had little to offer in the way of evidence. But why would the sheriff be looking into her break-in? They didn't have jurisdiction over problems in town. By the time she thought of that, though, it was too late to ask questions. The deputy asked Chet to step outside with him for a moment. Chet returned looking unaccountably pleased, but offered no explanation. She shrugged and went back to work.

∞

The only sounds on the street were the occasional rustle of some small animal risking a trip through the shrubbery and the faint whir of cars passing by on other streets. The one nearby streetlight flickered a pale yellow light. There was no moon.

The back door opened, and the man carefully looked around. Satisfied, he walked down the steps and opened the back of the camper shell on the pickup truck that was parked at the curb. He took another look around, then slipped back into the building. A few minutes later, he reappeared with a large brown paper bag, crossed the sidewalk and slipped the bag into the back of the truck. As he was closing the lid, a voice came out of the darkness behind him.

"That's far enough, son."

He spun around to see three police officers standing behind him. Where the hell had they come from? He drew himself up to his full height and faced them. "What's the problem?"

"We have a search warrant for the premises and for your truck." One officer held out the paper. "It would be easiest for all of us if you'd just let us into the building."

He grabbed the paper. The officer helpfully shone a flashlight on it. He had to stop himself from angrily batting the flashlight away. "I want my lawyer here before I let you guys do anything."

The officers looked at each other for a moment, then one of them nodded at the others. "Legally," the officer said, "you understand we can just go right in whether you like it or not—even break down the door if we need to."

The man glared at the officers, who looked at each other again in some kind of silent conference. Finally it seemed to be agreed. "Go ahead," said the officer, "suit yourself. We've got all night."

He pulled his phone out his pocket and flipped it open. As he turned to walk away, the officers closed ranks. "No, you do your calling right here. You're not going anywhere for a while."

"Fine! Whatever!" He punched buttons viciously. "Craig? Hey, sorry to bother you so late, but I've got some cops here with a search warrant and I don't want them going in without you being here. Can you come down? No, not my house. Yeah. No, don't give me that. I know you don't have to be here, but as much as I'm paying you, you get your ass over here now. Or I can just tell them... Right." He snapped the phone shut and turned to the officer who seemed to be in charge. "Can I at least sit down on the steps till he gets here?"

"No, right here is just fine. Keep your hands where we can see them."

"What? Am I under arrest?"

"No. Just a precaution. Standard procedure."

One of the officers spoke briefly into his radio, and after a few minutes two police cars pulled to the curb, one in front of and one behind the pickup truck. He considered his best course of action—demand answers from the cops? Play up the business of being wrongfully accused? In the end, he stood silent.

Twenty silent minutes later his lawyer arrived. The officers showed him the search warrant and the lawyer read through it quickly.

"You want to search the place for *what*? You've *got* to be kidding me."

"I don't think the judge would issue a warrant if we were kidding, Craig."

The lawyer stood silently for a moment, his jaw muscles tensed. Then he crumpled the papers and threw them to the ground. "God *damn* it." He looked at his client, who wasn't moving or looking at any of them. "Well, in that case, give them the goddamn keys and let them get this over with."

Hello Fall

Finally the day of the dance arrived. Ruth locked up the shop at noon, ate a quick lunch upstairs, changed into shorts and a tank top and walked over to the Veterans' Hall. Several members of the decorations committee were waiting for her. Six large cardboard cartons sat by the door. "What's that?" she asked.

"Decorations. Annie finally talked the discount store into donating them. Wasn't that nice? Now maybe we can lower the price of admission."

Ruth grinned. "No, let's keep the extra money for next year's dance."

"And next year's *other* people getting it organized."

After a few minutes, the Veterans' Club secretary arrived to open the doors. Ruth and the committee went through into the wonderful coolness inside and flipped on the lights. One of the men produced the sketches the committee had agreed on, and then everyone helped bring the cartons of streamers, balloons, paint, poster paper and other decorations inside the hall. The chairman of the decorations committee gathered everyone around to hear their assignments. "Where's Kyle?" she asked. "I thought he was going to be here to help with the stuff that needs to be put up high." Nobody knew. "Oh hell, I'll call him in a while if he doesn't show up."

Just as the last instructions were being given out, Eddie walked into the room and looked around uncertainly. He spotted Ruth and hurried over.

"Can I help out? I got some free time this afternoon and all."

"I... that's very nice of you, Eddie. Um, sure, if you'd like to help, why don't you check with those guys over there? I think they're going to be putting out the folding chairs in a little bit and they could use some extra hands for that."

"Thanks. I'll do that." He hustled away, leaving Ruth shaking her head in disbelief. Would wonders never cease?

Ladders were brought from the storage room and the people who weren't afraid of heights were assigned to string streamers. The rental company was due to arrive with tables, punch bowls and glasses in about an hour, so the alcove where the refreshments would be served had to be tidied up and decorated first. Ruth and two other women took on that chore. The others were assigned to put posters on the walls, sweep up where necessary, twist the crepe paper for streamers and blow up balloons. Ruth was pleased to see that the tank of helium was already there. The party store must have delivered it earlier. *Just one less source of gas to worry about*, she thought.

Everyone was chatting happily; someone brought in a portable boom box and put it on the floor and slipped in a CD of golden oldies from their high school days. The cheerful music echoed around the room and some of the people sang along as they worked. Ruth kept a wary eye on Eddie for the first half hour or so, but he seemed to be working right along with everyone else and being genuinely helpful, so eventually she relaxed and quit trying to keep track of his every move.

A few more people arrived and volunteered to pitch in. Soon there was a large group of people bustling around the hall. They seemed to be making a special effort to cooperate, and while people frequently asked Ruth for advice on this matter or that, no one asked her any personal questions. For the first time in weeks she felt relaxed.

She and her friends had just finished hanging a large banner that said "GOODBYE SUMMER, HELLO FALL" when the truck from the party supply store showed up. Ruth and the two women helped carry in several boxes full of punch cups, small paper plates, napkins and coffee cups as the men from the store set up three folding tables and draped clean white tablecloths over them, then brought in two large punchbowls.

When the tables and punchbowls were set up to Ruth's satisfaction she thanked the men, both of whom assured her they'd be back in time for the dance. "Have to see what this stuff looks like when it's being used," one said with a grin.

"I think you're more interested in the food than the tables," Ruth said with a wink, and the men joined in the laughter.

A few minutes later two men from the Veterans' Club showed up with a large coffee maker and another box of coffee cups. They went into the small kitchen in the back of the hall, filled the coffee maker and soon had it set up on one of the tables. "I don't know that anyone will want coffee this afternoon, but it's here for you all if you do. We'll be back later to refill it for the dance," one of the men told Ruth. She thanked him and the two men looked around, gave the decorations a thumbs-up, and left.

Astonishingly soon, it was past 4:00 and most of the streamers were hung. The refreshment tables had been decorated along with the alcove, and Ruth joined some other people in hanging streamers along the front of the bandstand and putting up another banner. Kyle still hadn't showed, but there were enough people who were at ease with heights that there was no problem. The band was due to arrive and start setting up any minute. Grace and five members of the refreshment committee arrived with armloads of chips, dips, and bottles of soda and ingredients for punch. Grace assured Ruth that her father would be along later with some special Mexican goodies as well. She brought several salad bowls from the kitchen and set them on the tables while her assistants put the perishables in the refrigerator. "I'll put the chips out later. If I do it now," she said, looking around at the crowd of workers, "there won't be any left for tonight."

"Everything looks great, Grace," Ruth said with a smile. "Why don't you guys lay out napkins and cups and get the tables ready. You're right, you better not put out any eats. I think we're all hungry enough to eat the tablecloth by now."

Grace was just about to answer when she spotted something over Ruth's shoulder. Her smile changed to a scowl. "What's she doing here?"

There was a sudden hush in the room. Ruth turned to see Jodi Diamante walking toward her. Ruth straightened her shoulders and lifted her head as Grace stepped up beside her, still scowling. Several of the people who had been unpacking plates and utensils walked up behind Ruth and Grace and stood silently watching.

Jodi stopped and looked around the room. "Well, what are you all staring at? I just came to help out with the dance."

Snickers echoed around the room. One man who was up on a ladder said "You can help by leaving town," under his breath but just loud enough to be heard. Jodi turned in his direction, then gave a sniff and turned back to Ruth.

"I came over to help out. That's all."

"We don't need your kind of help," Grace declared, firmly.

"I wasn't talking to you," Jodi sneered.

"Why don't you…" Grace began, but Ruth laid a hand on her arm and cut her off.

"Tell you what, Jodi," Ruth said pleasantly, "we're just about done here. Why don't you ask around and see if anyone needs help with what they're doing? If they do, then you can join right in. If they don't, I guess your…" she cleared her throat, "services won't be necessary this evening."

Jodi stood for a moment, staring at Ruth, considering. Then she said "Yeah, I'll do that. I'll just do that. Who knows, if we all pitch in, you might have time to go home and get ready for your hot date for the dance tonight, Ruth."

Grace drew breath as though to speak but Ruth touched her arm again and she subsided. Ruth stood looking at Jodi, silently, with a carefully neutral expression on her face, until finally Jodi turned around and walked over to a group of people who were setting up folding chairs around the outside of the room.

Ruth watched her go, amazed at how unruffled she felt inside. After a moment, Grace grabbed her arm and pulled her back in the direction of the kitchen.

"How could you just stand there and let her get away with that?" Grace whispered. "I would have told her off but good!"

"I know you would have, Grace, and thanks for standing up for me. But I just didn't want to justify all that snottiness with an answer. This way she doesn't have an opportunity to say anything more." Ruth looked through the door and watched as the chair-arranging group kept right on working, not acknowledging Jodi's presence at all. "I doubt she'll stick around much longer when she sees just how much people want her 'help.'"

"I guess you're right. But we were all having such a good time here before she messed it up."

"We can keep on having good times. Just pay no attention to her and enjoy."

A man looked around the corner of the kitchen door. "Ruth? We've got the band truck parked outside. Can we get some help with this stuff?"

"Sure, Emilio. Why don't you ask a couple of those guys out there; they'll be glad to help you."

"Thanks. We'll get set up first and then go have some supper, all right?"

"That sounds like a good idea for all of us."

The band members and their helpers carried in instrument cases, microphone stands, amplifiers and several boxes of miscellaneous equipment. After everything was deposited on the bandstand the group got to work plugging everything in and getting ready for the evening.

The various groups of workers finished up their tasks around the hall. Jodi walked from group to group but was rebuffed by every one. Finally she pulled a folding chair away from the wall and placed it near the bandstand, then grabbed a small paper plate from one of the refreshment tables and sat down and fanned herself as she watched the band. No one paid any attention to her. Grace nudged Ruth and whispered "You'd think she'd get the message."

Ruth looked over at Jodi, then went back to arranging paper napkins. "Some people never learn."

Finally everything seemed to be ready. Ruth washed her hands in the kitchen and pushed her hair back from her face. She went back into the hall and looked around. "You guys did a really great job," she said. "Why don't we lock up now and go get some supper and come back in an hour or so and finish whatever is left. I know you guys must be hungry."

"Sounds good, Ruth," several people said, and began putting away their tools and supplies. The crowd milled around for a few minutes and then people began to head for the exit. Ruth remembered Eddie and looked for him, but he was nowhere in sight. Oh well, maybe his burst of helpfulness had worn off while she wasn't looking.

The door to the outside swung open again and several people came striding through.

The sheriff was followed by four deputies and the chief of police. Then three police officers stepped through the door. A murmur of surprise went around the room, cut off by a collective gasp when two other people entered the room.

Adam Talbott and Lydia Caldwell.

The Last Thing on My Mind

Adam strode past Lydia and the officers and climbed up on the bandstand. It wasn't till Ruth backed into the wall with enough force to make her teeth snap together that she came to her senses. She staggered, regained her balance, whirled and ran into the kitchen so she could slip out the back. No chance. The door had a double-locked deadbolt and there was no key in sight. She growled and kicked the door as hard as she could. It hurt.

A chorus of angry shouts came from the main room. The noise echoed around the kitchen as Ruth fell back against the door, grabbed her foot and squeezed down on her throbbing toes.

"You got a lot of nerve, Talbott!" "You oughta be ridden out of town on a rail!" "Go back where you came from, you..." "Who the hell do you think you are?" Ruth dropped the foot and covered her ears. The sheriff had apparently gotten one of the band's microphones turned on and was trying to out-shout everyone and get them to settle down, which just made matters worse. The noise level was unreal.

She edged over to the doorway and peeked into the main room. The sheriff was up on the bandstand with

Adam and everyone else in the room had formed a growling, fist-waving mass in front of the stage. The chief of police was over by the exit with his radio pressed to one ear and his finger in the other. Adam was talking to one of the band members who stood with arms crossed, shaking his head, obviously saying "no" to something.

Nobody was looking her way. Good. She slipped out of the kitchen and sped along the back wall toward the door.

The sound of the crowd pulsed with her heartbeat. The short distance between the kitchen door and the exit seemed to stretch out for light-years. She reached the doors and slipped through, dashed down the short hallway and through the main door to the outside.

As she jogged toward home she heard a shout behind her.

"Ruth! Ruth! Please wait! Please!"

She stopped, whirled to see Lydia hurrying down the walk. After one brief, astonished moment of immobility Ruth spun back and ran faster.

"Ruth, please! Don't go! Please!" Lydia also began to run, hampered by her high-heeled shoes. "Ruth! *Oh!*" She tripped and went sprawling face down on the sidewalk.

Ruth heard the impact and turned to see Lydia slowly picking herself up, pale pink sleeveless dress covered with dust. She sighed and trudged back to where Lydia sat on the grass dabbing at one skinned knee with a handkerchief, stockings in tatters and both her shoes a yard away on the sidewalk. Ruth stood looking down at her for a moment. Finally she sighed again and said wearily, "What do you want, Lydia?"

Lydia pressed the handkerchief to a bleeding elbow and winced, then looked up at Ruth. "Ruth, could you sit down here by me for just a minute? It hurts my eyes to look up into the sky like this. Please?"

Ruth lowered herself to sit cross-legged on the grass, but not too close to Lydia. "All right, Lydia, what?"

"Ruth, I... Please come back. Adam has things to say that you should hear. He told me what happened the night he left, and I know how you must feel..."

"Cut the crap, Lydia," Ruth snapped. "You couldn't begin to 'know how I must feel.' Just say what you have to say and then you leave me the hell alone from now on."

Lydia dabbed at her elbow and winced again. "All I meant was..." She bit her lip. "All right. I'm sorry. No more comments on your feelings, I promise. I'd just like to ask you to come back with me and listen to what Adam has to say. Will you please at least do that?" She pressed the bloodstained handkerchief to her knee again.

Ruth looked away. What on earth could Adam possibly say now that would matter? But still, if Lydia felt it was important enough to come chasing after her and ruin her precious outfit... "All right, Lydia. I'll listen. But that's all. After I hear Adam's song and dance routine that's the end of it. I don't want to see either of you ever again. You can have my building and everything in it. I'll be out of town as fast as I can manage it and believe me, if you two know what's good for you you'll do the same."

"Ruth, I don't think you..." Lydia closed her mouth. "I'm sorry. Never mind. Thank you for agreeing to listen. Let's go back inside." She struggled to her feet, but Ruth made no move to help her. Lydia picked up her shoes, looked down at her already shredded stockings, shrugged and started walking, carrying the shoes. If the sidewalk was hot, she gave no sign.

As the two women re-entered the hall, the sheriff was still up on the stage trying to get the crowd under control. The chief of police had moved to stand just outside the building so he could hear his radio better. He nodded to them as they went inside. The deputies were near the rows of folding chairs and the officers were moving around, trying to get people to settle down. Adam stood at the back of the bandstand. The sheriff was saying "...and I want you all to just listen now. I know what you all think, and I thought it myself till yesterday, but we've discovered a couple things I think you all need to hear." An angry mutter came from the crowd. "Yeah, I know. But you'll think differently after you've heard this. You all go sit down now and listen."

Footsteps echoed in the hall behind Ruth. She turned to see Eddie running in, with Chet puffing along in his wake. Eddie waved one hand in the air. "Ruth! Ruth! I gotta talk to you! Please!" She took a few steps down the hallway toward him. He ran up to her, reached out to take her hand.

Ruth backed up a step. "What on earth? What is it, Eddie?"

Chet came up behind his nephew. "Durn fool kid was waiting for me..." he panted "...when I got home from the market." Said... we gotta get here right away."

"Ruth, I want to testify! I already told the cops she paid us to break the window." He dug in the front pocket of his jeans and pulled out a handful of crumpled bills. "Here, it's all I got. Take it. To pay for the glass. Please."

Ruth put both hands to her head and squeezed her eyes shut. What on earth was going on? She stepped back and bumped into someone. Her eyes opened. Lydia put out a steadying hand. All Ruth could do was shake her head. "Eddie... I... can we talk about this later? I just... we can work it out, whatever it is. But not now, OK?"

Eddie's hand dropped to his side. Chet put an arm around his shoulders and leaned on him, still trying to get his breath. "Son, I don't know... what's up, but..."

The noise level in the room behind them dropped precipitously. Ruth walked unsteadily through what felt like shimmering fog to the doorway into the room. Most of the people had turned to sit down in the folding chairs, but Jodi and a few others still stood in front of the bandstand. The sheriff shooed them all away. Lydia started toward the bandstand, still carrying her shoes. Ruth folded her arms tightly across her chest and leaned against the wall for support; Chet and Eddie stood beside her on her left. Lydia looked over her shoulder, hesitated, then turned and came back to stand beside Ruth on the other side. "I promise you this will be worth your while," she whispered. Ruth just shook her head.

The sheriff blew into the microphone. It was working. "I want you all to listen to Talbott, now. What he's going to tell you is the truth." The crowd booed. The sheriff scowled at them, put his hands on his hips and stared till the noise finally died away. "I mean it now, you folks listen."

Adam stepped up to the front of the stage and took the microphone. "Thank you, Sheriff Carter." The sheriff nodded and stepped back behind Adam. Adam cleared his throat.

"I know what you all think of me right now" —angry mutters and a few hisses from the crowd— "and I don't blame you for thinking it. I haven't been straight with any of you from the very beginning. It's probably a worthless gesture for me to apologize for that, but I do. Sincerely."

"Oh sure!" yelled Jodi, and the crowd joined in with its own angry shouts. "Tell us about it!" "What a crock!" "G'wan, go back where you came from!" "Beat it, Talbott!" The sheriff jumped down off the bandstand and walked toward the crowd. The voices subsided to a mutter.

Adam waved a hand in acknowledgement. "Whoever broke into our office seems to have gotten into some papers that gave you all a good idea of what we'd intended to do. Since I knew I couldn't keep the papers from circulating, I asked the police to concentrate on finding out who was responsible for the break-in. It probably would have been easier if my partner or I had been able to look through the files carefully to see what was taken..."

A shout from the crowd. "Yeah, but you ran!" Loud applause and a few shrill whistles followed. People looked at each other and nodded in emphatic agreement. Adam's face flushed red and he looked down at the floor.

The applause died away. Adam sighed and looked back at the townspeople. "Yes, I did. That was the dumbest thing I ever did in my life. At the time I had my reasons" — derisive laughter from the crowd— "but obviously I wasn't thinking straight. If you all will bear with me, I'll tell you why I did something that stupid. After I talk about a couple other stupid things that some of *you* were responsible for." The crowd stilled; people looked at each other. Now what?

"Chief Clifford knew right from the beginning that there was a connection between the break-in at Electronic Wizardry and the break-in at my place. But the police department didn't find any evidence to confirm that at first. Then someone came forward—never mind who it was, but

I want to thank that person and I plan to pay them a reward—and that led to an investigation of someone else who lives outside the city limits. That's where the sheriff's department came in." People muttered and shifted in their seats. Adam let them rustle for a moment.

"Seems someone recently bought some illegally high-powered walkie-talkies. He and someone else were testing them out and some county residents with CB radios happened to overhear them. One of the voices was pretty recognizable. The CB owners talked with the sheriff."

Adam looked around the room. "I see Duane Haldeman isn't here right now. Maybe he's at his parents' house, maybe not. But there are a couple deputies out there with a search warrant so I suppose we'd all better hope for his sake that someone is there to let them in." Astonished whispers from the crowd.

"In addition, the police have heard about at least two sets of photocopies of papers from my office. They've got a pretty good idea of who has them, and why. And they have a pretty good idea of who was behind the break-ins, and why. They have a search warrant for someone else's house as well, and I can see that person definitely isn't going to be there to open the door for them. It doesn't matter. In a minute or two I believe the police will have just about all the evidence they need to make an arrest."

The crowd murmured and people looked around at each other. Jodi quietly got up and moved toward the exit, but as she passed behind one of the deputies he said softly, "I don't think you want to do that, Jodi." He took her firmly by the arm and tried to lead her back to her seat.

"Get your hands off me, you pea-brained gorilla!" Jodi struggled and tried to pry the man's hand from her arm, but he was too strong. "Let me go! Let go of me or I'll sue every last one of you for everything you've got! Damn it, let me go!" She kicked at the deputy and tried to bite his hand, but he easily fended her off. And by that time, two officers, the other deputies and the sheriff had crossed the floor.

"Jodi, you best settle down or we'll have to put you in handcuffs." There was just the faintest edge of menace in the sheriff's voice. "Or maybe we'll just arrest you right now for assaulting an officer. If you didn't do anything, I guarantee you can sue us for whatever you want. But I'd advise you to stick around and listen to this. It's very interesting."

Jodi swore, struggled for a moment more, then subsided. The deputy released her and she wrenched her arm away. Glaring at the men around her, she ostentatiously brushed herself off where the deputy had touched her. Then she marched over to a chair, head held high. "All right, Sheriff, tell Mr. Dirtbag Talbott he can continue with his little dog and pony show. But I'll tell you this: when he's done, I'm calling my lawyer and you're going to be sorry."

The sheriff looked at her with amusement, and then gestured to Adam to continue. Two of the deputies took up positions between Jodi and the exit. The officers went back to their places in the crowd.

Adam nodded. "Thank you, Sheriff. As I was saying, the police and the sheriff's department traced the copies from my office back to their original source, a person who's sitting in this room at the moment. That person spread some of the copies around town and was the leader of the group who tried to confront me in Ruth Peyton's apartment to..." he cleared his throat, "demand some answers. That person has also been behind certain other acts of, shall we say, malicious mischief over the past couple weeks."

He looked at Jodi. "I know you didn't make all those phone calls to my answering machine, but you did make at least one, the day after the break-in. And since so many of the other calls were similar I have reason to believe that you told those people what to say."

"Don't make me laugh!"

Adam gave her an icy smile. "I wouldn't dream of it. But several of those phone calls were made from people's home phones, and my Caller ID box has a big memory."

"Got a super box from your girlfriend?" Jodi curled her lip. The people around her looked at her in shocked silence. She waved a hand airily at Adam. "Go on with your little story, funny boy."

"Thank you, I will." People shifted and rustled in their seats and the sheriff held up a hand for silence. A few newcomers came through the doors and stopped. The police chief's radio crackled and squawked, clearly audible across the room, and he brought it up to his ear and listened.

"As I was saying," Adam continued in a mild, conversational tone, "there's a trail of evidence that leads back to one person, and although there's no proof—yet—that that person did any of the actual breaking in, there's a lot of evidence that indicates that that person was behind the whole thing. And that's not all." He glanced around the room, but apparently did not see the person he was looking for. "When I first got here, there was a lot of talk about someone selling pot in town. I'm aware of the rumors that tied me to that, but those rumors were way off base. The people who were behind that have also been located, and funny thing, Jodi's part of that, too."

Silence, and then an agitated buzz of conversation. Adam let it go for a few moments and then continued. "Someone did some very fine detective work. And asked some very good questions about why there was so much electrical interference in one part of town. Well, it turns out that an amateur electrician was very lucky not to have been killed by the pot drying setup he created... in the basement of Kyle Feed and Seed."

Shock and disbelief from the crowd.

"Yes," said Adam. "A complete hydroponic setup, to grow high grade pot plants. If the Rube Goldberg dryer arrangement hadn't been spitting static into everything for blocks around, they might have kept growing there for a long time. I couldn't believe it either, but the police now have Kyle, Craig Nakamura and Jack Bicknell in custody and they believe they'll find more evidence at Jodi's house."

The chief of police approached the stage. Adam handed down the microphone.

Chief Clifford cleared his throat. "I just got word that the antique radio that was stolen from Ruth Peyton's store was found out in Duane's parents' garage, and Duane has some very interesting things to say about how and why it got to be there. Officers, if you will." He waved a hand at the men standing near Jodi. "Jodi Diamante, you're under arrest for..."

Adam hastily interrupted. "Just a minute, Chief. If you don't mind, I have one more thing to say." The officers who had moved in on Jodi stood still. Adam reached down and took the microphone back from the chief. "Caldwell & Talbott won't press charges against anyone for the break-in." Astonished murmurs from the crowd. Jodi glared at Adam but said nothing. Adam waved a hand in Ruth's direction. "I don't know whether Ruth will go along with this or not—the damage at her place was a lot more extensive than it was at ours, and she has a perfect right to see the folks who broke her window pay for it—but at the moment, my partner and I are not interested in prosecution. The drug charges should be more than enough."

The crowd erupted into confusion. Ruth leaned back hard against the wall for support, wishing she were anywhere, anywhere else. Lydia patted her on the arm. She pulled the arm away.

Lydia drew back a pace. "I'm sorry, Ruth. We couldn't get hold of you to let you know what was coming."

"What... what the hell are you talking about, Lydia?"

"Adam tried to call you at least once a day all last week, and I tried to call you at least a dozen times over the last two days, but you were never home. Or... not answering the phone? We both thought that this was too important to just leave a message on the machine." Lydia looked uncertain. Ruth folded her arms across her chest and waited for the other woman to continue. "After Adam heard Chet's message on our office phone he knew better than to call the shop, and when I called, Chet wouldn't let me through to you on the shop phone. I'm sorry, but I didn't know of any other way to reach you. We thought... well, you don't have email and I thought you'd probably just tear up a letter."

Chet stepped forward and shook a fist at Lydia, who took another quick step back. "You bet I wouldn't let you through. That girl took enough guff from you two crooks to last a lifetime. Now you let her be, you hear me?" Eddie put a restraining hand on his uncle's shoulder, but moved up to stand beside him just the same.

The noise from the crowd died down as Adam raised a hand for silence. Chet shrugged Eddie's hand off but subsided, and the two men went back to lean against the wall again.

Once he had everyone's attention again, Adam continued. "Can we all sit down now? I'd like to talk with you all for just a bit. About me. And once I'm done, you all can decide what you want to do to me, and I'll accept whatever it is. I... let me tell you a story." People muttered, shifted feet, resettled themselves in chairs. Adam sat down on the edge of the stage and looked at the floor. Finally the room got quiet and he looked up. "This is probably the toughest thing I've ever had to do in my life, so please forgive me if I don't make much sense. But I have to explain. For myself as much as for anyone else."

He put the microphone down for a minute and wiped his hands on his pants legs, then picked it up again. "When my family moved to Lyric, about all I ever told anyone was that we'd come from Atlanta. My dad took the job with the community college here and my parents got involved in all the faculty stuff and I went to school and made a lot of friends. But I'll bet people wondered why I never invited anyone over to my house. And why my parents never bothered to get to know any of the neighbors and almost never showed up at anything that didn't have to do with the college.

"My parents... my parents were alcoholics. I wouldn't invite anyone over because I never knew if my mom was going to get silly and fall all over someone or my dad was going to offer you guys a stiff drink as long as he was having one. Or if one or the other of them was going to be

passed out in the living room. And they never went anywhere because they were usually so far in the bag..." His
voice caught. He blinked, wiped his eyes with the back of
his hand, took a deep breath.

"We came here because my dad had run out of options. He had tenure and they couldn't fire him, but he
was showing up for his classes half sloshed and... well, the
administrators made it quite clear that they'd make life
hell for him if he didn't find somewhere else to go. They
said they'd give him a good recommendation. But I think
maybe my dad's reputation had gotten around. It took
him a long time to find the job here. I guess nobody else
wanted to take a chance.

"So here we were in this nice small town. Small town
neighbors help each other out, don't they?" He looked
around the room in mute appeal. The people in the audience murmured, looked at each other. "Doesn't everyone
in a small town help when people need it?" Nods and
whispers from the crowd.

"I... nobody helped *me*!" His voice went up an octave
and cracked. He put a fist to his mouth and coughed painfully. "My parents were drinking themselves to death and
I was running the house and... and here was this lovely
small town where neighbor helps neighbor and nobody
ever helped me! Nobody took my parents aside and told
them about AA. Nobody threw my dad in jail when he
drove the car up on the courthouse lawn. Nobody suggested my mom get some help after she got looped at the
faculty reception at the country club and fell into the
punchbowl. They just looked the other way and let her go
on drinking."

He looked around, found Ted in the crowd, waved a
hand at him. "You guys might have wondered why I didn't

want to go into the dining room after we played golf that day. It was because I thought everyone would remember... everyone would still be talking about it, my mom falling into the punchbowl with her best dress on.

"How I hated you all. I was living in hell." He choked, took a handkerchief out of his back pocket and dabbed at his eyes. The room was absolutely still. He pressed the handkerchief to his mouth until it stopped quivering.

"Well. When I graduated I got out of here as fast as I could get and I swore I'd never come back till I could show you all. I wanted to own this town, be the richest man in it and tell you all to go to hell. So I worked hard, made a bunch of money and then I came back to Lyric and I started looking for places to buy. I snooped around. I wanted to get a bunch of people together with enough money to back me up on anything I wanted to do. And I'm ashamed to admit that I used my partner's company as my stepping stone. I misled her and lied to her about why we were going to Lyric. She believed me. She had no way of knowing what was really on my mind. It took me a long time to convince her to forgive me for that."

Angry mutters from the crowd. "I know. I know. You folks couldn't think less of me than I think of myself. But let me tell you something else. I came back here expecting everyone to remember what happened all those years ago. I expected to hear stories about my parents and be reminded of every horrible moment. And I expected to get a huge thrill out of rubbing people's noses in..." He stopped, took a deep breath, exhaled. "Well, of course it didn't happen that way. Because people didn't remember the bad things. Or if they did they were kind enough not to mention any of it. Nobody brought up the past. People... well, some people anyway... were glad to see me again. That just staggered me.

"A lot of people who have alcoholic parents can't count on anything being the same from day to day, and our parents embarrass us so often that we think everyone notices every stupid, drunken thing..." He coughed again. "Well. It took a long time for it to dawn on me that every-one else in town had just shrugged those things off or completely forgotten them or maybe had worse problems of their own. And my parents didn't have friends, they just weren't the friendly type, they refused to get to know any of our neighbors... oh God..." He choked.

Adam stood up, forced his shoulders back, leaned his head way back and gave a shaky sigh. "Here I'd been nurs-ing this grand dream of revenge all these years. What an idiot I was. But by the time I finally came to my senses I'd already gone too far." He sat down again.

"Ruth tried to get through to me. But I... I thought I knew better... I remembered things the way I wanted to." He looked around at the stunned, silent audience. "There's not much I can do to make up for the trouble I tried to cause. And I know an apology isn't going to be even half-way adequate. But I do apologize. I... I can't change the past. But I didn't ask for help. So I have to accept the blame too." He put the microphone down, wiped his hands again, looked at the floor. The crowd started to murmur softly.

His voice carried without amplification. "Just one last thing, and then I'm going to ask you to decide what I ought to do. I want to give Ruth Peyton a special apology. I wouldn't even play straight with her, even though I told her I'd be honest. And I owed her more than anyone else. Do you want to know why? It was because I finally realized

I was just so happy to be back with her that nothing else mattered much at all. And I was afraid if she found out what I was up to she'd never come near me again. Of course, how I expected to keep on seeing her after everyone found out... God, I was such an idiot."

He turned to look at Ruth, who stood frozen in place against the back wall. His voice caught as he continued, "I know I did a lousy job of showing you that I cared, Ruth, and..." he stopped for a moment to get his emotions under control again. "And I promise you, here in front of everyone, I'll never do anything to hurt you, ever again."

People muttered and shifted in their seats to look at Ruth, who stared fixedly at the floor and said nothing. Finally Adam picked up the microphone and continued.

"Yes, I ran out of Ruth's apartment that night. All I could think of was that there was a mob down there and they might hurt Ruth if they came barging into her apartment looking for me. I thought if I ducked out the back—I thought that fire escape would make a lot of noise—everyone would go chasing me and leave Ruth alone. I swear to you that that's all I had in mind when I ran. When I saw that only a couple of people were following me I should have stopped. I should have marched right back and taken what was coming to me. I should have..." He looked down and cleared his throat.

"Let me tell you why I didn't. It wasn't till that very moment that it *finally* dawned on me what an ass I was. And at that point all I could think of was undoing the damage I'd already done. I knew I'd never be able to get back into my office without the mob storming in there, so I just took off and kept going back to Chicago. I didn't have much time. A lot of projects had already been set in motion. I knew I'd have to work fast, and without a lynch mob breathing down my neck while I did it. That's why I left."

He stood up. "And let me tell you something else. I'm grateful to Jodi and her friends for doing what they did." The crowd erupted. Jodi began to laugh hysterically. Adam held up a hand and raised his voice to be heard. "Let me finish! Let me finish!" When the noise level dropped he said, "I'm grateful, because they taught me a lesson and I needed it. That's why I'm not going to press charges." The crowd erupted again.

More people came through the entrance doors. It seemed to Ruth as though the whole town was packed into the hall. Some of the people who had been there all along got up and ran to tell their friends what had happened. Some quickly dialed their phones. The buzz of agitated conversations swirled around Ruth. Why couldn't she just beam herself out of this awful, buzzing room and back to her own apartment where she could be alone and safe?

Lydia touched her on the arm and said "Do you see why I wanted you to hear this?" But Ruth wasn't listening. The sound of the crowd was beginning to throb with her heartbeat; she was light-headed and dizzy and ready to slide right onto the floor. Slowly it dawned on her that someone was calling her name. She looked up. Chet and Eddie had moved forward and stood like twin sentinels, fists clenched. Adam was behind them, holding his hands out, palms up. "Ruth?" The crowd quieted down; people were watching her. She bit her lip. *Now what?* It was getting very hard to breathe. She raised a shaky hand and wiped her forehead.

"Ruth? Can you possibly forgive me again?" One left-over tear slowly made its way down Adam's cheek. Ruth turned her face away.

"I..." her mouth was dry. She gulped, pushed her tongue against her teeth, swallowed. "I... I don't want to deal with this right now, right here. I can't."

"Ruth? Would this help?" He got down on his knees on the floor, held out both hands.

Ruth closed her eyes and shook her head. When she opened her eyes he was still on the floor. She leaned back against the wall and looked up at the ceiling. "What, Adam, you want me to see that you... you *groveled*? You are *really* pushing your luck."

There was a long silence. And then she just couldn't help it. She started to laugh. Weak-kneed, she slid to the floor and whooped. "He *groveled!*" she kept saying between gasps for air. "Oh my God!"

Adam scooted toward her on his knees. Chet blocked his way and scowled down at him. "You must be outta your mind, boy."

"Yep, Chet, I probably am. Let me through. I can't get up fast enough to keep you and Eddie from killing me if I try anything funny. Really."

Chet considered for a moment. "What do you think, Eddie, do we let the man through?"

"Only if he keeps... groveling." Eddie shot Chet a big grin.

"You got yerself a deal. Grovel, boy." Laughter from the crowd.

Adam scooted forward again and reached Ruth, who had subsided to tight-throated giggles. She looked at him and wiped the tears out of her eyes, then pointed a shaky finger. "You *groveled!*" Which set her off all over again. She fell weakly forward in the direction of her pointing finger. Adam gathered her into his arms and held tight.

ᨀᨘ

Two hours later, the music echoed around the walls of the ladies' room as Ruth splashed cold water on her face. As she turned to get a paper towel to dry herself off, Eleanor patted her on the back. "Come on, Ruthie, you can't stay in here forever. Adam is out there and if you keep him waiting much longer I bet he charges in here after you."

Ruth managed a smile. "Yeah, that would be a sight, wouldn't it? Maybe we could fix it so he'd get some toilet paper stuck to his shoe on the way out." The smile faded. "I... I still don't know what to think. He's put me on such a roller coaster..."

"I know. God, I could just kick myself for thinking that this afternoon was such a great time to take the kids to the lake. I missed the event of the century! Why do I do these things! But now you look here, even though I wasn't around to personally knock his block off, this time he's got half the town to keep an eye on him and the other half just a few phone calls away."

Ruth looked at her reflection again. No change. "The problem is that they're all going to be keeping an eye on me too, and I look terrible, Eleanor."

Eleanor took her by the arm. "No, you don't. You're fine. Your hair is fine. Your dress is fine. A couple of fast dances and you'll be glowing. Now come on!"

As the door swung shut behind them and the music swelled Ruth had to fight back the urge to turn and run right back to the sanctuary of the ladies' room. At the end of the short hallway, Adam held out his hand. Eleanor breezed past him and into the swirling crowd.

Wordlessly Ruth put her hand in Adam's. They looked at each other for one long moment. It wasn't all right yet, but the promise was there.

Finally he cleared his throat. "Would you like to dance? Seems a shame to come to an end-of-summer dance and stand around all night."

"I... yes."

Holding hands, they walked toward the dance floor. And as though it had been arranged in advance, at that moment the band started playing a soft, slow tune. Adam gathered Ruth into his arms. After a minute of silent rhythm, Adam whispered "Now that I've groveled, do you think maybe someday you can forgive me?"

"Well... it was a pretty impressive grovel, I must admit." She grinned, but then got serious again. "Adam, much as I'd like to, I just can't wipe the slate clean in an instant. You of all people should understand that."

She felt him sigh. "Yes. But as long as you're willing to give me a chance, that's all I ask."

"I think I can manage that." She felt him relax.

"Do you suppose," he said after a moment, "that the grapevine would ever quit grape-ing if I tried to kiss you right here on the dance floor?"

"I doubt it very much."

"Ah."

"Doesn't mean you can't try it, though."

Epilogue

November

Ruth laid the silverware on her table and stepped back. Everything looked perfect. The new peach tablecloth and napkins were just the right color to set off the arrangement of chrysanthemums and daisies that bloomed from a silver bowl in the center of the table. She'd even found candles that matched the tablecloth perfectly. With a satisfied smile, she went to check on the progress of dinner.

As she closed the oven door she heard footsteps on the stairs. She wiped her hands on a towel and was halfway to the door by the time Adam's knock came. He put two brown paper bags down on the floor and greeted her with a kiss.

"Boy, does that smell good. I've changed my mind—I don't wonder why you talked me out of taking you out to dinner tonight. What's cooking?"

"Lasagna, mostly." She closed the front door as Adam took the bags into the kitchen. "What's that?"

"Oh, just a little something for dessert." He held up his hand to forestall her protest. "I know, I know, but this

316

is something special. Can't have you doing all the work on your own birthday. Now, how soon is dinner?"

"Whenever the timer goes off."

"We'll have time for this, then," he said, taking a bottle of sparkling apple juice out of one of the bags and heading into the kitchen to get two glasses. He held the bottle over the sink and twisted; the cork came out with a resounding POP! and some of the juice fizzed out over his hand. "Damn near as good as champagne," he grinned as he poured. He handed Ruth a wineglass, then, as his glass softly chimed against hers, said "To you, Ruth. And... to us."

Ruth smiled, raised her glass and sipped. The bubbles tickled her nose. She looked up at Adam.

He smiled back at her, then took her hand and led her out into the living room. Setting his glass down on one of the small tables, he gently drew her down into his lap.

"Aren't you going to take your jacket off?" she asked as she carefully set her glass on the floor and snuggled up against his shoulder.

"In a minute. I have something in the pocket here that I didn't want to get lost." He squirmed a bit, wiggling his left hand into his jacket pocket and then out again holding a small red velvet box. "Happy birthday."

Ruth sat up, then slowly reached for the box. It opened to reveal a heart-shaped diamond pendant. "Oh, Adam..."

"Hope this is better than that cheap old locket. Do you still have that?"

She burst out laughing. "Would you believe I flushed it down the toilet?"

"What? Did you really?"

"No, of course not. But I have no idea where it got to. Who knows, maybe Rick buried it in the back yard."

"I bought this right here in the jewelry store on the square so everyone would know where I got it. I special ordered it and swore everyone to secrecy just to make sure the news got spread all over town."

Ruth laughed so hard she nearly slid off his lap. Eventually she wiped her eyes and gave Adam a kiss. "That's perfect. Absolutely perfect."

"Here, turn around and I'll fasten the chain for you." Ruth did her best to turn around. "Just a sec, I never could figure out how these stupid clasps work. There we go." He slid the chain around her neck and clasped it together in the back. "Go look in the mirror." Without a word, Ruth went into her bedroom to look. After a moment, Adam followed her.

"Oh, Adam, it's beautiful."

"Would it be too horribly cliche'd to say 'And so are you'?"

"Definitely." She turned and smiled at him. "But you can say it anyway, if you want."

A few minutes of peaceful silence passed. Then Adam said softly "I have another present for you."

"Another one? Surely it can't be better than this," she said with a chuckle.

"Well, if you'll go sit down for a minute and let me get it for you, you can judge for yourself."

"This had really better be good," she said, as she returned to the living room and her favorite chair. He went to the kitchen and rummaged in a bag. "I want you to stand up now, turn around and close your eyes."

"I'm not sure I'm willing to go along with this." But she followed the directions. After a moment she heard footsteps. Something soft and heavy draped over her shoulders. Her eyes flew open and she looked down, then started to laugh. She slipped her arms into the sleeves of the oversized letter jacket, pushed the cuffs up and turned, still laughing, to hug Adam and bury her face against his chest. "How on earth did you manage to get one of these?"

He chuckled. "Oh, it took a fair amount of arm-twisting, but I finally talked the coach into it. What do you think, does it fit as well as the other one did?"

She stepped back and looked down, considering. The jacket's lower hem came halfway to her knees and the sleeves threatened to push back down over her hands. The orange and black letter L on the left side was so new that little tufts of fuzz still clung to it. She pulled the front of the jacket together, leaving nearly enough room for two of her inside it. "Yeah," she giggled, "just like the other one. But is this yours or mine?"

"Yours, of course. But I'm hoping you'll let me wear it once in a while. That is, if you can keep it out from under your brother's truck."

"I have no idea when Rick will get leave, or whether he'll come here, so you've got at least a little time before he can run over it again. After that, though, no guarantees."

"Well, Rick and I will have to discuss that. I'm too out of shape to mess with a sailor, so I'll have to make sure I can duck and run. Or try diplomacy. It's working with Chet, anyway—he hasn't thrown me out of the workshop for at least a week." He grinned. "And if nothing else, Rick still owes me for the other jacket."

"Don't push your luck," she laughed.

"Actually," Adam said, moving closer, "speaking of jackets, I was just thinking that a jacket like that is pretty warm. Much too warm to wear indoors, if you know what I mean."

She looked at him in mock innocence. "Oh, I don't know, these fall days can get unexpectedly cold. I think I'd better wear it for a while, just to be sure."

He gathered her into his arms. "These days can get unexpectedly warm, too, you know." He kissed the back of her neck and she shivered.

"See, I'm shivering. Cold." she said breathlessly.

"Ah, then I think we'd better do something to warm you up." His soft whiskers tickled their way up her throat, and his mouth found hers.

After a long, breathless moment she pulled back just enough to whisper "I think maybe I'm just a little bit warmer. Are you?"

"Hot," he murmured. His hands came up under the jacket and caressed her back. She brought her hands up between them and began to unbutton his soft flannel shirt. "What about supper?"

"Hmmm? Supper? Oh, supper. Well... Let me go turn the oven off; I think maybe it'll keep..."

A short time later, the living room was empty and the oversized letter jacket lay crumpled in a heap on the floor.

Author's note

I'd especially like to thank John Woram, good writer, good friend, who has always been endlessly patient in explaining to me How Things Work.

My daughter "Blinkie" greatly improved the text by wielding her red pencil with skill and vigor, and super editor Deniz Bevan caught all the mistakes that got past the rest of us.

I'd also like to thank Diane Trout and the late and sorely missed George Brickner, who made it possible for me to use the awesome Scrivener to write books with, and my husband Jim and son Daniel who put up with me when my mind was so full of plot permutations that I forgot just about everything else I was supposed to be doing.

Some people might recognize a certain amount of similarity between the fictional town of Lyric and one of my favorite places on earth, Fairfield, Iowa (where a building much like Ruth's really does stand on the northwest corner of the square). However, Lyric has plenty of elements that were inspired by other places I have lived, and almost all its inhabitants are strictly imaginary, not based on anyone who ever lived in Fairfield (or anywhere else, for that matter). The fictional Chet Walker was inspired by a man who really was a mentor to younger people learning electronics. The original "Chet" (who did not live in Fairfield) has long since passed away, but his skills and his outlook on life and work live on.

The story of Lyric and its inhabitants will continue in *Dutchman's Puzzle*.

www.ingramcontent.com/pod-product-compliance
Lightning Source LLC
Chambersburg PA
CBHW020336180626
46812CB00001B/232